The drunken man stumbled toward me, his fingers closing upon the ribbons of my hat.

Suddenly the stranger I had noticed across the street ran toward me and grabbed my assailant by the neck and sent him sprawling into the gutter.

In the next moment I felt myself lifted in two strong arms. My rescuer's face was very close to mine, and for one strange instant I looked up into eyes intensely blue and felt in me a sudden sense of destiny. To love or to hate—one or the other. No woman could ever be indifferent to such a man.

SKYE
CAMERON

Phyllis A. Whitney

FAWCETT CREST • NEW YORK

SKYE CAMERON

THIS BOOK CONTAINS THE COMPLETE TEXT OF
THE ORIGINAL HARDCOVER EDITION.

Published by Fawcett Crest Books, a unit of CBS Publications,
the Consumer Publishing Division of CBS Inc., by arrange-
ment with Hawthorn Books, Inc.

Copyright © 1957 by Phyllis A. Whitney.

ISBN: 0-449-24100-9

Printed in the United States of America

22 21 20 19 18 17 16 15 14 13

One

It did not begin in New Orleans at all, though that is where it came to a climax. It began on a soft spring day in the little New England town where I had grown up. A day of apple blossoms and warm golden sun, when we could believe for the first time that the long winter was really past. So calm and bright a day to be so filled with disaster.

I had no knowledge then of my enemy. I had never heard of a man from Leadville whose name was Justin Law. In that year of 1880 I was twenty-two—which was getting on for marrying—but I knew that I would marry soon, for I was in love with Tom Gilman, and he with me. My only rival was my mother. But this time—oh surely this time—Tom was mine.

If you are to understand this story, it will be necessary to understand my feeling about my mother. That is, insofar as I am able to understand it myself. It is very strange to so love and so hate a person from one breath to another as I have loved and hated my mother.

Who could not love her and wish her well and trust her anew, when she seemed at once so lovely and guileless and herself utterly trusting? Yet she was also a born coquette, adept at those feminine wiles so natural and appealing in southern women, though constantly shocking to the New England-bred. It was my father's delight, and also his doom, that he loved her with so deep and tolerant a love that he suffered her actions as one might suffer the flittings of an iridescent dragonfly, with no thought of controlling its flight. I had little in me of such tolerant love that day early in May when I went down to the apple orchard to revel in its scents and delicate hues.

But first I must tell you my name so there may be a beginning of acquaintance between us. It is Skye—Skye Cameron. There are some who think this a strange name, but I am proud to be named for that far misty isle in the Hebrides, where my father, Bruce Cameron, was born and grew to young manhood. I am proud of everything that ties me to my father, but I have always been afraid of those things in me that are my mother's.

Not that I ever resembled her outwardly, for hers is the dark beauty of the New Orleans Creole, blue-black hair, and eyes the warm velvet hue of brown pansies. She is not very tall and her bones are slight, so that she gives the impression of being delicate and fragile. Many have had the impulse to protect her from all that is harsh and hurtful—even those who know she does not wilt easily.

I am taller than she, and my own bones are larger, giving me the look of one who is strong and solidly planted. My hair is a wild red color, of which I have been desperately ashamed, for it is far from a fashionable hue. There are matching red freckles across my nose to mar me further. I can remember the way her friends would commiserate with Mama over my unfortunate hair, and I know it distressed her. She could pucker my skin with lemon juice in futile efforts to control my freckles, but there was nothing she could do about my startling hair. Papa said I was a red-gold Scottish lassie and for her to let me be. But as I grew older I learned to bind my hair severely back and hide its length and weight in the confines of a snood.

Mama did not approve of the severity either. She said I wore both my hair and my Creole mouth in too prim a line. My mouth was hers, and it troubled me. I wanted no soft, full lips that could go easily tremulous, or widen in lilting gaiety until a dimple was pressed into my cheek. I did not want to win men to me with that strange magic that was my mother's. I wanted respect and a granting of my intelligence—not blind adoration which noted only exterior grace. Later Justin Law was to call me in scorn a Puritan, though by that time I had come to recognize the dangerous fires that could burn within me, smothering all Puritan coolness. In New England, however, I had only impatience for what I regarded as light-minded in my mother and would not emulate myself.

Oh, I knew the spells she could weave! I had watched them all my life. Those lavish parties she loved to give, shocking our frugal neighbors, since my father's salary as schoolmaster scarcely allowed for such entertaining. But when some brilliant piece of writing by Bruce Cameron would appear in a magazine, he would likely as not bestow the money he received upon my mother and she would squander it gaily on a party. Every child in town fawned

6

on me as my birthday drew near, wanting to be invited, knowing that my mother's parties were like no others seen in that part of the country. She could laugh like the youngest one there, and take their hands in dancing games, tease and enchant them. And afterwards, when we were replete with ice and those delicious confections she made of brown sugar and pecans, so strange to the northern tongue, she would gather us all about her and tell us wonderful stories.

She had married my father and come to the North shortly before the war and had returned to New Orleans only once during the carpetbagger government. But she could make us shiver with tales of the time when "Beast" Butler ruled the city. She could make us hate the wicked Yankees who had waged war upon her beloved Crescent City, and revel in her accounts of the bravery of New Orleans women, the gallantry of its men. Even I, who had heard these tales so many times, fell under her spell.

But later when we ran outside to play and were away from her witchery, it was I who recovered first in helpless anger. I can remember shaking a ten-year-old boy in fury when I was only nine. "Don't be so stupid!" I raged at him. "Don't you see—*we* are the Yankees she hates! *We* are the villains of her stories!" But they could never see that and only thought me crazy-wild.

Oh, I know how eaten I was with jealousy in those childhood days. Because, while I never admitted it to myself, I longed to have my friends crowd about me, admire me, love me—as they did my mother. Yet while I yearned I held myself apart and could not reach out to them as I longed to do. Papa said my eyes could be as blue-gray as Loch Dunvegan on a rare day when the mists drew apart, but mostly, I'm afraid, I made my eyes chill with the thoughts I hid behind them.

You must not think that Louise, my mother, was not a good mother to me. She loved me warmly, even while she despaired over me. And later, when young men came to the house she welcomed them and sang my praises till they were weary. Looking at her, they forgot to look at me, forgot her married state and the thirty-eight years she wore so lightly. She could not bear it otherwise. If a man looked at her without admiration, she must fly at once to a mirror to search for wrinkles and gray hairs.

All the while I dreamed of a stranger. A man who would be as strong and tall as my father. But unlike my father he would not care for my mother's sort of woman. He would

7

want a woman like me—someone with depths my mother never dreamed of—or so I wanted to think in my vain young fantasies.

Tom Gilman came to town as a stranger. I met him away from home and we grew to be friends. He was neither tall nor strong, but rather shy, with a thin, sensitive face and an unhappy past. He needed me as no one had ever needed me before. I could comfort him and listen to him, talk with him, as with no one else my own age. Surely this must be the love I had longed for and dreamed about.

Papa was less sure. Sometimes I felt that he did not wholly approve of Tom Gilman, but wanted to give me every opportunity to know my own heart. For once he was almost unkind to Mama. He would whisk her away when Tom came to call on me, and even scold her gently when she wanted to tell him of my housewifely virtues. For a little while I had Tom to myself. Or so I thought.

Then I went down to the apple orchard that day and found them there. My mother sat on the warm green earth, with dandelions springing up about her. Indeed, she held one in her fingers. Tom Gilman lay with his head in her lap, staring dreamily up through apple boughs while she stroked his cheek with a yellow dandelion. She was all pity for him. I knew that in the moment I stood staring at them. How could she not pity him, how could she not be kind to this poor young man who had fallen in love with her and could not have her because she was forever my father's. That was the strange thing I had always to recognize, the thing that made my father's life bearable. There seemed to be no falseness in her, no betrayal of his love. At least there was none in those New England days.

They did not see me and I fled back to the house—straight into my father's arms. I sobbed against his broad chest as I had not done since I was a child and he held me fiercely, soothing and calling me "lassie," as only he could say the word. Through my stormy weeping he learned what had happened. For the first time that I could remember, I saw him angry with my mother.

He strode down to the orchard, though I begged him not to, and he sent Tom packing. What he said to Mama I will never know, but he frightened her, for she went weeping into the house, sick with what she regarded as bitter injustice. Of course Tom would marry me, she wailed—who else? And she never understood that I could never again want him.

8

It was his anger that was my father's undoing. Anger did not come to him easily and when it did it was an earth-shaking thing. It would have been better if he had beaten Tom—better perhaps for them both. But that was not his way. So all the dark, stormy fury was unreleased and must be drained out of him through physical labor.

For all his intellectual interests, his teaching and his writing, Papa loved to work with his hands. He indulged in a bit of farming and kept our small house in repair himself. Such labor gave him both physical satisfaction and time to think, he said. On this day he had been mending shingles on the roof, atop a high ladder, and when my mother had gone into the house, he went back to his work. He was a man of sanity and good sense; a man of wise caution under ordinary circumstances. But that day poison flowed through him, driving him to rage, making him uncertain of his movements.

I had gone to my own room, to sit there dully, staring at the walls, feeling that my life had somehow come to an end. It was not only Tom who was gone; it was my hope and my courage. The ladder went up past my window and I will never forget my stunned horror when it tilted, teetered for a moment, then crashed to the ground, carrying my father with it.

A moment later my scream must have echoed through the house, for my mother heard and went past me in the hall, her face white with fear as she rushed downstairs and out into the yard. My own trembling legs would not carry me so quickly and by the time I reached the place where he had fallen, Mama knelt beside him, murmuring his name over and over, "Bruce! Bruce, my darling." Papa's eyes were closed and he did not speak or move, did not respond to the ministering of her hands. She looked up at me, her eyes smoky-dark in her white face.

My father's body did not die that day and we did not know till later the thing which had happened to his spirit. Our doctor came and did what he could. On later visits he grew increasingly grave. It was probable, he said, that my father would never walk again. It was probable that all his splendid manhood must lie inert in a bed for whatever years of life remained to him. An injury to the spine had left his legs useless.

I can still remember that dreadful afternoon when the doctor told my mother the truth. She stood in the bedroom doorway, listening to his soft mumble. I had pulled a stool near the bed to be close to Papa, and neither of us could hear the words he was saying. But we could see Mama's face and hear the despair in her voice.

"What is to become of me if this is true?" she cried.

We heard the doctor's tones then clearly enough. "Madam," he said, "it is your husband about whom I am concerned. I will be here to see him again day after tomorrow. Good day, Mrs. Cameron."

Mama did not show him to the door. She turned back to us, shaken and trembling. "It isn't true!" she cried. "It can't be true!"

Papa's lips barely moved. "Tell me what he said, Louise."

Mama was too shattered to withstand his plea, though I think she should not have told him until he was stronger. He listened until she was done, then closed his eyes and turned his head to the wall. He lay like that for the remainder of the day and would not speak to us. His courage might not have failed him for himself, but I think he gave up at that moment because of my mother. He had failed her and he wanted only to die.

Mama grew thin with worry in the weeks that followed. She could cook gruels and broths to tempt any invalid's appetite, but nothing had prepared her to take on responsibility as head of a family. She had been bred to lean on a man for guidance and now the man lay helpless in bed, his vigor gone, his power of decision as paralyzed as his legs.

The most frightening thing to me was the fact that we seemed unable to reach him in any way. He spoke no word of complaint, but once I saw his eyes follow my mother in agony as she went out of the room and the knowledge of his inner suffering brought me to my knees beside his bed in tears.

"It was my fault that this happened!" I sobbed. "If I had not gone down to the orchard that day . . ."

He spoke to me in the new, colorless tone that had become his since the accident. " 'Tis no one's fault but mine."

Though I wept on, my head close to his on the pillow, no comforting hand reached out to touch my hair as it would have done before. I was so near to him that I could hear the catch in his light breathing, yet he was as far from me as the distant blue mountains I could see from his window.

It was Mama at length who made the decision. Or rather, it was made for her by her older brother who lived in New Orleans. I knew little of my uncle, Robert Tourneau, for my mother had never spoken of him with affection. I knew that her parents had died in a yellow fever epidemic when she was nine, and that she had been raised by a maiden aunt who had since died, and by her brother Robert, eleven years older than she. For all her love of New Orleans, she had been glad to marry my father and leave the home that belonged to her brother.

Now, however, in her need, she had written to Robert Tourneau. In the good days she had spent my father's savings prodigally. Now all income had stopped with Papa's injury and there was no one else to whom she could turn. I had proposed teaching school myself, but Mama grew indignant at the very thought. No daughter of hers should so demean herself. I must remember that I was half Creole and that Creole ladies did not work for a living. The fact that such work was preferable to starving made no slightest impression on my mother. Robert Tourneau, she pointed out, was a most successful lawyer who had recouped his losses in the fifteen years since the war. He also owned a shipping firm which ran steamboats and barges up and down the Mississippi. He was wealthy and would help us. Certainly no Creole would ever fail a member of his own family.

Uncle Robert did not fail us. He wrote what I felt was a most generous and courteous letter. Both he and his wife Natalie wanted us to make our home with them for the time being. Perhaps his own personal physician could do more for Bruce than northern doctors had. Uncle Robert had great confidence in him. At least we would have time in New Orleans to decide about the future. There was an order enclosed for sufficient money to cover our transportation south.

Mama seemed unreasonably indignant over the letter. "Why does he qualify the invitation?" she demanded. "That house is my home as well as his! He is only doing his duty."

I said nothing, but I determined not to have my opinion of this newly found Creole uncle beclouded by my mother's prejudice. I meant to go to New Orleans with an open mind, prepared to like the man who was coming to our aid in this moment of great need.

Mama read his letter aloud to Papa and her voice trembled in the reading. "We must go," she said. "There is no other way."

Papa's voice was weak, hardly more than a whisper. "As I recall, you bear your brother little love."

"I love New Orleans," Mama said, and now there was a hint of longing behind the words.

Papa closed his eyes and I saw something which hurt me

11

more than all that had gone before. From one closed lid a tear coursed across his cheek and into the pillow. I turned away quickly and went out of the room. This breaking up of my father I could not bear to see. He had been a man of great courage. Now there was no will left in him—only weakness. Overnight he had crumbled and that was a frightful, an appalling thing to see.

For myself, I wanted to get away from the town where I had grown up. Looking back I could remember only the hurtful things which had happened to me there. Loneliness was an aching in me that would not lessen in these surroundings. Perhaps, in going to New Orleans, I would leave my unhappy self behind, as a locust sheds its shell. And perhaps some southern doctor might be able to help Papa after all. Perhaps a warmer climate would be kind to him, as a New England winter could not be.

I worked with a will to help Mama make her uncertain decisions and get our little house sold, our belongings packed. And while I worked I dreamed a little about the life to come. New Orleans meant escape to me, but it meant other things as well. The city on the crescent curve of the Mississippi was part of my heritage. Now the stories my mother had told me rose up vividly to possess my imagination and excite my fancy. My mother's home, Uncle Robert's home, was in the Vieux Carré—*le Vieux Carré de la Ville*, the old French Quarter of the town. And Mama said there was nothing like the "Old Square" in all America. For her the Quarter was the heart of New Orleans. There life was gay and gracious, men were gentlemen and women ladies. No finer people had ever lived than the Creoles, according to my mother, who felt all Northerners were crude and dull by comparison. I could not feel akin to New Orleans myself, as I often felt akin to the gray little island of Skye. But perhaps this kinship would come and I would discover a new being in that old city.

The Creoles, I knew, had been given this name to distinguish children of the French and Spanish colonials who had been born in New Orleans. They were a rapturously romantic and dashing people, though from what I gathered, their golden days had been at a peak before the war. I was curious to know them, and to discover what, if anything, of the Creole existed in me.

Then, too, a conception of Robert Tourneau, built partly from my mother's words, partly from my own dreams, began at this time to take fire in my imagination. I could see my uncle as a handsome and compelling figure—a truly romantic Creole. There would be strength and power in this man—qualities which had gone out of my life with the crippling of my father. My uncle would be able to solve our problems and open for me such doors as I had never stepped through before.

Now the days which carried me toward New Orleans brought with them a sense of destiny and I looked forward eagerly to the first meeting with my uncle.

Two ✿

Our train to New Orleans was delayed several times along the way and we arrived late in the evening. During the trip my mother grew tense with anxiety, unlike her usual gay and confident self. Her going home seemed far from joyful. Even her appearance was neglected.

When we reached the station, she descended from the car to look for help, all wilted wine-red plumes, her frock crushed and untidy. I in my drab brown foulard, which I'd felt was more suitable to the journey, stayed beside my father. Before Mama returned, a young man entered our car. The moment he saw my father stretched upon his berth, he approached and bowed to Papa and me.

"Mademoiselle Cameron? Monsieur Cameron? I am Courtney Law and I work for Monsieur Tourneau. I am here to place myself at your service."

That was the first time I heard the name of Law. Since then it has seemed to me that a signal should have chimed through my being, warning me that something of great consequence to my life had begun at the very mention of that name.

But Courtney's identity meant nothing to me that night and my meeting with the man Justin still lay in the future.

Mama returned, not having found her brother in the station, and Courtney presented himself to her. Uncle Robert, it seemed, had come to meet us earlier, but when it was

13

learned that the train would be very late, he had asked his young clerk to await our arrival.

Courtney Law was as handsome a young man as I had ever seen, with the black hair and flashing dark eyes of the Creole, for all that his name was hardly French. Mama was relieved to have help, but for once she was surprisingly indifferent to an attractive man. All her concern seemed to rest upon my father, and her face was so drawn with anxiety that she seemed far older than she was.

Mr. Law assured us that he had brought help, and then he turned to me once more. I was surprised to see his eyes light up with interest as they met mine. He would return at once, he said, and hurried away. Mama fluttered anxiously over my father and said she hoped the young man would be quick. We had endured enough on this journey.

In a few minutes he was back with Jasper, the Tourneau coachman, a dark-skinned Negro who wore his boots, his long-tailed coat and his tall hat with a flamboyant air. He and the yard boy, who had come to assist him, carried Papa to the carriage, with Courtney Law giving orders and supervising the move. Quite evidently he expected Mama and me to be helpless about such matters.

In the carriage Papa was propped against pillows, his useless legs stretched out on one of the small drop seats in front. Mama sat beside him and I don't know whether she clung to him for her own comfort or for his. My father was white-faced and I feared that his pain was great, though he let no sound escape his lips. I sat next to my mother, with Mr. Law opposite me on a second drop seat.

The night was warm, but dark and windy, with gray clouds racing across a half-moon. This was New Orleans at last, but it was I, not my mother, who felt excitement and interest in all the sights and sounds about us. I doubt if Mama let her glance stray twice outside the carriage.

Courtney Law had the quick perception to see that my mother wanted only to be quiet and care for my father, so he addressed himself to me as the carriage rolled over cobblestones. In the shifting light cast by street lamps I could study his face anew and I wondered about him. How did a man with such a name come to have the sensitive face of a French poet? There was a blood mixture, of course, with the Creole dominating. Certainly his manners were more polished than any I had ever seen in a man, and his speech was attractive, with the touch of a French accent to the words.

He identified points of interest we passed and I sensed

his pride in this city. When we reached the Vieux Carré I was aware of narrow streets, straight as lines on cross-ruled paper. The moon had vanished and the houses stretched dark between street lamps. If they noted our echoing passage at all, they looked at us warily from behind dark shutters, withdrawn and secret, as if they judged us strangers. There was an odor I did not like and I knew it came from the deep open gutters that lined each street.

The carriage stopped at last before an iron gate that guarded an arched stone passageway. The *allée* was enclosed, like a tunnel through the lower level of the house. Courtney Law sprang out of the carriage and hurried to the great cast-iron knocker beside the gate. Then he returned to help Mama and me from the carriage.

In the dim illumination cast by lanterns which hung from the vaulted ceiling of the passageway, I could see the woman who came to open the gate in response to the clamor of the knocker. She was a tall, light-skinned Negro woman in a guinea-blue dress, with a blue tignon tied about her head. She carried herself with an air of pride in which there was nothing servile.

"Delphine!" Mama cried. "You are still here?"

"Yes, Mam'zelle Loulou," the woman said, "this is my home." Her words bore a faint reproach, as if to chide my mother for her surprise.

She gave a sharp order to Jasper, who in turn commanded the yard boy, Henri. My father was lifted from the carriage and carried into the passageway. We followed and the gate clanged shut behind us, locked by Delphine.

Courtney Law walked beside me, shaking his head in sorrow over my father's condition. "He will receive the best of care in this house, mam'zelle," he said. "Do not concern yourself. M'sieu Robert does nothing in a small way."

I caught the ring of admiration and respect in his voice as he spoke of my uncle and my sense of anticipation increased.

Jasper and Henri carried my father with some difficulty in the curving, enclosed flight of stairs that rose from the end of the passageway. Mama followed anxiously after, her steps slow and her face pale and strained. I was concerned lest my father be hurt, but big Jasper was very strong and they carried him gently.

From the gallery above I could hear Aunt Natalie's pleasant voice greeting my mother, speaking warmly to Papa, directing the way. When I reached the top of the

15

first flight she gave my hands a squeeze of welcome and kissed me on the cheek. I had a quick impression of a plump little woman in black, with a round face that made up in amiability what it lacked in beauty. Then she waved us toward the parlor with an apology and asked us to be comfortable while Papa was settled in his room.

Mama spoke quickly and I was again aware of her uneasiness and anxiety. "No—if you please. I must go with my husband. Skye, you will stay to meet my brother and make my apologies, please." She moved her hands in a vague gesture and hurried after Papa. I knew she was only too glad to postpone her meeting with Uncle Robert and I felt a little scornful for her foolish dread.

Aunt Natalie let her go and spoke to Courtney. "Please attend this young lady," she said. "And perhaps you will inform my husband that our guests have arrived."

Courtney seemed gallantly pleased with his assignment as he led me toward the parlor.

The second floor had a wide hallway which ran from courtyard to street, with two rooms opening off either side. I was to learn that the Tourneau house was somewhat unusual in its construction. Most Creole homes had outside hallways that were not a real part of the living quarters. Mr. Law indicated a room on the right, across the hall from what was plainly the dining room.

"Please make yourself comfortable, mam'zelle," he said. "M'sieu Robert had much work to do this evening. I will call him from his downstairs office."

He went off and I looked eagerly about. This room was clearly the lived-in section of a long double parlor. Folding doors, now ajar, separated it from the more formal, less frequently used first parlor. After the cramped quarters of the train, it was good to stand up and move about. I stepped to the double doors and looked in to see what a Creole first parlor was like. Each room had its own small fireplace and marble mantel, its individual furniture, but the first parlor was far more elaborately and luxuriously furnished than the second. Its rosewood sofa was covered in handsome blue brocade and there were little gilded chairs, surely from France. A huge, gilt-framed mirror over the mantel reflected a crystal chandelier, and lovely figurines in bronze and ivory stood on the shelves of the corner whatnot.

Oddly enough, no sumptuous draperies hung beside the tall windows that ran across the street end of the room, and

16

instead of the beautiful rugs I should have expected, reed matting had been laid upon the floors.

From where I stood I could glimpse the door of a darkened room directly across the hall from this one. Wedges of moonlight cutting through shutters showed me the welcome sight of bookcases crowded with volumes. That was the library. Certainly a room I must look into at the first opportunity. But now I retreated to a sofa in the other parlor and seated myself to wait.

Before long I heard footsteps in the hallway and looked up eagerly. Courtney stood back to allow my uncle to precede him into the room and I saw Robert Tourneau for the first time.

He stood motionless in the doorway for just a moment and I had the swift impression of a dark-visaged man with a tuft of black beard on his chin. He was tall, erect, distinguished, and there was somehow an aura of darkness about him, due perhaps to his dark suit and hair and eyes. Then he smiled and came toward me and the somber impression vanished. He had the finely chiseled nose of an aristocrat and his eyes, deep-set beneath level brows, seemed to brighten at the sight of me. He was fully as handsome and impressive a man as I had expected.

I gave him my hand and he bowed over it gracefully, drew me from my chair and looked at me. "So this is Skye," he said and I heard that low-toned melodious voice for the first time.

Suddenly I was conscious of my shabby brown foulard and my brown hat that did not sufficiently hide red hair that would undoubtedly seem strange and out of place in New Orleans. But if there was any criticism in my uncle's look, he did not reveal it.

I explained quickly that Mama had gone to see my father settled and would join us shortly.

"Good," he said "You must both be weary from your trip and will be anxious to retire."

I shook my head, smiling. "I've wanted so much to see your New Orleans—to see the Vieux Carré. And to meet my—my family."

Clearly he was pleased. "And now that you've had a glimpse of the Quarter?"

"I'm going to like it," I said confidently.

"You'll do more than like it," Courtney put in and I glanced at him in surprise. So compelling was the presence of my uncle that I had forgotten the young man was still

17

there. "Perhaps," he went on, "I may be permitted to show you something of it, Mam'zelle Skye?"

My uncle nodded approvingly before I could answer. "An excellent idea. It is time this young woman came home to her own. It is *your* New Orleans as well, my dear."

I found myself drawn to him, further discounting my mother's dubious warnings. So quickly had he forgiven what he must regard as my foreign blood, and accepted me as belonging to New Orleans. He turned to the young man beside him with a courteous bow and thanked him for his assistance that evening. Courtney murmured that he must be on his way. He bade us both good evening, gave me another look in which interest had plainly kindled and went away, leaving me surprised and a little confused. I could only presume that this was the typical manner of the southern gentleman, for whom I had heard great praise from my mother.

Aunt Natalie appeared in the door from the courtyard gallery, but Mama was not with her. She took my hands again and welcomed me. Her movements were serene, but I noted that she gave Robert a quick look that seemed to have something of apology in it. It was evident that she was considerably younger than her husband. He had not married her as a young man.

"Your sister Louise is most charming," she told him. "But the trip has tired her. She hopes you will forgive her for retiring at once."

Uncle Robert raised dark eyebrows. "A disappointment. I've not seen my sister for many years."

"She was not feeling well toward the end of the trip," I put in hastily, not wanting my uncle to suspect any discourtesy to him behind my mother's actions. After all, he was being more than generous to us and it did seem that Mama might have waited long enough to say good evening and thank him. "We are very grateful to you," I went on. "My mother will want to tell you herself tomorrow."

His small neat beard reminded me of a picture my mother had once shown me of General Beauregard, a Creole whom she greatly admired. My uncle had a habit of stroking his beard when he was faintly amused, and his fingers touched it now. He merely bowed in response to my words, and I had the feeling that he saw through my effort to dissemble about my mother. No one, I suspected, would ever fool Uncle Robert for long, and I respected him for his keen perception.

But now Aunt Natalie was taking me in hand. "Come,

18

my child. I know you must be weary. Your uncle will excuse you, I'm sure. Now that your mama and papa are settled, I will show you to your room. The hour is late—you must get your rest."

Uncle Robert took my hand again for a moment and his dark gaze held my own compellingly. "I think you will be happy here, my dear," he told me, and I began to feel that with my uncle's help happiness would indeed once more be possible. Not in any way had this first meeting with him disappointed me. Most problems, I felt, would slip away when Uncle Robert took them in hand. He was a man to inspire confidence.

I thanked him and said good night. Aunt Natalie led the way onto the rear gallery. The house reached its arms about the courtyard on three sides, three stories high, with a separate, lower building rising at the back. This, I knew, was the pattern of most houses in the Quarter, built not by the French, but by the Spanish after most of the French houses had burned down. Once the rear buildings had undoubtedly been slave quarters.

Aunt Natalie motioned to the left of the court. "Our small daughter Caroline has her room in that wing, and once also the little son whom we lost. Ah, how Caro wept tonight that she could not remain up until you came. Caro has only eight years, and is sometimes thoughtless, as is the way of the young. Our infant Tina is of course in the nursery upstairs, close to me. This way, if you please."

We moved along the gallery to the right, our way lighted by a lamp in the courtyard below and by radiance from windows opening upon the gallery. My mother and father had been given adjoining rooms in this gallery wing, and my own room was at the very end. Its door cut across the gallery and I went up two steps into it, pausing with a sense of delight. If I could not have mountains on my horizon, it was at least something to have so lovely a corner room overlooking a New Orleans courtyard.

"I hope you will be comfortable, my dear," said Aunt Natalie. "Delphine will bring you hot water in a moment. That bed should make anyone sleep. Seignouret made them very large, you know. Be careful to tuck in the mosquito *barre* all around, once you are in bed. Good dreams to you."

She closed the door and left me alone. I looked about with interest and increasing satisfaction. The bed's two rear posters reached clear to a curved half-tester that extended above it, to which the mosquito *barre* was attached.

The posts at the foot of the bed were not so tall and each ended in a carved knob. It was a grand bed, noble in its proportions. A footstool with two steps would enable me to get easily onto that high mattress.

There was the usual marble-topped washstand with a china bowl painted in a moss-green design. The charming dressing table also had a marble top. But of equal importance with the bed was a huge armoire, far larger than any wardrobe I had ever seen. I thought in apology of the meager and undistinguished costumes I would hang within its cavernous depths. Such a piece of furniture seemed to indicate the lavish extent of the Creole wardrobe.

I took off my hat and laid it on a shelf of the armoire. Then I drew from my hair the heavy bone pins that pressed into my scalp and in relief shook the long coil free from its knot. I loved the feel of it over my hands, but I turned my back on all mirrors so that I need see no more of its color than I had to. The strands felt silky and alive to my touch— it might have been beautiful hair had it been blue-black like my mother's or even a warm brown color like Papa's.

When Delphine tapped on my door, I tried to smooth my hair back before she entered. I had forgotten that she was to bring me hot water. She carried a big china pitcher across to the washstand with the air of a queen bearing jewels, and barely gave me a glance in passing. Her carriage was as fine as that of any Creole lady and while she must have been in her fifties, she still bore evidence of the beauty which had been hers as a girl. Her skin was no darker than that of any woman who had been long in the sun. A warm, rich color, with a tint of dark rose at the cheekbones.

"Is there anything you wish, mam'zelle?" she asked, placing fluffy, scented towels over the rail of the stand.

My interest in Delphine was growing. Papa had always been against slavery and I had grown up with a sympathy for the Negro cause. This woman must be the daughter of slaves, must have been bron into slavery herself. Yet she spoke like no colored woman I had known in the North. Jasper's accent was, I imagined, more typical of the southern Negro. The yard boy had chattered a strange patois I could not understand. But Delphine spoke correct English with an accent as French as that of Natalie Tourneau.

"Nothing, thank you," I said. Then, as she moved toward the door, I added, "Tell me, Delphine—where are you from?"

She gave me a clear, direct look. "New Orleans is the

20

city of my birth, mam'zelle," she said and went quickly from the room.

My curiosity was whetted, for I shared with my father an interest in people that always made life entertaining. Already under this roof existed several little puzzles we would enjoy unraveling in a sympathetic manner.

"We," I had thought to myself, and winced, remembering. My father no longer took an interest in the world around him, as he had once done in so lively and analytical a fashion.

At the thought of my father, I decided to bid him good night before I went to sleep. I found a band of ribbon in my portmanteau and bound my hair back at my neck. Then I stepped again onto the narrow gallery that ran above the court at this second level.

When I rapped on the door of the next room, my mother opened it and she appeared to be vexed.

"How like Robert to put us in a wing that is used for business agents and persons of that type, instead of where we belong in the house proper!"

Her readiness to criticize her brother seemed to me unreasonable.

"My room is most comfortable," I told her. "Uncle Robert has been very kind."

"It is not a matter of comfort," Mama said tartly, "but of social importance. However, there is nothing we can do if this is Robert's decision. Is there anything you want, Skye?"

"Only to tell Papa good night," I said. "How is he now?"

"He was in considerable pain," she said. "Natalie sent Delphine with something to help him. He is already asleep. Perhaps tomorrow he will feel better."

I said good night to her then and she went along the gallery to her own room. When she had gone I stood for a moment with my hand on the gallery rail, looking down into the darkness of the courtyard. The gas lamp had been extinguished and I could not make out the nature of the foliage which made dark shapes below me, but I heard the play of a fountain, caught the soft rustle of leaves as a breeze came through the arched passageway from the street. A delicate perfume rose from a vine that climbed a courtyard wall nearby and I experienced suddenly a feeling of yearning delight. The mingling of warm, tropical June scents rose toward me in a heady wave, almost a tangible force, assaulting my senses.

The strange longing was so strong within me that I reached my hand to the vine beside the gallery and plucked a tiny rosette of fragrant white. The blossom's sweetness clung to my fingers, scented the very night about me. I touched it to my lips and suddenly understood the longing which possessed me. Such a night was made for lovers' arms, for the clinging of lovers' lips. It was my own hungry youth that called out in loneliness. But that was what I had hoped to escape in New Orleans.

I flung the blossom from me and went quickly back to my room. There I turned down the oil lamp and undressed with faint moonlight now and again slanting through the two windows of my corner room. I climbed into the bed and saw that its one decorative touch was a great "S" carved high on the mahogany of the headboard. Kneeling I could trace the carving with my fingers.

"S" for Seignouret, perhaps? My Aunt Natalie had spoken the name almost with reverence. Yet it was one I had never heard. As best I could I tucked the mosquito *barre* around the edge of the bed and found that in New Orleans even mosquito netting was hemmed with fine, handmade lace.

There was so much to learn about this city in which I must now live. But I must be careful in the learning. I did not want to go too fast. Already I had been betrayed into a sweet, sad longing that frightened me a little. I must not altogether lose my identity. I must not be too easily seduced by soft southern air and the scent of flowers. Perhaps the Creole in me was something against which I must be on guard.

Three ☀

The next morning I was awakened early by a stir of sound from the courtyard. Birds were singing and there was a muted chatter of voices as servants moved about their tasks, already polishing, cleaning, trimming shrubbery. Somewhere above the baby Tina woke and wailed.

While I stretched and yawned in my bed, wishing I might sleep the morning away, a young Negro maid brought me a tray on which a china chocolate pot gave off an odor, not of chocolate, but of coffee.

"Le p'tit noir," she said and then chattered something at me in the same tongue the yard boy had spoken—a strange mixture that sounded something like French, but was not. Fortunately she threw in enough English words so that I could make occasional sense of what she was saying. I gathered that the coffee was to wake me up, but that I was to have breakfast on the gallery with "M'sieu Robear" in not later than a half hour.

My uncle's name in itself was enough to rouse me. If he expected me at the table, I did not want to be late.

The first sip of coffee nearly choked me. It was thick on my tongue as syrup, and fiercely strong and bitter. So thick was it that it left a dark stain inside the cup. I managed a few swallows before I gave up. If this was the famous coffee of New Orleans it was not for my pallid northern tongue. But even those sips wakened me.

For all the cool, early morning breeze at my windows, the sky was already blue and bright overhead with the promise of heat to come. The clothes in my portmanteau needed the attention of a flatiron, but I had been too weary last night to trouble about them. There was nothing for it but to wear again my brown foulard and change to something fresh later on.

As I sat before the marble-topped dressing table, binding back my hair, I wished vainly that I might conceal it under a tignon such as Delphine had worn. I had a feeling that no Creole would approve the color of my hair.

And surely, without my hat, my hair was the first thing my uncle noticed as I approached the table on the gallery, where he already breakfasted with Aunt Natalie. I saw his eyes rest upon it briefly, then turn away. He rose as I came toward him and pulled out the chair at my place, seated me with the air of a man to whom small courtesies were second nature.

"Good morning, Skye," he said. "You slept well, I hope?"

I told him that I had indeed and took my place at the table. Aunt Natalie looked plumper than ever in a black gown cut in the fashionable princess line and fastened clear to the throat with tiny pearl buttons. Her smile was friendly, but like a good Creole wife, she kept her eye on her husband for a lead in all that she said or did.

The breakfast was a heavy one, with fried rounds of veal and gravy, corn grits dotted with butter, hot biscuits, thin buckwheat cakes and brown sugar. Of course there were quantities more of the bitter coffee, though now it was permissible to dilute it and drink it *au lait.*

My uncle seemed preoccupied this morning with the affairs of the day ahead of him and there was little conversation. I had just buttered a second fleecy biscuit when Mama came out upon the gallery and hurried toward us. She looked nervous again and ill-at-ease, but when Uncle Robert rose, she held out a hand to him with a pretty air of apology.

"Good morning, Robert," she said. "It's good to see you looking so well. We're most grateful for your hospitality. I'm sorry I overslept."

He returned her greeting gravely and seated her next to him. It was probable, I thought, that he had been a little hurt by her lack of any wish to see him last night. He asked about my father and conveyed sympathy. His own physician would call upon him this afternoon. We need have no concern—everything possible would be done to assure Bruce Cameron's recovery. He went on then to speak of another matter.

"Courtney Law, the young man whom you met last night, and who works as an apprentice clerk in my office, must take you both for a drive about New Orleans on Sunday afternoon. If that is convenient for you. I'm sure, Louise, that you will want to reacquaint yourself with the city of your birth, and your daughter has already shown herself eager to know our section of town."

Perhaps in her preoccupation and anxiety last night, Mama had not paid much attention to Courtney's name. Now, at mention of it, she glanced up quickly, though she did not speak. To cover a silence I felt was somewhat rude on her part, I expressed eagerness for the outing and hoped Uncle Robert would consider that it came from both Mama and me. But my uncle, I think, was not deceived and he sipped his coffee in thoughtful silence.

As I ate my second biscuit, I looked over the railing into the courtyard. At this early morning hour it was still shady and cool, and now all the lush growth was visible. There were banana trees with long shaggy green leaves, and a slender clump of bamboo in one corner. Wisteria grew up a trellised wall, its lavender petals gone now, the fronds thick and in full leaf. A vine bore the small rosettes of Grand Duke jasmine—the flower I had plucked last night. But the night spell had vanished and this was no more than a charming Creole courtyard.

It was paved with faded orange brick and in its center a small fountain played merrily. I could see the glint of darting goldfish in the water, and all around the fountain's edge were small red flowerpots, abloom with plants. The odors from the street did not penetrate here and all was clean and sweetly smelling. No wonder the houses of the Vieux Carré turned their backs upon the world and centered their living about these lovely courtyards.

"Your daughter," said Uncle Robert suddenly to my mother, "does not reveal her Creole blood to any outward extent."

"I resemble my father," I said quickly, not wanting him to disapprove of me for what I could not help. "My Scottish grandmother had red hair."

He smiled and stroked his beard, amused by my quick defense. "It is nothing we can very well change. But your name—that is something else. I find it a harsh name, Louise. One can do nothing to soften it. Has she no second name we can use?"

Mama shook her head, and though his tone was pleasant enough, she looked more chastened than I had ever seen her. This morning she wore a light-colored frock, creamy as her skin, with only a touch of rosy ribbon for accent. I thought she looked very pretty and young, but it was in vain that she fluttered appealing lashes at her brother. He, at least, was one man who was immune to her charm, and I could not help liking him for it.

"Skye was her father's choice as a name," my mother said. "I wanted to please him. And he felt that no lesser name should come between Cameron and Skye."

My uncle's shrug was French and expressive. "Ah, well. I would never choose to name a girl child for a chilly Scottish island, but the deed is done. And I am pleased with the girl, if not with the name." He flashed me a smile as charming as my mother's could be, when she felt like smiling. There was, after all, some resemblance between these two, I decided in surprise.

Uncle Robert finished his breakfast before the rest of us and excused himself from the table.

"I must get downstairs to the office," he told his wife. "I have an important case coming up in court this morning and there is work to be done." He glanced briefly at Mama. "Please tell your husband that I will visit him later today."

He was almost as tall as my father, when he rose, but his shoulders, though he held them well, were less broad. One felt there might be steel in his back, rather than muscle. Again I had an impression of strength and power. Strength was a quality I greatly admired and to find it in my uncle to such a degree gave me a reassuring sense of safety here in his house.

Mama sighed as he disappeared down the curving stairway at the far end of the gallery. "My brother hasn't changed in the least," she murmured. "Or if he has, the iron has bitten even more deeply."

Aunt Natalie said nothing, but I felt impelled to take issue with such criticism. "A man without iron in him is hardly a man," I said.

"What a child she is!" Mama laughed lightly and smiled at Aunt Natalie. "At Skye's age one is always an authority on men."

There was no answering her. I was beginning to suspect that my mother's inclination to prejudice against Uncle Robert was based on the fact that he was one man she could not wind about her fingers.

Aunt Natalie had relaxed visibly at her husband's going. "Don't mind, Loulou. He is a brilliant, busy man, with much to worry him. He has been through great trouble since the war, as, heaven knows, we all have."

"This Courtney Law who met us last night," my mother said, "—do I know his family? I seem to remember the name."

"You need not hesitate," my aunt said, laughing a little. "All that is long ago. The families are most excellent friends. But you are right—the name is the one you recall. They still live in the Garden District. It is to Robert's credit that he has been exceedingly kind where little kindness was due."

The conversation had taken a mysterious turn and I was about to ask a question, when Aunt Natalie fixed me with her placid gaze.

"Are there no men in the North?" she asked my mother. "That this daughter of yours goes unmarried? We must do something about this, now that you have returned to New Orleans."

"I hope you will," Mama said guilelessly, not looking at me. "I'm afraid Skye has grown too particular about young men for her own good."

Aunt Natalie seemed aghast. "You don't mean that you leave it to the child to arrange such matters herself? Where is your good sense, Loulou? The young lack the experience to act with wisdom in such matters. But now that she is here—"

I couldn't listen to such talk. I didn't want to be rude, but Aunt Natalie, and my mother too, must understand that I would not have such Creole ways thrust upon me.

"I believe Mama married my father for love," I said. "And I hope to marry for love too."

Aunt Natalie was plainly shocked, but before she could continue, her attention was fortunately distracted. A little girl had slipped out of a room on the gallery wing opposite ours. She came toward us like a small bird darting, and there was about her something bright as quicksilver. It lay perhaps in the sunny color of her dress, in the brilliance of her smile and the straight whiteness of her teeth, for her hair and eyes were dark as her father's. She was thin and quick and very lively. Even when she stood at the table beside me, it was as if everything about her continued to dance. Her gaze flitted quickly over my mother and then rested on me, and I knew it was my hair that held her attention.

She was, however, a well-bred Creole child, for all that she was only eight. She waited for her mother's introduction, curtsied politely and bade us *bon matin*. Only then did she give in to what must have been an imperative impulse and darted a hand toward my hair. I felt her small fingers touch lightly as butterfly wings, even as her mother cried out in reproof.

"But it is beautiful!" Caro said. "Like fire in the sunset. Yet smooth as silk and without burning."

"You will apologize to your cousin," said Aunt Natalie in shocked tones. "One does not touch another's person, or make comment on the appearance. Think what your papa would say!"

Caro said softly. "Papa is not here. But I am sorry if I have offended you, Cousin Skye." She smiled at me winsomely and added in mischief, "I would have touched it anyway. I could not help myself."

I loved her at once, this little girl, and I was glad that my hair had won me a friend.

"I'm on my way to school, Maman," she said. "Jasper is waiting for me now." She told us good-by before darting off in the quick way that was characteristically hers.

Aunt Natalie explained that Robert did not approve of the company of children at daytime meals, so Caro was served alone. At suppertime, unless there were guests, it was necessary that she learn to conduct herself well in adult company—which meant speaking not at all and behaving like a young lady of good family.

Our meal had come to an end and I asked Mama if it would be possible to visit Papa for a little while.

She shook her head. "Not yet, Skye. He was still asleep when I looked in. It's best to let him be."

"Then," I suggested as we rose from the table, "I'd like to go for a walk this morning and see something of the Vieux Carré. Later I must iron my clothes and—"

Aunt Natalie broke in on my words. "Delphine will of course see that the chambermaid takes care of your frocks. As for walking—my husband does not wish the unmarried ladies of his household to be seen on the street unattended. Fortunately, young Courtney will come Sunday afternoon —day after tomorrow—to take you and your mother for a drive. Then you will have your wish to see something of our city."

Already the growing heat of the day was making itself felt and Mama fanned herself languidly with her handkerchief. "I don't really care to go driving. I've no desire at all to go out in the streets of New Orleans."

I looked at her in surprise. "But you've always spoken with such enthusiasm about the Vieux Carré."

"It is different now," she said sadly. "There is nothing to look forward to. Nothing that matters."

This was again the listless woman she had turned into on the train, and she was someone I did not know. I glanced in distress at Aunt Natalie and she misunderstood my look.

"Don't concern yourself, my child. You shall have your drive about town. If necessary Delphine may go with you as chaperone."

That wasn't what I had meant, but it startled me further. The edict that I must not go out alone in New Orleans seemed overly protective. At home I walked about as I pleased, and my parents thought nothing of it. Now, it seemed, I must not even go for a drive in public with a young man without taking Delphine along. None of this was to my taste and I saw no reason why I should be forced into so strict a Creole pattern when this had never been my way of life. However, there was nothing I could do about these matters now. Later, perhaps, I would speak to my uncle about them. He had shown sympathy and friendliness toward me and I felt he would not be difficult to talk to.

Now, for want of anything better to do, I went to my

room and laid upon my bed the few dresses I owned which would be suitable for the New Orleans summer. I looked at them with some distaste and wondered what I might wear for the drive with Courtney Law. Somehow my interest in the outing had increased since I knew my mother would not be with us. Perhaps deep in my consciousness there had been a knowledge of how it would be if she came on the ride too.

I could understand that last night in her utterly weary and distressed state, she would give no thought to any man, however attractive. She had not troubled about her appearance, as she had at the start of the trip, nor had she taken time to be charming to Courtney Law as I was sure she would normally have done. This morning at breakfast, she had made a faint try with my uncle, but now she seemed to have given up again. And though I did not like to see her thus, I could not help but know that the drive would be more pleasant for me because of her absence. It would be something to fill the emptiness to have a man as attractive as Courtney Law bowing over my hand and behaving as though he thought me lovely and desirable. After all, I had come here to escape my former self. Who could know at this point whether Courtney might not figure in this change?

When I'd done what I could about my clothes I went to my father's room. My mother was just coming out and she whispered to me that I must try to cheer him. I tapped on the door and went in.

A bed stood beside the window that opened on the gallery and my father lay upon it, his lean length covered by a sheet. Against the pillow I saw the gray that had crept into his brown hair, the marks which pain had creased beside his mouth. But his color was better than I had seen it since the accident. A long sleep had apparently been good for him.

I tried to put a cheery note into my voice as I greeted him and asked if he had enjoyed a Creole breakfast. At least he did not turn his head away in broken despair, but looked at me with eyes that were steady enough.

"I can still taste the coffee," he said dryly.

This was almost a joke; it was certainly an effort and I laughed with a catch in my voice. "You're looking much better this morning, Papa. I was afraid the long trip might leave you weary for days."

The lines about his mouth seemed to deepen. "I had

hoped the trip would be harder on me than it was," he said grimly.

I seated myself on a wooden stool near his bed and leaned forward to take his hand in mine. This was the nearest he had come to speaking the thing I feared, the thing I had sensed in his mind ever since he learned he could not hope for recovery. My father, who possessed so much strength and wisdom for others, had none left for himself.

For a while he was still, as if his thoughts had turned far from me. Yet when he spoke, I saw that he had been thinking of me all the time.

"Skye, lassie," he said, "I've not brought this up since—since that day. But tell me now, girl, what of Tom Gilman? What of your feeling for him?"

His words caused me no more than a twinge of hurt and I knew by now that it was due more to hurt pride than to my love for Tom. But I could not altogether meet Papa's gaze. I hid my face against his arm and spoke softly.

"I'm glad I found out in time. What you did was best for me, and for him too. It is Mama I find hard to forgive. She drew him to her, though he never mattered to her at all. You are her only love, Papa."

"She should be released from any love for me." He spoke the words so softly that I hardly caught them.

I raised my head. "What do you mean?"

"No matter for now," he told me. "It's glad I am, lassie, that you were mistaken about Tom Gilman. There'll come a better man for you."

I made myself smile. "Of course! I shall become a ravishing southern belle—wait and see!"

"That's my girl," he said.

He was still weary and his eyelids closed. I longed for the old companionship when I had been able to tell him what I thought and felt, I would have liked now to talk about the restrictions which Creole custom placed upon my actions, and ask him how I might escape them. But plainly he wanted me to go away. Remembering the room with book-filled shelves I'd glimpsed across from the parlor, I asked if he would like something to read. It would be fine if he took an interest in books again. But he still had no wish for them, and I went away and left him alone.

With time on my hands and nothing to do, I decided to look into the library myself. The door to the room stood open and the bookshelves were more clearly visible than they had been by moonlight the night before. I walked in without hesitation and looked about me.

To my surprise this room was even more sumptuously furnished than the first parlor across the hall. Here the wine-red draperies had not been taken down for summer, and the flowered Aubusson carpet was soft beneath my feet. The Napoleonic influence was especially marked, for there was an Egyptian touch to the cornices. The elaborate plaster rosette on the ceiling above the gilded bronze chandelier was formed of Sphinxes' heads, delicately touched with color. Double doors separated the study from the dining room, but they stood apart now to allow for ventilation, with curtains hung in the opening for privacy.

I forgot the bookshelves for the moment because the room was something of a museum. Collectors' items graced every small table, hung upon the walls, stood on whatnots in the corners. Satsuma from old Japan, a Chinese Buddha carved in jade, a wall tapestry from medieval France.

Crossed on the wall beside the tapestry were two swords of unusual design. The blade of each had three grooved sides and tapered nastily from hilt to point. Dueling swords? I wondered, recalling New Orleans' romantic history in the field of dueling.

As I stood absorbed, I heard footsteps in the hall outside and Uncle Robert came suddenly into the room, closing the door behind him. He did not see me at once, but walked directly to a massive mahogany desk, set near the shutters to the street gallery. He unlocked the drop leaf and began searching through papers on the desk. I coughed discreetly to reveal my presence and he started and looked around at me.

"Your library coaxed me in," I explained. "I thought I might find something to read. But the room is filled with so many fascinating things that I forgot about books."

He turned from his desk and faced me. Near him was a small rosewood table with an enormous silver warming cover set upon it. Uncle Robert's fingers sought the silver knob and toyed with it absently. For just an instant I had the feeling that he was not pleased to find me in this room. Then he flashed his winning smile and I realized that I had only startled him. He came forward graciously and took my arm, and I was aware again of the low, musical quality of his voice.

"I'm pleased that you like my study, Skye. You are, I see, admiring my swords."

"I wondered if they were dueling swords," I said.

He reached for one of the weapons and took it almost lovingly into his hands. Then in a flash he stepped lithely to the center of the room and set the blade whipping in strokes too lightning-swift for the eye to follow. His skill in fencing was clearly superb.

"That," he said, as he replaced the weapon upon its rack, "is a *colichemarde*—the finest of all dueling swords."

Next he turned to a black leather case upon a table beneath the crossed swords. Opening a silver clasp he turned back the cover of the case lined in green velvet, and I saw that within lay a brace of handsome, silver-mounted pistols.

My mother had told me of how skilled the men of New Orleans had been before the war in the art of dueling. In the cemeteries many tombs bore the legend *Mort sur le champ d'honneur*. Men had fought with pistols beneath the Dueling Oaks in City Park, she said, in Audubon Park as well, and earlier with swords here in the Vieux Carré in St. Anthony's Close. Her stories had left me breathless, as a fairy tale might. Now with my own eyes I saw cold steel upon the wall, and the murderous look of pistols, meant not for military battle, or for the defense of a house against marauders, but weapons intended solely for dueling. The reality seemed suddenly less romantic. I looked into my uncle's face and saw a dark light in his eyes.

"Have you ever fought a duel, Uncle Robert?" I asked.

"Dueling is against the law. I myself was a member of the committee organized to call a halt to the settling of quarrels by means of the duel. Though I must admit that not all of those who joined the committee have abstained from resorting to the pistol. They are, of course, to be condemned."

"Then you disapprove of dueling, Uncle Robert?"

He looked beyond me, as if into the past. "There was a time in the past when the *Code Duello* had real meaning in this city. There was a day when the *Maîtres d'Armes*, the best of fencing masters, taught every gentleman to defend his honor. But when the Americans came they were a clumsy lot who could duel only with pistols. The rapier went out of fashion. Butchers without skill or honor sought to settle their differences with strange weapons. It was better to let an honored custom die, than to see it debased by those of low blood."

I wished I might have seen Robert Tourneau as a young man. What a dashing, romantic young blade he must have been. There seemed few such men in our time, few whose strength a woman could admire.

The subject of the duel's decline had apparently depressed him. He turned from me and went to his desk, searching for the papers he had come to fetch. I sensed that I did not belong in this room and moved quietly toward the door. He came at once to open it for me and just before it blocked my view, I caught sight of a small portrait which hung in a dim corner behind the door. No more than a glimpse did I have of the delicate, warmly colored face of a lovely young girl. It was a haunting, wistful face and I'd have liked a closer look at the portrait, but my uncle had opened the door and there was nothing to do but go.

He bowed me out with his usual courtesy. "Let me know whenever you want reading matter and I'll be glad to make my library available to you."

I thanked him and found myself standing in the hallway —with no book in my hands.

Four   ✸

That first day in New Orleans seemed a long one. I went downstairs to admire the courtyard and in daytime I was able to appreciate for the first time the utter grace of the curved stairway that ran from the third floor down to its enclosed opening on the passageway below. Off the arched *allée* of the porte-cochere several doors opened, leading into my uncle's office. In New Orleans most men of the professions had their offices below their living quarters. The dampness, in any event, would be too great downstairs for living comfort.

Probably Courtney Law was in one of those rooms now and I was tempted to look in upon him. But I had already trespassed once this morning, so I turned instead to the courtyard. But while such a court is lovely to look upon and pleasant to sit in during the cool of morning and evening, it can be explored rather quickly and once more I had time on my hands. I walked to the gate that now stood open, and looked out.

What a lively scene the street offered! Drays and carriages, handcarts and brightly dressed colored women with baskets on their heads, all mingled in the gaudy, noisy excitement of Chartres Street. With the morning sun still low in the sky, the narrow streets of the Quarter were still shady and reasonably cool. I was strongly tempted to walk through the Tourneau gate and go my own way, exploring as I pleased. But this was my first day in New Orleans and I decided reluctantly that I had better be on my best behavior.

Only our meals broke the monotony of the long hot day. The dinner meal at noonday was pleasant and leisurely. Uncle Robert had gone to the courthouse and was dining out, so my mother came to the table. At supper that night, however, she pleaded a headache and did not appear.

In the evening Uncle Robert was no longer preoccupied, but pleased with the way his affairs had gone that day. A case had been concluded and won, and as a consequence he was relaxed, his conversation rapier-quick and stimulating. Even small Caro, who sat erect at the table on a backless stool, to teach her spine good habits, listened with respectful attention.

The dining room had great charm and grace in my eyes that night. It was high-ceilinged and spacious, with the usual elaborate plaster rosette, from the center of which hung a glittering chandelier, dripping with crystal and ashine with lighted candles. We dined entirely by candlelight— branched candelabrum on the high sideboard, and more silver candlesticks on the table. The silver tureen which held the gumbo of shrimp and okra and tomato, reflected myriad lights in its gleaming surface.

My uncle considered gas an unpleasant light and would not have it used except in his office and in the courtyard. So oil lamps and candles were still in use throughout the house.

Closed shutters had sheltered the rooms all day and now cool air from the courtyard stirred pleasantly through the rooms. I could feel its breath on my cheeks and around my ankles. Again there were no draperies, no rugs, but only matting on the floor. Aunt Natalie explained that it was the custom to strip the rooms for summertime living, and thus keep them refreshingly cool. During the winter rugs would be put down right over the matting. Only in his study did my uncle refuse to give up the luxury of rugs and draperies. But Uncle Robert never minded the heat. He preferred it any time, he said, to the damp cold of winter.

The meal had come nearly to an end when there was an unexpected interruption. Delphine slipped quietly into the room and stood at Uncle Robert's elbow. He looked up at her, nodding permission for her to speak.

"It is M'sieu Courtney. He has returned from his mother's house and is most *distrait*. He wishes to see you at once, m'sieu."

Uncle Robert did not look altogether pleased. "We do not interrupt a meal with unpleasantness. Surely his affairs will keep. Show the boy upstairs and have a place set for him. He can join us for dessert, and we will talk later."

Delphine hesitated as if she wanted to say more. Then she bowed her head and went away. Courtney came running upstairs before a place had been set, and while he restrained himself with an effort and managed to walk into the room at a decorous pace, it was plain that he was upset.

He murmured his apologies to Aunt Natalie, Caro and me, and went straight to the head of the table to speak to my uncle. He did not seem to see the long-fingered hand Uncle Robert raised to stop him, but burst at once into words.

"Forgive me, m'sieu. It is most urgent. My mother has sent me here. It concerns my brother Justin. He has returned to New Orleans. Indeed, m'sieu, he has moved into our house today, though my mother has no wish to have him there."

I looked at Uncle Robert and saw that this news, whatever it signified, was of concern to him too. His lips tightened into a thin line and, pushing his serviette aside, he rose from the table.

"You will excuse me, madame?" he said to his wife, bowed courteously to me and to his small daughter, then led Courtney from the room. They went into the study at the front of the house, and beyond the curtains which divided study and dining room, I heard the double doors being closed.

Aunt Natalie sighed and spooned her blancmange. "What a shame that Courtney could not allow my husband to finish his dinner in peace. I'm sure I don't know what this can be about. The brother has been away from New Orleans for many years."

Caro, released from the restraint of her father's presence, bounced on her stool. "He has been in prison, Maman! He is the one who is a murderer, is he not?"

Aunt Natalie shook her head in reproof. "You must not say such violent things, Caroline. These are not matters for the attention of a *jeune fille.*"

"But once I heard Papa tell you that this man has a—a criminal record," said Caro, with a bird-quick glance at me to make sure I was impressed with her knowledge. "So what can he be but a thief or a murderer?"

"Voilà tout!" cried Aunt Natalie. "Not another word!" She clasped her hands in a despairing gesture and rolled her eyes heavenward. "Until you have the years to be sensible, you must not listen to adult conversation."

Caro subsided and gave her attention to her dessert. But her bright dark eyes continued to watch me across the table, to see how I responded to her startling information.

Aunt Natalie went on calmly. "Poor Aurore, Courtney's mother, will be most disturbed. What happened long ago was very sad for her, and this will bring it all back. At the beginning of the war Harry Law, her husband, fled from the South. Aurore is a second cousin of my husband and if it had not been for Robert's quick action, Harry might have been put in prison here, perhaps shot as a spy. For Aurore's sake, Robert helped him to escape—though of course this was not known except by members of the family. It entailed much risk for Robert."

"So Aurore was left with two children to raise by herself?" I asked.

"No—one child only. Justin is seven years older than Courtney—he was about ten or eleven at the time—and he chose to go with his father. Harry Law died some years later, far away in Colorado. The older son has never returned to New Orleans until now. After this long abandonment and with the poor reputation he has gained for himself, his presence will hardly be welcome to Aurore and Courtney."

Uncle Robert and Courtney returned to the table just then, and the young man was prevailed upon to sit down and join us in dessert. My uncle took only coffee. He was plainly shaken. His lips were pressed tight at the corners and once his cup clattered in the saucer as he set it down. What had happened that could so disturb a man like Robert Tourneau? I wondered.

Courtney at length roused himself and turned to me with the same attentive manner I had noted before. He was, he said, looking forward to escorting me about the Vieux Carré Sunday afternoon. I told him how happy I'd be to go, and our words broke the strained silence that had settled upon the table. While we finished our meal, Aunt Natalie, Courtney and I talked idly of unimportant matters. My uncle, darkly preoccupied with his own thoughts, made no effort to join in.

Viewed across the table, Courtney Law seemed even better-looking than I had thought him before. On the walls of this very room were several family portraits and I had observed that the women were extraordinarily beautiful, the men handsome in a way not at all like the more rugged good looks of northern men. Courtney bore a strong resemblance to these gently distinguished Creole portraits. His manners were charming and courteous. He could pay every lady, including young Caro, quick compliments that carried the ring of sincerity. His respect and admiration for my uncle was evident in every look he turned Uncle Robert's way, and I liked that in him. He was an altogether admirable and attractive young man and I could look forward to going out with him.

When the meal ended and Courtney went downstairs, Delphine returned to the dining room just as the rest of us were leaving. She spoke softly, urgently to Uncle Robert and I caught a phrase or two.

"It is true indeed that he is back, m'sieu . . . a great brute of a man . . . uncouth, rude . . . the yellow hair of the barbarian."

I was curious about all this, but I could not very well linger in order to listen. Once more I went to my room to consider my meager wardrobe. Never wanting to seem in competition with my mother, I had not troubled much about clothes in the past. My single white muslin might be suitable for the Sunday drive with Courtney, but it was old-fashioned in style, with no bustle and too much fullness in the hemline. But it would have to do, since it was at least better than the brown foulard.

While I was considering the possibility of a bit of ribbon to trim the frock's plainness, Mama came tapping on my door and I invited her in. It was her first visit to my room, but she hardly looked about as she sat down in the little rocker.

"Robert's doctor came to see Bruce this afternoon and Robert came with him." She sighed and fell silent.

I tossed aside the bands of green ribbon I'd been toying with. "What did the doctor say?"

Mama shrugged. "Nothing. He shook his head like a black raven and looked lugubrious. I think his visit did your father little good. If anything, those two made him feel more helpless than before."

"Perhaps one of us should be with him now—" I began.

"He wants no one," Mama said. "He is sunk in apathy and wants only to be left alone. There seems no way to reach him."

She gave me a quick, frightened look and I felt sorry for her. Always she had relied upon her husband for guidance, trusted his judgment. Even when she flouted it at times, she always ended by doing whatever Papa wished. Now her small bark was without a rudder.

"We mustn't worry," I told her gently. "We must give him time to recover from the trip, accustom himself to a new setting."

My mother twisted her hands together. "But there is no time! Skye, what is to become of us?"

"It seems to me that we're very lucky," I pointed out. "Uncle Robert has made us welcome in his home and I'm sure he will do everything he can for Papa. There's nothing to be concerned about."

"You don't know Robert! If the whim should move him he would turn us out with never a qualm. He has always disliked me. I have no reason to think he has changed now."

I felt she was biased in her judgment and being exceedingly unfair. She was so quick to distrust anyone who did not spoil and flatter her that I could not credit her fears. Uncle Robert had shown that he was ready to like me, and that he would be content to have us here for as long as we chose to stay. But there was no use in arguing this with my mother.

"If only Bruce would write again!" Mama went on. "But he won't even look at a book. Sometimes I think he has turned against me. Perhaps he blames me for his fall."

"That would never be his way," I told her quickly. "Perhaps you blame yourself."

But she would not be cornered into such an admission. She roused herself and moved about the room, looking at its furnishings for the first time. My dressing table caught her attention and she went over to examine it more closely.

"Skye, this palisander dressing table is the very one I used in this house as a little girl! It was a gift from my father that I prized a great deal. He was a true connoisseur of the beautiful and many of the things he purchased are to be seen in this house. Natalie says that Robert continues the tradition. Though in a different way. As impoverished

38

families move from the Quarter and are forced to sell their treasures, Robert buys them up."

She made a little face at the thought and stroked her fingers gently over the cool marble, touched the carving of the rosewood frame that held the mirror. I could well imagine her as a girl sitting before this dressing table, studying her own reflected image as I had studied mine. Momentarily the years between us fell away and I touched her hand lightly.

"Let's ask Delphine if it can be moved into your room," I said. "If it will give you pleasure—"

She shook her head quickly. "No! I don't want to remember." Then she bent toward the glass and stared at her image, suddenly startled and disbelieving. "How dreadfully old I have become. Those puffs under my eyes—and there are a hundred new lines!"

"That's nonsense," I assured her. "You've only to get enough sleep and dress yourself and you'll be as beautiful as ever. It's not so easy for me. I haven't your gifts to start with. I'm to go driving with Courtney Law Sunday afternoon, and this is all I have to wear."

She turned in distaste from the telltale mirror. "That's right. He's to show you the Vieux Carré, is he not? She picked up the plain muslin dress and looked at it with a practical eye. "It isn't too bad. Not fashionable, perhaps, but the straight lines of the bodice suit you. No ribbon though. You are not the type for ribbon, as I am. If only you would do something more interesting with your hair."

I didn't want to change my hair. It was as I chose to wear it because severity at least minimized its dreadful color.

"Don't worry about me. This drive is of no importance anyway," I said, not wanting her to suspect that I'd begun to look forward to it a little. "After all, this young man is merely taking me for a drive because Uncle Robert wishes him to be courteous."

She nodded thoughtfully, turning the dress about in her hands. "Yes, that is plain. In fact Robert dropped a word or two to me. This Courtney Law—he comes in part from a good family, in spite of the bad blood on the Law side. Aurore is a LeMaitre—an excellent Creole family. And Harry Law brought considerable wealth to the marriage."

I stared at her. "What are you implying?"

"Of course!" she cried and dropped once more into the rocker. By this time something of her natural gaiety had returned and she clapped her hands like a delighted child. "Now I see what my brother intends! If you can find a husband of wealth, Skye, all our problems will be solved and we needn't be dependent upon Robert. Leave it to him to think of that!"

How exasperating she could be! This notion, I knew, had come to her on the inspiration of the moment, yet she would now twist and turn and try to make me believe it was my uncle's wish. Whatever happened, I did not mean to have her thrust me into a loveless marriage. Nor did I mean to let her blame Uncle Robert for the plans I knew were suddenly running through her clever little head. How I felt about Courtney I could not possibly know as yet, nor how he might come to feel about me. This was something which must be allowed its own course and not be bruised by hasty, clumsy hands.

But Mama had the bit between her teeth and she was running on, enchanted by her own notion.

"Listen to me, Skye! Harry Law built Aurore a home in the Garden District—very large and beautiful. I have danced at balls there as a girl. Harry was an American and he would have invested his money well."

There was no stopping her, and I contained my irritation. "I understand that Harry abandoned his wife and never came back," I pointed out. "Perhaps he took his money with him."

"He went away only to save his life," Mama said. "And obviously, since Aurore still keeps up the house in the Garden District, he left her well off. In any event, Courtney must have inherited part of his father's wealth."

I climbed up the little stepladder and plumped myself down in the middle of the bed. "You're building castles of mist. When they blow away you'll have nothing at all."

"But I tell you," Mama cried in true Creole excitement, "I remember them together—Harry and Aurore. I never understood what men could see in her, and of course she was older than I—but it was a case of true love. Harry would have cared for her well. After all, did he not take her away from my brother Robert?"

This caught my attention. "You mean Uncle Robert was interested in Courtney's mother?"

"Interested? They were affianced! All the wedding plans were made. When the American took her right out from under Robert's nose, it was the great *scandale* of the season."

This was a new glimpse of my uncle and I winced at thought of the pain he must have suffered. No wonder he had not married as a young man. It must have taken him a long while to recover from such a blow. Now I could admire him all the more for his forgiveness of Aurore and his kindness to the young man who was her son. I tried to put my thought into words.

"At least it's to Uncle Robert's credit that he has held no grudge, has even been generous enough to give Courtney a place in his office. A man must be big to forgive so magnanimously."

"Robert never forgives anyone for anything," Mama said and all her spite toward her brother seemed to ring in her words.

But I remembered the portrait of a lovely young girl which hung on the wall of my uncle's office and knew that more sentiment could move him than my mother dreamed. Was that portrait the Aurore LeMaitre of long ago? Mama's rancor against Uncle Robert colored all her thinking toward him. She would never see him in a favorable light. My sympathy lay with him—this man who had lost his love to another, and who was our friend. Our only friend.

"Anyway all this past history doesn't matter now," I said. "Courtney is a pleasant young man and I shall go driving with him, well chaperoned. But he is not likely to be interested in me with so many Creole beauties around. Or I in him for that matter." Which, I felt, should make my position clear and conceal any mild interest that might be stirring in me.

My mother left her chair and walked thoughtfully to the door. "Perhaps I should go with you, after all. Perhaps I can do more for you than you are willing to do for yourself."

I held my breath and waited. If I opposed her, she would surely come, for she could never bear to have anyone tell her no. But as I watched her face, despair came into it again and I knew she was thinking of my father. Whether or not I found a wealthy husband would not help her if she could not rouse Papa again to some interest in life.

She shook her head sadly. "I don't want to leave your father. Nor do I want to see the Vieux Carré until I feel stronger. There is too much to remember."

So I was safe for the moment from her interference. When she left my room I began to plan for Sunday by myself, mightily relieved.

Five ❦

When the day came it was bright and warm, a lovely afternoon for a drive. Mama took a special interest in my appearance and I knew she was still thinking in terms of a wealthy husband who was to save us all from want. I didn't argue with her, but quietly went my own way. Courtney, if he were to like me, would have to like me as I was. This, at least, I had clarified to myself in the intervening hours.

Courtney's arrival was prompt and Delphine came with us in the carriage, wearing one of those blue dresses, freshly laundered and starched, that seemed to be her uniform. Her tignon, bound neatly over its high, concealed comb, gave her the air of one wearing a crown.

Courtney handed me into the carriage and opened for me the little white parasol I'd borrowed from Mama. He looked quite the dandy this afternoon in his light gray trousers, gray vest and darker gray coat. His top hat was of fine Parisian felt and he doffed it gracefully.

"White becomes you, mam'zelle," he said as he sat beside me in the carriage.

Delphine took the drop seat, and seemed to see and hear nothing. Courtney paid no attention to her after a first greeting and talked as though she were not there at all. I, however, could not forget her, sitting opposite us, straight and remote, her skin like pale gold in the sunlight. She was, I felt sure, missing nothing, for all that she looked past us and seemed not to attend what we were saying.

My mother's words about marriage had taken a little of the edge off my pleasure in the day. I liked Courtney and could not help but respond to his attentive gallantry, as any woman would. But I wanted our friendship to grow naturally and my mother's words had made me self-conscious. However, as the carriage rolled along the busy street, I began to have a sense of release, almost of escape. Even in these few days my bonds had begun to chafe and I found it pleasant, though a little unsettling, to be taking the air in the company of so personable a young man.

There is something naturally ardent about the eyes of the Creole. I had noted the same warmth of expression in portraits on the walls of my uncle's house. One had the feeling that with these men love was the business of the day and that they enjoyed nothing more than playing a romantic role. Courtney was no exception.

He did not forget that he was taking me on a tour of the Vieux Carré, but he made it clear that even as he spoke of the scenes about us, he looked upon me as a man does upon an attractive woman. When I spoke, his eyes followed the movement of my lips and my hands with an air of being entranced. It was an air to which I was unaccustomed and I had none of my mother's skill in fluttering withdrawal or provoking advance. He went too fast for me. Disconcerted, I fixed my attention upon the scene outside the carriage and tried not to meet Courtney's interested gaze. I did not know him yet, and I meant to have no more of falling in love without some assurance first that the man was worth loving.

Fortunately for my equanimity, the passing scene was intensely interesting. The Vieux Carré, I found to my surprise, was open for business on Sunday. On every hand vendors paraded the walks, calling their wares in French, or in that strange mixed patois I did not understand. Their musical calls mingled with the sound of horses' hooves, the jouncing of wheels over pavement, the shouts of teamsters.

As we drove past the tightly set little houses, with their square façades, I found more interest in them by day than in my previous glimpse at night. They were bright in the sunlight—pale pink and cream, light blue, sometimes gray or green, seldom white. Often the colors added up to a warm mixture that had no name, but which must result from the gentle weathering of the seasons. Except when a house was the French type of cottage, there were always balconies of green or black iron, and the delicate cast-iron lacework gave the flat little buildings an air of grace and distinction. Mama had told me that the handwrought iron of LaFitte's day was growing rare. But to my eyes the cast iron seemed equally beautiful.

I tried to look up and forget the open gutters that ran beside every walk. They had been sluiced down this morning, and apparently sun and wind helped as scavengers, for the odors seemed less offensive.

Courtney set himself to interest and entertain me, but I

43

soon became aware that in spite of his surface attention, something in him was withdrawn and there was a preoccupation behind his words. Realizing this I relaxed and paid heed to the scene about me.

The squares we traversed—for they were squares in New Orleans, not blocks—had, he explained, really been little islands in the early days, surrounded as often as not by water. Early settlers had called the paths along these *ilets* banquettes, and thus the sidewalks of New Orleans were still named. This end of Chartres Street was the more elegant, he assured me. Toward Canal it was like Royal Street, almost wholly a commercial thoroughfare.

"Your Tante Natalie would prefer a house on the more fashionable Esplanade, but M'sieu Robert's home was built long ago by the Tourneaus and he would as soon think of cutting off a hand as of moving elsewhere. Your uncle, mam'zelle, has great pride of family."

"You think a great deal of Uncle Robert, don't you?" I asked.

He nodded gravely. "We owe him much, my mother and I. You have heard, perhaps, the story of my father?"

"A little of it," I admitted.

His eyes darkened. "It is no secret, mam'zelle. Had it not been for M'sieu Robert we would have faced great disgrace. I don't know what my mother would have done had her husband been shot as a spy."

It occurred to me that this might have been rather hard on Harry Law too, but I did not say so.

"Like others," Courtney continued, "we invested in Confederate bonds during the war. Afterwards, when they became worthless, we had little left. Had it not been for your uncle, who felt the responsibility of the family tie, we might have fared badly." He spoke rather stiffly now, like a man who wanted the facts to be made quite clear, yet endeavored to retain his personal pride in spite of the existing truth.

I nodded sympathetically, but could not help smiling to myself. What a blow this would be for Mama's clever plans! To find that Courtney Law, after all, would not make me a wealthy husband. And how it showed up her pretense that this idea stemmed from my uncle, who of course knew that Courtney was no catch, financially speaking. Released from the possibility of being pushed into his arms, I could feel more comfortable, more natural with him. Courtney and I were both poverty-stricken. We could like each other for ourselves alone, and already I was liking him.

"Perhaps now that your brother has returned to New Orleans," I said casually, "some of the burden will be eased for your mother."

"We want nothing from that one!" Courtney said sharply. "The only time my mother wrote to ask for help after the war, we were refused on the pretense that my father had nothing. He even asked impertinent questions. When he died we learned about it only in a roundabout way. Yet now Justin returns to town as the owner of a fabulous Leadville silver mine and has the effrontery to move into our house as though it were his own!"

"If your mother doesn't want him in the house, can't she ask him to leave?" I inquired.

"She did so at once. I, too, have requested him to leave the house. But in his uncouth way he has laughed at us and invited us to put him out if we wish him to go. He speaks much nonsense about finding his roots. As if such as he could ever have roots in our soil!"

Courtney looked at his hands—the long-fingered hands of a gentleman; uncalloused hands which might hold the reins of a horse, but would never be used for physical violence. I could hardly see Courtney putting his brother forcibly from the house.

"Last night," Courtney went on, "this man came to the gaming tables at L'Oiseau d'Or here in the Vieux Carré, and threw down his money as if he scattered pebbles on a beach. I saw with my own eyes the fantastic winnings he made, while the rest of us lost. Madame Pollock, who is the proprietress of the establishment, finally requested him to leave."

"And did he?"

"In his own good time he gathered up his winnings and went out, laughing at us."

A picture of this barbarian from the West was beginning to take form in my mind. An uncouth blond giant, wealthy and ruthless. A man whose appearance in town had somehow shaken Uncle Robert as I would not have believed possible. The picture made me curious and I wondered when I would have a chance to see this man for myself.

Courtney had fallen silent, unhappy in his own thoughts. I stole a look at Delphine, but she sat like a statue opposite us. Quite clearly she was there to lend propriety to the occasion and nothing more. But I was not deceived. I knew how watchful she could be, how little she missed. Probably she was tucking away our entire conversation in order to report it to Uncle Robert later. It would be just as well to get away from the subject of Justin Law, which so disturbed my uncle.

I remarked on an old building we were passing. Windows with heavy cypress blinds were set deep in thick walls and the patina of soft gray age lay upon it.

Courtney made an effort to throw off his gloomy thoughts. "That was formerly the convent of the Ursuline nuns. It is one of the oldest buildings in New Orleans. Forgive me, mam'zelle, for intruding my personal problems. It was my intention to make the afternoon interesting for you." Now his eyes rested on me again in a way that was bold and warm, and not unpleasing.

"I'm enjoying every moment of it," I told him quickly. And added, with a sly look at Delphine, "In the North I've been accustomed to walk about as I please. Here I find that Creole life is likely to imprison a woman."

Courtney frowned at the thought of my wandering the streets of the Vieux Carré alone. "*Jamais*, mam'zelle. Never must you walk about alone. The French Quarter has grown increasingly rough since the war. It returns a little to the wildness of the early days. Never would it be advisable for a young lady of good family to venture out alone. You might well be insulted. So many of *les bonnes familles* have moved away. The section is filled with too much of what the Americans call riffraff."

I could hardly take his words seriously. The teeming streets about us seemed too busy to be anything but safe. And it was clear that many of the *gentils* mixed with the variegated throng. But my attention had been caught by a term I had heard used strangely since coming to New Orleans.

"Why do you say 'Americans,' as if you were not one of us?"

"It is a term we have grown accustomed to." Courtney's shrug was expressive. "We mean, I suppose, strangers from other states. Particularly Northerners. The Creole has never resigned himself to being anything but French and Spanish."

Apparently Courtney ignored his own American blood and considered himself wholly Creole. And I, of course, due to my upbringing, would be considered wholly American.

We drove past the beautiful St. Louis Cathedral, flanked by the old buildings of the Presbytère and the Cabildo, and Courtney told me they had been built long ago by the wealthy Dan Almonaster upon the smouldering ruins of the French city.

46

Across Chartres Street was Jackson Square—once the old Place d'Armes of New Orleans. And stretching along each side of the Square, Courtney explained eagerly, were the most romantic buildings of all. The Pontalba apartments, which had been built by Micaela Almonaster de Pontalba, Don Almonaster's colorful daughter.

Courtney glanced at me slyly and then away. "In a certain manner you remind me of Micaela. But naturally a young woman like yourself would not be interested in that lady's unconventional history."

Of course this interested me at once and I urged him to explain. He told me she she had lived a dramatic and extravagant life abroad for many years, and when she returned to New Orleans in 1848 she had been dismayed to find business moving away from the French Quarter and too many Creole families leaving the section. The Baroness had thrown her great wealth into plans for beautifying Jackson Square and building these apartments on either side along St. Ann and St. Peter Streets. Their construction was inspired by the Palais Royal buildings in Paris, and she intended them to support the architecturally beautiful buildings her father had erected.

Courtney shook his head sadly. "For a time some of the best Creole families lived in the apartments, and some still do. But sections have been sold to outsiders and are falling into neglect and disrepair. It is to be regretted."

"But why do I remind you of Micaela?" I asked, still tantalized.

He bent toward me, his eyes warm, laughing. "One day perhaps I shall tell you, mam'zelle. But it will be on a day when you do not wear a hat."

Delphine moved, coughed faintly and I glanced at her quickly, found her look upon me in a strange appraising way. But her eyes evaded mine and I knew there was some undercurrent here I did not understand. And I could not coquette with Courtney by coaxing him to explain.

We drove on around the Square and then turned back toward home. To my disappointment the river was hidden from view by the levee and the dock sheds. Over the sheds rose the masts of ships, well above the town. I determined that one of these days I must walk up there and have a look at the river.

Courtney asked a few polite questions about the North and I tried to give him a picture of the little New England town in which I had grown up. I felt as I talked, however, that my words interested him little and that his attention was given to watching me, rather than listening to what I said. And I could not tell whether the afternoon had been a success or not. I wanted this young man to like me, wanted to like him, but we belonged to different worlds and we had not yet found the way to bridge the gap of strangeness between us.

When we reached the Tourneau house, Courtney helped me out, bowed over my hand most courteously, and thanked me for the afternoon. Nevertheless, I sensed a disappointment in him. For that reason I was all the more surprised when he spoke again just before I went through the gate.

"My mother has been most interested in hearing of your visit to New Orleans," he said. "She would like me to bring you to call on her, if you care to do so."

"Of course," I said. "I'd love to visit her." And I tried to smile at him warmly to make up for the lack he might have felt in me.

When I went upstairs to my room, Mama was waiting at the door to pounce upon me.

"Tell me all about your drive!" she cried. "How did you like the young man?"

"I like him very well," I told her coolly. "But you might as well know that neither he nor his mother have the wealth you imagined. All that was lost during the war."

Mama regarded me in dismay. "Ah, the war, the war!" she murmured.

I knew she felt she had been robbed anew through the wickedness of the North.

"But then," she went on, half to herself, "I cannot understand why Robert—"

I spoke impatiently. "You're mistaken in thinking Uncle Robert had any special intention behind throwing Courtney and me together. This was your idea, not his."

But never would she admit being caught in one of her little fabrications. She shrugged as if the matter were of no consequence and went out of my room.

Six ❄

On Monday morning, after breakfast, Aunt Natalie said she would be happy to have my company on a trip to market, if I cared to come with her. I was only too eager for further exploration of the Vieux Carrè. Especially when I learned that Aunt Natalie liked to make her market trips afoot, accompanied by Delphine.

I wore again my old brown foulard and was glad enough to put on my brown hat in order to hide my hair from the stares of New Orleans.

Again the streets teemed with an activity one hardly dreamed of from the seclusion of hidden courtyards. Delphine walked behind us, decorously carrying a large reed basket, and my aunt paid her no attention. Once, when I stole a backward look, I saw that the woman walked as proudly as though she led a procession and she seemed to have only scorn for lesser colored folk whom we passed along the way. I found myself wondering what report she might have given Uncle Robert about my drive with Courtney yesterday.

When we reached Jackson Square, we turned toward the river, walking beside the high iron fence that surrounded the Square. I could glimpse tropical foliage within and walks with inviting benches. When I had persuaded the Tourneaus to permit me out alone, I would come here and explore the Square, sit in the sunshine on one of those benches. I knew from my mother's tales that this had been the old Place d'Armes of history. New Orleans had changed flags several times on this ground.

But now Aunt Natalie led the way toward the somewhat tumbled-down sheds of the old French Market on ahead. It was necessary, she pointed out, to make the most of the cool of the morning. The day already promised to be sultry and warm.

To me the market was a delight. Its stands of brilliant flowers and exotic foodstuffs offered rich color on every

49

hand. There were bright piles of pomegranites, golden mangoes, bananas both red and yellow, with the contrasting hues of vegetables in stalls next to them. There were odors too—of fish and spices and coffee, and the ever-present dankish smell of the great river. Everywhere women were doing their early morning shopping and there was much good-natured arguing and bargaining going on all around us. Parrots squawked in their cages, chickens clucked. Piles of crabs crawled upon one another, waving their claws aloft. In the street wagons clattered by and drivers shouted. It was a place that teemed with life and excitement. I had been shut in long enough to respond to it eagerly.

Aunt Natalie attended at once to the serious business in hand. She pursed her plump mouth as she concentrated on a basketful of strangely shaped squashes, then spoke rapidly in French to the vendor. At length a selection was deposited in Delphine's capacious basket, and we went on. Often she consulted the colored woman, whose judgment she clearly relied upon. On occasion she turned aside to indulge in a friendly exchange of talk with ladies of her acquaintance.

Shopping, it appeared, was to be a lengthy affair and the market beckoned me to explore further. Gradually I let distance grow between Aunt Natalie, Delphine and me, so that I could wander more freely. I watched the Indian squaws who sat on blankets selling powdered filé—ground-up bay leaves, sassafras roots and goodness knows what, for the making of gumbo filé. A woman nearby noted me as a stranger and explained what it was.

Twice I circled the long arcaded market, with its slate roof slanting shedlike over the flagstone banquettes. During that time Aunt Natalie and Delphine moved no more than three stalls. Now they were studying the comparative excellence of tiny river shrimp. Did not Delphine agree that these would be delectable for gumbo? Delphine agreed solemnly and I found myself smiling. I lacked, I fear, the patience to move so slowly when it came to filling a market basket. I would have bought eagerly from all that was luscious and appetizing, figuring out later what to do with my booty. But that was hardly the housewifely Creole way.

Since my two chaperones paid little attention to me, letting me wander as I pleased, I took the opportunity to leave the market shed at the far end and walked toward the opening of a narrow street that beckoned me with its strangeness. Other streets of the Quarter buzzed with the sounds of men and women going about the business of the day. There was laughter, the chatter of voices, the echo of horses' hooves. But this short, narrow street seemed empty and deserted. Even in the sunlight there was something hushed and guarded about it.

Curious to know its secret, I stepped on the flagstones laid across an open gutter and followed the banquette past tightly closed shutters and archways that seemed like dark caves. Here the glimpsed courtyards were neglected and weed-grown. The faint air of decay that haunted the entire Quarter gave way to signs of real dilapidation. Here a shutter hung awry, there a wall crumbled to ruin. Why? I wondered. What sickness ailed this street? Why should it stand deserted, while others rushed with life? Where were its inmates on this bright and golden morning?

As I walked along I was startled by a sound like a muffled scream in one of the houses. It was choked off so quickly, however, that I could not be sure I had heard it and blamed an uneasy imagination. I had begun to feel that so secretive a street must hide some great iniquity.

Halfway along the square I became suddenly aware that a man was watching me. I had not seen him because he leaned against a wall, half hidden in the shadow of an arch. The broad hatbrim pulled over his eyes hid his face and he puffed lazily at a cigarette. When I came opposite him, he pushed the hat carelessly back on his forehead, the better to stare at me, and in the brief glance I gave him I saw that he looked for some reason amused.

Since I was well within sight and hearing of the bustling market, I refused to be made nervous by a stranger who stared at me in bold insolence. Giving him not another glance, I wandered on, looking about me with what I hoped was the air of a lady at ease and idly curious about her surroundings. Probably it was my hair again which attracted attention. I was accustomed to amusement from those who knew no better, and it was likely that such a deviation from the normal would be all the more noticed in brunette New Orleans. I would, I decided, walk to the end of the square, then return to the market at a leisurely pace. I would not under any circumstance notice the rude fellow who watched me.

The street retained its secretive quiet until I had reached the curb at the end of the square, and turned to retrace my steps. Then a green-shuttered door on my side of the street was thrust open and a man stumbled down the two steps to the street. He was red-faced and disheveled. By his

garb and the tattooing on his arms, I knew him for a seaman. The reek of alcohol was evident even from where I
stood. I expected him to reel out of my way across the street
in the same direction in which he was headed.

Unfortunately, however, I was close enough to catch his
attention and he saw me and spat out a stream of unclean
words. Before I could cross the street, he stumbled toward
me and reached out a hand to catch my arm. I turned to
escape his filthy grasp, stumbled on the rough banquette
and fell to my knees. His fingers closed upon the ribbons
of my hat. He pulled it from my head with a cry of glee and
tossed it into the gutter. Then he reached for me again.

In my fright, I did not know that the man across the
street had intervened until he caught my assailant by the
scruff of the neck and wrenched him away from me. Moving
as calmly as though he brushed at a fly, he pushed one big
hand into the seaman's face and sent him sprawling across
the deep gutter. In the next moment I felt myself lifted in
two strong arms. My rescuer's face was very close to mine
and for one strange instant I looked up into eyes intensely
blue and felt in me a sudden sense of destiny. To love, or
to hate—one or the other. No woman could ever be indifferent to such a man.

Then he set me upon my feet, removed his hat and
bowed to me politely, though I sensed a hint of laughter
beneath his courtesy. He was unbelievably tall and broad
of shoulders—a giant of a fellow. And in this town of dark-
haired men and women, he had a curly thatch of yellow
hair, thick and shining in the sun. His chin, I thought, was
made of iron, and there was a straight hard look to his
mouth, despite the grin that lifted one corner. The words
"blond barbarian" rang in my mind and I wondered if this
was the man of whom I had heard so much—Justin Law,
the brother of Courtney.

"Did he hurt you?" he asked curtly.

"He—he just frightened me," I faltered. I could feel my
hair slipping over my shoulders and with hands that still
betrayed me by shaking, I tried to gather it up, thrust back
its pins and regain some semblance of dignity. My rescuer
regarded me with bold eyes which paid me no pretty compliments, but made me aware that I was a woman.

"What do you expect if you walk on Gallatin Street?"
he asked. "It's a good thing most of its denizens sleep by
day and prowl by night."

"I—I don't know anything about the street," I admitted,

wondering why I should trouble to apologize for my presence.

He turned his back on me and walked to the banquette's edge where the seaman sprawled half into the gutter, and hauled the fellow out.

"Be on your way," he said. "You've had worse tumbles than this one."

The sailor took the opportunity to get out of reach as quickly as possible. My rescuer stared ruefully into the gutter.

"If you wish," he said over his shoulder to me, "I can fish out your bonnet. But I doubt that you'll care to wear it again."

I shuddered. "Please let it go. It was an—an old one anyway. And thank you for coming to my aid." I turned to walk away. For some reason I had an impulse to flight. It was as if some instinct told me that if I stayed within reach of this man I was lost. But I had no choice for he came with me.

"I'll see you back to the market—if that's where you've wandered from," he told me. He did not offer his arm as a gentleman like Courtney would have done, nor did he pay the slightest attention to my protest that I could certainly walk that distance alone.

He strode beside me in silence and I was sharply aware of the force and strength of the man. One could sense the vibrant life that flowed into his walk, into the vigorous swing of his long arms. If this was Justin Law, then I knew neither Courtney nor Uncle Robert would approve of my being in his company, yet I could do nothing but go with him.

Not until I saw Delphine coming toward us from the opening to the street did I think of the explanations I must now make. Delphine's face registered thorough disapproval. My Aunt Natalie was a kindly soul and her displeasure would not last long. But there was something formidable about Delphine. She had left her market basket behind and her hands were crossed severely at her waist. The guinea-blue dress swished about her feet with the firmness of her steps. A few yards away she stopped, waiting for me to reach her, as a nurse might wait for a truant child. The pause gave her still greater advantage and made me feel a suppliant for forgiveness.

"Well!" said the man beside me. "This is an interesting turn of events. You have a duenna of some note, it seems."

I saw then that Delphine was paying no further attention to me, the real culprit. Her eyes, as close to black as any

53

eyes can be, were fixed coldly upon my escort, whom she had undoubtedly recognized.

"As I live and breathe it's Delphine!" he said as we reached her. "I don't suppose you'll remember me, since I must have been about ten years old the last time you saw me. But I've not forgotten you—and I'd say you're not a day older."

She looked at him stonily. "Nineteen years have passed, m'sieu, but I do not forget your face. Come, Mam'zelle Skye, your aunt concerns herself with your absence. Good day, m'sieu."

He fell back then, beaten at last, and I could hardly resist the impulse to turn my head and look back at him. Only Delphine's presence saved me from so weak a gesture. As I walked back to the market with the tall, silent colored woman following me, I felt as cowed as a guilty child.

She did not speak until we were across the busy street that ran beside the market. Then she murmured, as if to herself, "It is a black wind that blows that one back to town."

"Is that Justin Law?" I asked. "He spoke as if he had lived in New Orleans, but he certainly hasn't the appearance of a Creole."

She seemed lost in her own thoughts, so she did not hear me. Which was not, of course, so discourteous as deliberately not answering.

Aunt Natalie stood at the curb with her basket at her feet, watching our approach anxiously.

"My dear child!" she cried as we reached her. "But how disarrayed you are! And where is your hat? What can have happened?"

I explained quickly that a drunken sailor had snatched my hat from my head and I'd had difficulty escaping him. I said nothing about my rescuer, waiting to see what Delphine might offer. But Delphine had picked up the basket again, now overflowing with foodstuffs. As we turned toward Chartres Street she followed us in regal silence. As I realized later it was not to Aunt Natalie that she felt it her duty to report my conduct and my encounter with that vigorous, golden-haired giant of a fellow.

My aunt chattered despairingly as we walked. "My child, never must you wander off like that again. I thought you safely in the market. Gallatin Street is a place of great wickedness. Men have been murdered there. And of course no woman is safe amid such evil, even in the daytime."

I had no desire to visit Gallatin Street again, but I found

myself wondering what *he* had been doing there—lounging in that archway with a devil of amusement in his eyes. Already I was beginning to think of the answers I might have given him, of how I might have put him in his place. It was regrettable that the right words all suggested themselves too late.

When we reached home I went to my room to restore both my appearance and my equanimity. The dust of the town could be washed from my face and I could comb my hair back smoothly. But somehow I could not brush away the feeling of strong hands lifting me from my knees, could not escape my remembrance of how brightly blue his eyes had been. How brightly mocking! I was angry again at the mockery, so that my cheeks flushed and my breath came quickly.

I wished I might go to my father's room and tell him about the encounter. But Papa and I were no longer close, as once we had been. He might be disturbed by what had happened and he was no longer the one to whom I could turn when my thoughts churned with confusion.

Could I talk to Uncle Robert? I wondered. I did not know him well, it was true, but he had been kindly and sympathetic on the occasions when we had spoken together. At that moment I had a longing and need for fatherly council.

However, at the noon meal that day Uncle Robert was preoccupied with his business affairs and the burden of conversation was carried lightly by Aunt Natalie, who talked to us about Tina, the baby, and by my mother, who had at last roused herself enough to come to the table. Immediately after the meal my uncle went off to court and there was no opportunity to talk to him.

In the afternoon I took some sewing into Papa's room and sat beside his bed. Mama was reading aloud to him, but I think he did not listen, sunk in apathy too deep for interest in what went on about him. At length he seemed to fall asleep and Mama looked at me sadly as she closed her book. I was weary of mending and I took my work back to my own room. It was there that Delphine found me.

She held a milliner's box in her hands and once more the look of disapproval was in her eyes.

"Mam'zelle has had the opportunity to order a new hat?" she inquired.

I shook my head, puzzled. "Why, no, Delphine. Of course not. I haven't been out of the house."

She thrust the small round box toward me. "Nevertheless,

this has been delivered in your name, mam'zelle. There is, perhaps, some mistake?"

"There must be," I said. I took the box and carried it to the bed, not knowing what to make of it. As Delphine said, it was a mistake. But how odd that a milliner should send a hat mistakenly in my name—a name that was scarcely known in New Orleans. Perhaps there would be something inside that would solve the mystery.

I untied the ribbon that held the lid in place, while Delphine watched me, making no move to leave. When the cardboard lid was off I turned back the tissue paper to reveal the most beautiful little hat I had ever seen. It was small in circumference and rather shallow in the crown, and it was made of a pale fern-green material. There were soft ruchings about the crown and graceful little fronds, almost fernlike in their pattern, circling the brim. Plainly it was a hat that would go well with red hair and I recognized the fact at once.

I set it on the bed, a little excited now, and searched through the tissue for a card, a note—anything which would reveal the identity of the sender.

"You must return it at once, mam'zelle," said Delphine from the doorway. "It is not proper to receive such a gift."

"Return it to whom?" I asked, dumping out tissue upon my bed. "There's nothing here to tell me who has sent it."

But I knew, of course. In my heart I knew, just as Delphine knew. Who in all New Orleans was aware of the fact that this morning I had lost my hat through a rude encounter on Gallatin Street? Who else but the man I was sure was Justin Law. It had been enough for him that he had seen me with Delphine. He must have made inquiries, found out my name and then gone to a milliner's for a hat that would suit my shade of hair. It was hard to keep from showing my delight, and of course I must not smile in the face of Delphine's disapproval.

"Only a barbarian would send such a gift to a lady, mam'zelle," Delphine said sternly.

I did not want to listen to her. Suddenly I wanted to keep this little hat more than I'd ever wanted any piece of clothing in my life. Even though I never wore it, I wanted its possession, and I suspected that everyone in this house, once the details were known, would be in league to take it away from me.

"I don't know what you're talking about," I said, and carried the hat over to my dressing table. There I sat upon the stool and looked at myself in the mirror. The little hat was so beautiful that I was almost afraid to set it upon my head. What if it looked wrong on me? What if I spoiled its perfection? I closed my eyes and set the hat upon my head, trying to feel the rightness of its position with my fingers.

When I opened my eyes and looked again in the mirror, I saw that Delphine had come to stand behind me. I could see her face past me in the glass and I had to move to block her out so that I could judge whether or not the hat suited me.

It did not. The color was right, it was true. But the hat was feminine and fascinating—and I was not. It sat upon my drawn-back hair incongruously and it was not the hat that failed, but I.

"There are many milliners to be found in the Vieux Carré," Delphine said coaxingly. "Madame Natalie will have one make you a hat that will be just for you. But first one must change the wearing of the hair. A softer line, perhaps—"

I snatched the hat from my head. This was the sort of thing I heard constantly from my mother and I was weary of it. Always she was bent on turning me into an imitation of herself. And I knew that would only emphasize the contrast between us. Somehow I'd had the fleeting notion that the fern-green hat might transform me, make me attractive in a way that was not my mother's. It had not done so and I could have wept foolishly in my disillusionment.

Delphine took the hat from me and carried it to the bed. There she returned the tissue paper to the box and made a little nest of it to receive the hat.

"I will send Jasper back to the milliner with this, mam'zelle. There is no need to trouble oneself. The matter will be cared for properly."

But before she could return the bit of ferny stuff to the box, I sprang up and snatched it from her. I hung it upon a lower knob of my four-poster bed and stood back to admire it.

"Return the box, if you like!" I cried. "But I shall keep the hat. If I can't wear it, I can at least look at it. That bedpost looks well in it. Better than I."

Delphine shrugged eloquently, as though I had taken leave of my senses. She picked up the box, replacing its lid.

"M'sieu Robert will decide, mam'zelle," she told me coldly and went out of the room.

When she'd gone I shut the door after her and curtsied to the bedpost, so gaily dressed and fashionable. "Don't worry," I said. "We'll keep it between us—you and I!"

I flung myself on the bed and gave up the afternoon to wasteful dreaming. He had held me in his arms and looked into my eyes and I could not forget him. He had laughed at me and almost scolded me—but he had seen me as a woman. Not in Courtney's practiced way which was probably something to be turned upon every woman, but because in that moment I had been an individual to Justin Law. He had seen a girl who had lost her hat, and he had gone out of his way to do this lovely, surprising thing.

I was no meek little Creole girl to be pushed around by Delphine or anyone else. My Scottish dander was up and I meant to keep the hat whether it became me or not.

Seven ❧

Uncle Robert turned no questioning look upon me at supper that night, so I could only suppose that Delphine had not as yet disclosed my adventures of the day. I planned to get to him first, if possible, and tell my own story, but when the meal was over he left the table and went at once to his study, closing the door. My chance was gone, but now there seemed no urgency.

For the moment all was serene. Mama, as yet, knew nothing about the hat, and she went again to Papa's room, seeming a little restless. Caro played with her dolls on the courtyard gallery outside the parlor. I sat at a small desk, writing a letter to an old friend at home, listening with one ear to Caro's imaginative chatter a few feet away from me. She was playing an elaborate game of Carnival and her favorite doll was to be a Queen of Comus.

Amused, I put down my pen to listen. How many times I had heard my mother tell wonderful Carnival stories. She always spoke with hushed respect, as of a royal court, rather than one that was make-believe. The traditions of Carnival and of Mardi Gras, its final day of climax, were something New Orleans women grew up with from childhood. I had heard my mother date the happenings in her life by certain years of Carnival. She always said she would have been a queen the very next year, if she had not married Papa and gone to live in the North. And I was inclined to believe her.

Now here it was again—the Carnival play, with a little girl and her dolls. So entertained was I by listening to Caro that I did not hear Delphine's step until she stood beside me.

"Mam'zelle Skye," she said, "M'sieu Robert wishes to see you. In his study, if you please."

I sensed a faint satisfaction in her tone. She had been quicker than I in gaining my uncle's ear. I could not hold it against her. Loyalty to Uncle Robert in all his affairs undoubtedly came first in her eyes. I must seem to her a child to be chastised until I could fit decorously into Creole ways.

"Thank you," I said, folding my notepaper and wiping my pen in an unhurried manner. "I will go to him presently." That at least gave me an air of dismissing the summons as unimportant.

Delphine went silently away and Caro, who had paused in her playing to listen, came in from the gallery to stand beside me in obvious sympathy.

"A little while ago I peeked in at Papa through the curtains in the dining room," she whispered. "He was studying his chess set, Cousin Skye. That means it is very serious. Have you done something naughty, cousin?"

I gave her a quick hug in thanks for her sympathy. "Only a little naughty," I said, and rose from my chair. This, after all, was the opportunity I had wanted. Now I could make a request for freedom of movement. After all, I had not been raised in so protected a manner and it wasn't in the least necessary in my case. In fact, I could explain everything— except the hat.

It seemed a long way down the hall to the door of my uncle's study. The little hat still hung upon my bedpost and I loved its every frill. But I did not know what to say about it to Uncle Robert.

When I tapped, he called to me to enter and I stepped again into that sumptuous room that was his study. My uncle rose at once and drew a chair close to his desk for me. Again I was aware of the silky Aubusson beneath my feet.

"Please sit down, my dear," he said and waited for me to take the chair before he returned to one at his desk.

Remembering Caro's words, I looked about for the game of chess, but saw no chessboard in evidence. Again that small table of the rosewood they called palisander stood near his desk, the large silver warming cover concealing its top. Probably Uncle Robert was given to working late at night, and this was here for the purpose of protecting evening suppers.

Uncle Robert regarded me thoughtfully. "Delphine has told me of the unfortunate incident this morning when you wandered away from the market."

"I'm sorry she has," I said, "because I had wanted to tell you about it myself."

His nod was kindly. "I'm glad you feel that way. And I would still like to hear your account, my dear."

I told him briefly that I had not realized the reputation of the street and had regarded myself as being so close to the market that I was perfectly safe. But the drunken seaman had taken me by surprise and I would have been in a difficult position if it had not been for the man who had rescued me.

I did not mention Justin Law by name. For some reason I wanted to hold back my suspicion of his identity.

Uncle Robert listened gravely, his manner attentive and sympathetic. When I had finished my story, he nodded again.

"Yes, that is as Delphine reported it. But you must remember, Skye, that a young lady of good family does not wander into scandalous adventures. In the future I hope you will be circumspect enough never to be caught in so unfortunate a position."

"I hope so too," I said. And then added boldly, "But I am not always a circumspect person. I'm not even sure that I always want to be. Does that shock you very much, Uncle Robert?"

He smoothed his small dark beard in amusement. "It does not shock me, but I must confess that it worries me a little. For instance, this man who rescued you—"

"He was very kind," I said quickly. "I don't know what I would have done without him. And he went out of his way to see me back to the market and safely into Delphine's hands."

"That was most generous of him, I'm sure," said Uncle Robert, but now all trace of amusement was gone from his voice. "Perhaps I had better tell you about this man, my dear. Since I am not at all certain why he is here in New Orleans, or what trouble he means to make, it is better that you be forewarned. Delphine, of course, knew his identity. The man is Courtney's brother, Justin Law."

There was no point in dissembling now. And I was curious

to learn everything I could about this man. "Yes," I admitted, "I thought as much. I had heard him described."

"You must realize," Uncle Robert went on quickly, "that Courtney and he have nothing in common. They have not seen each other since they were children. This man has grown up away from civilizing influences and is rough and crude in his ways. According to Courtney, poor Madame Law is ill over what has happened. She no longer considers him her son."

It seemed to me that everyone was being rather hard on the older brother. As a child he had shown courage enough to follow his father—who had probably not wanted to leave wife and home. He had grown up under circumstances he could not help and if he lacked the Creole polish, he was not altogether to blame. It was my father's belief that the customs of other places and other people should be treated with tolerance and some effort at understanding, even when they differed from ours.

"Why are you so hard on Mr. Law when you don't really know him?" I asked.

Uncle Robert reached long aristocratic fingers toward a cinnabar box on his desk and toyed with the cover idly. For a long moment he seemed lost in his own thoughts, as if he were deciding how much to tell me. As he played with the red box, his fingers sprang the catch on the lid and it flew open, revealing handsome ivory and ebony chess pieces within. He picked up a black pawn and tossed it absently in his palm, and I recalled Caro's reference to chess.

"Which are you, Uncle Robert?" I asked on sudden impulse. "The white or the black?"

He gave me a quick amused look and then reached out to lift the silver cover from the palisander table. Beneath it a chessboard had been set, with a game in progress. Having expected to see wine and biscuits, I regarded it in surprise. I had often played chess with my father and I saw that this game had been arranged according to no rules I knew. The black king was in a strongly protected position and his men were moving in to trap the white queen. But there was one factor which made the entire game nonsense, as far as I could see.

I glanced at my uncle curiously. "There's no white king. How can you play a chess game without two kings?"

His smile turned faintly sardonic. "In the days before the war I had the honor of playing chess many times with the greatest player who ever lived—Paul Morphy of Creole

61

New Orleans. I have always regarded the game as a superior mental exercise. And I am quite conversant with its rules."

He reached again to the cinnabar box and selected a figure from among the discarded pieces. The set had apparently been made by an Oriental artist and the figure was a beautifully carved ivory statuette in long Chinese robes.

"The white king is dead," said my uncle and tossed the piece carelessly back in the box. Then he smiled without rancor at my bewilderment. "Some men think best when they take a long walk, others while they read, or play a game of dominoes. For me a chessboard clarifies my thinking, enables me to make my plans visually. The rules, under such circumstances, are my own."

He replaced the silver cover upon the table and I saw that it fitted into a groove which had been cut in the table's surface, and hid the entire chessboard.

"The cover," Uncle Robert said, "is for the purpose of keeping the board safe from the careless hands of servants who are dusting. No one lifts it from the table except myself."

For just an instant I felt chilled. Did those pawns and knights and castles represent men and women whose lives my uncle wished to manipulate? I remembered what my mother had said of his love of power. But these were unpleasant thoughts and I did not want to entertain them about my uncle.

Now he leaned back in his chair and regarded me affably, his fingers playing with the gold chain that looped across his vest. He was not, as I found, a particularly relaxed person. His hands were wont to move often, not only in an expressive French way as he talked, but even when they might have been at rest.

"I am glad that you are a young woman of spirit," he said, and his tone was the kindly one I liked in him. "I find your independence of thought admirable, providing it is restrained behind a womanly exterior. You are, after all, of marriageable age, my dear, and I hope you will forgive me for speaking frankly. Your marriage is something we must consider."

I was glad of the opening. It would be possible now to tell him how I felt about marriage. Perhaps I might even find in him an ally against my mother's maneuvering.

"Several people have spoken to me about marrying since I've come to New Orleans," I began. "But I feel—"

He raised a long forefinger reassuringly. "There is no need for precipitant action. However, you are a young woman of good family and from this house you should be able to step into a most favorable marriage."

"Thank you for your concern, Uncle Robert," I said, "but I don't expect to think of marriage for some time. I'm not a very good catch, you know. My father can give me no dowry."

"That is of no great consequence." Again his hands moved, this time in a small gesture of dismissal. "In New Orleans we place a greater emphasis on family than we do on wealth, my dear. I am sure there will be many young men who will be eager to press their suit. Already you have won the admiration of my ward, Courtney. And it is not impossible that there will be something of a dowry forthcoming when you marry."

A twinge of uncertainty ran through me at his mention of Courtney. Had I after all misjudged my mother?

Uncle Robert took my silence for the confusion of gratitude. "Why should I not do this for so charming a niece? Providing, of course, that your marriage is suitable. But there is no point in discussing such matters now. You must be properly introduced to society this fall. When you appear in a box at the French Opera—which is the way in which we present our debutantes—you will, I'm sure, have suitors by the score. And until the time of your marriage you and your parents will of course be most welcome to stay in this house."

I could relax again and dismiss the suspicion which had stirred in me. Uncle Robert had spoken of Courtney only in passing. He was thinking in general terms of the future, with only my own good at heart. And that, of course, I could not resent. In fact, such concern gave me again the feeling of being somehow protected and safe in this house. Safe even from my mother. And that was a feeling I had seldom experienced before.

Uncle Robert rose and I knew the interview was at an end, though there had still be no mention of the hat Justin Law had sent me. I moved toward the door and Uncle Robert came to open it for me. Again I glimpsed the portrait that hung in this inconspicuous corner and wished that I might ask him whether it had been painted of Madame Aurore Law as a girl. But of course I did not dare.

"Remember, my dear," he said, laying an affectionate hand on my arm, "—no more adventures on Gallatin Street."

"Of course not," I promised. "But if I see Mr. Law again, I cannot be discourteous to him."

"Naturally," he said, "a lady is never discourteous to a *gentleman*." His implication was clear.

"But if this man comes of good family—?" I said.

My uncle put an arm gently about my shoulders. "These are matters beyond your understanding, Skye, and you need not trouble yourself about them. It is enough to know that Justin Law has been in prison for many years for a crime of violence. Only fortune saved him from a hanging. His reputation is evil to an extent that a young woman like yourself cannot possibly dream."

I recalled Caro's excited words as she bounced on her stool that day in the dining room. So she had been right, after all. But I had to hear this from my uncle's lips to believe what I did not want to believe.

"Is it true that he is a murderer?" I asked him directly.

"It is true," Uncle Robert said. "A man so debased has no right to speak to a respectable woman, no matter what the circumstances."

I wondered fleetingly if it would have been better to let me be mauled and insulted by a drunken sailor.

"Remember," Uncle Robert said with some perception, "that the scoundrel often has a dashing way with women. He can seem deceptively attractive. But his sort can bring only misery and unhappiness. Don't forget that, Skye."

His look had softened and I felt that he spoke to me as a father would speak to his daughter. I knew his warning must be justified and I nodded silently as I turned away. Behind me I heard the soft closing of the door.

The things he had said about Justin Law left me unexpectedly sick and shaken. Far more shaken than I liked to admit. It hurt me to consider that a man who could play so delightful a prank with a little green hat could cruelly take another man's life. Yet I knew there was violence in him. I had seen it in his handling of that sailor. I had felt it myself. I must give him no further thought. Perhaps that was why Uncle Robert had not embarrassed me by speaking of the hat. He expected me to do the proper thing, once I was in possession of a true knowledge of Justin Law.

He was right, of course. The hat must be returned at once to the milliner from whom it had come.

I hurried to my room, meaning to take the hat at once from its post and thrust it into its nest of tissue. But no bit of green fancy perched upon the post. The carved knob was as bald as though it had never boasted so stylish a covering for its polished top.

Delphine had come into my room in my absence and taken it away, I thought angrily. And that I would not have! I might give the order myself to have the hat returned, but I would not have Delphine take matters into her own hands. She might feel it her privilege and duty to run the rest of the family, but she was not going to run me.

I returned to the gallery and saw at once what I had failed to see before. On the courtyard gallery outside the doors of the second parlor, where Caro had been playing a while ago, stood Delphine. There was something still and almost secretive about her attitude. I saw that she stood half hidden, watching something that went on in the parlor.

Softly I followed the gallery around its turn and was upon her before she saw me coming.

"You had no business taking my hat!" I told her in a low voice.

I must have surprised her, but she did not start or even turn her head. "Your maman does not change, Mam'zelle Skye," she said and made a small gesture toward the parlor.

Quickly I stepped to the door and looked in. Over the mantelpiece hung a long, gilt-framed mirror, tilted somewhat to reflect the room. Before it my mother postured, tilting her head this way and that, admiring herself. Admiring the small green hat perched so becomingly upon her black hair.

A sense of outrage shook me, and at the same time a sense of helplessness. My impulse was to snatch the hat from her head and run off with it. It was mine. The most beautiful thing I had ever owned. And yet it was not mine and I didn't want it. I didn't want anything sent me by a man so evil as Justin Law.

"Stop whispering out there, you two," Mama said, "and come tell me how I look."

I held back the confusion of my feelings and went into the room. Delphine came silently with me. There was no escaping the fact that the fern-green hat became my mother, even though her hair was black and the hat had been destined for red. As she dipped and twirled about the room I knew she was herself again and that she had thrown off the depression and lassitude that had held her since she had returned to this house of her childhood.

She seemed not to notice that neither Delphine nor I made any comment on her appearance. Quite evidently she was sufficiently pleased with herself.

"Imagine my surprise," she said, "when I went to your

room just now and found this charming little hat upon the bedpost. Where did you get it, Skye?"

I glanced sidelong at the woman beside me. "Delphine brought it to me," I said cooly. "After all, I lost a hat this morning."

"But this is not your type," Mama cried. "Never, never! Skye, I will loan you a hat when you need one—or you can prevail upon Aunt Natalie to get you another. But this one I must have. This hat was made for me!"

I waited a moment to see what Delphine would say or do. But she did not look at me, and she said not a word.

Mama danced over to me and kissed me lightly on the cheek. "Look—look how foolishly it sits on your red head—" and she plucked it off and set it rakishly on my straight-drawn hair. I would have shaken my head free of it, hating her ridicule and knowing she was right, but she took the hat back quickly, lest it be harmed.

"Give it to me, Skye," she wheedled. "You know it's not right for you."

What did it matter? I hadn't intended to keep it anyway. If it pleased her so, she might as well be the one to wear it.

"Keep it, if you like," I said, and my words sounded angry in my ears.

But Mama did not notice. She said she must go show it to Papa at once and flew out of the room and across the gallery.

I looked at Delphine. "Why didn't you tell Uncle Robert about the hat?"

She moved away from me. "It is not necessary to disturb M'sieu Robert with trivial matters."

"I see," I told her, but I did not in the least. Something had made Delphine hold her hand from her original intent, and I could not know what it was.

She paused in the doorway and looked back at me tentatively. "If mam'zelle would dress her hair in a different style, the hat would become her better than it does Mam'zelle Loulou.

"It doesn't matter," I said. "I'm not going to wear it anyway and I like my hair as it is. . . . Delphine, you knew my mother as a girl in this house, didn't you?"

"Yes, mam'zelle." She turned from the door without another word and went about her business. Yet I had the surprising impression that she was shaken by some anger which included me as well as my mother.

Eight ✺

In the week that followed I found no opportunity to get out of the house alone. My uncle's warnings had, for the time being, dampened my enthusiasm for opposing the edicts of the house. Yet I still wanted to go my own way without incurring too much displeasure.

More than once I visited the market with Aunt Natalie and Delphine. But though the Vieux Carré is small—hardly more than a mile square—I did not again glimpse Justin Law. About this I had a curious reaction. The things my uncle had told me of the man should have held me chilled and disdainful of him. Yet I still thought of him more often than I liked, and on occasions when I glimpsed in the distance a man of his size, I found my rebel heart all too ready to quicken with anticipation. Though I fought it with all that was reasonable in me, an eagerness to see him again began to fill my being. I told myself sternly that I wanted only to test my own impression of the man against what my uncle had told me and be convinced as Uncle Robert wished me to be. But my heart was not concerned with reason and took a wayward bent of its own.

Since the talk my father had with Uncle Robert, he had scarcely roused himself. It was as if he had given up completely. The Creole doctor had come again, but he offered no more hope than had our doctor at home, and I doubt if Papa paid much attention to his words. Even in these few days he had wasted and his only desire was to be let alone. Of us all, only Delphine was able to get him to eat. Sometimes she brought him a bowl of strengthening soup made from chicken and okra and tomatoes. She would raise him in the bed, place the bowl calmly in his hands and then stand beside him, implacable as fate until he had every bit of it down. Yet when Mama or I brought him food, tried to coax him, he would not touch it.

Once I stopped Delphine on the gallery as she came from Papa's room with an empty bowl in her hands.

"How do you persuade him to eat, Delphine?" I asked. "He will touch nothing for Mama and me."

Delphine could be mannerly, yet at the same time convey more with her fine dark eyes than she put into words. "He is a man, Mam'zelle Skye. I treat him as one and expect him to act as one." She bowed her tignoned head courteously and went by me on the gallery. I sensed wisdom in what she said, but I could not stand beside my father's bed and feel anything but heartbreak and pity. He had become no longer a man, but only a helpless child.

The languid summer life of a Creole household enveloped us. We made the most of early morning in a courtyard still shaded and delightfully green and cool. But when the sun climbed high enough to pierce the shade, the very bricks burned in its glare and humid heat enveloped us. Then we retreated behind the shelter of our slanted blinds, with fans and cool liquids to drink. There were mornings when I found insects in my shoes on rising and dampness touched everything. Even the sheets upon my bed were often clammy to the touch. With evening we threw open our windows to the courtyard once more and welcomed any breeze that wafted through the passageway from the street.

It was a quiet, somnolent life and I began to long for something to happen. Assurances that the gay season began at summer's end did not comfort me. I did not want to live with brooding thoughts and longings until then. I wanted to be alive *now*.

Since the drive we had taken that Sunday, I had only glimpsed Courtney going and coming in my uncle's office. Though he always gave me the warmly interested look which was second nature to him, there was no conversation between us until one day when I stood in the courtyard, watching the goldfish dart through the waters of the fountain.

Courtney, coming down the steps from an office door, saw me there and came to join me.

"I have wished to see you, mam'zelle. I reproach myself that there has been no opportunity. Would you do me the honor to visit my mother's house on Saturday afternoon? Perhaps your Tante Natalie and your mother would enjoy the drive too. And if there are several ladies to speak with my mother—" He smiled meaningly and I knew he hoped there might be an opportunity to see me alone.

At once I was eager to go. I would enjoy Courtney's company and the way he treated me. But the thought leapt unbidden to my mind that I might see Justin as well. At

68

once I was impatient with my own wayward whims. Courtney was someone I liked. Now that no one was thrusting him upon me, I could take pleasure in being with him. I could even wonder if something more than friendship might develop between us, if ever we got a chance to know each other in this world of chaperones.

I told him readily that I would be pleased to visit his mother and then, perversely, I went a step further, dissembling.

"Has Uncle Robert given his permission for me to visit your house? I mean there is the matter of your brother Justin."

"That is why we've chosen Saturday afternoon," Courtney said. "This intruder in our household will be away on that day. For his convenience he has taken rooms in the Vieux Carré, and sometimes he does not come to our house for days at a time."

I did not like the twinge of disappointment that went through me. It was growing difficult to live with the two women I seemed to be. Which was I—the sensible one who knew danger when she saw it and stepped back, or the giddy moth who dashed foolishly toward the flame? Never had there been this division of mind and emotion in me before and I did not know how to control it.

"There has been no reconciliation then between your brother and you?" I asked Courtney quickly, to cover my own confused reaction.

"But certainly not, mam'zelle," he said. "There can never be such a thing."

I had an impulse to tell him what had happened that day on Gallatin Street, to tell him that I had already met his brother, but I knew that would only disturb him. When Courtney returned to his work in the office, I went upstairs to announce the invitation to Aunt Natalie and my mother.

Both were uncertain and I did not know until Saturday morning whether one or both ladies would accompany me. Then Aunt Natalie excused herself. Tina was feverish and she must stay with the baby. So it was Mama who decided to go.

That morning when I stood talking to her in the doorway of her room, she seemed restless and as eager for change as I.

"It will be a pleasant day for a drive to the Garden District," she said. "I haven't been there since I was a young girl. I'm looking forward to it."

"Is it all right to leave Papa alone for that long?" I asked.

She shook her head sadly. "He cares little whether I come or go, Skye. And I must have some gaiety in my life—I can't live without it." Already she had opened her armoire and was searching through the frocks that hung there. "You will love the Garden District," she said over her shoulder.

"Is that where the Americans settled when they came to New Orleans?" I asked.

"That's right. The Creoles wouldn't mix with them in the beginning. So the newcomers took over the Faubourg Ste. Marie, uptown from Canal Street. They built their own city, with big houses and beautiful gardens. Though it's a strange thing, Skye—while the Americans were strong and forceful, and scornful of the Creole's frivolity, yet in the end those who stayed took up the Creole way of life. Even today, New Orleans is more a Creole city than it is American."

She had found a cool, ruffly white dress that contrasted with her dark beauty and she took it out of the armoire and laid it upon the bed. "This will do nicely for so warm a day. And I'll wear the little green hat, Skye. I've gone nowhere yet where I could wear it. Do dress yourself up attractively, *chérie.*"

The moment I learned she meant to wear the green hat, something contrary possessed me. I knew exactly how lovely she would look and I suspected that this time she might put herself out to charm Courtney as she had not done before. I knew very well that I couldn't compete with her in appearance, and I didn't want to. I would be myself and we would see which one Courtney preferred. I wanted no man who could judge only by exterior furbelows.

So, when the time came, I put on my old brown dress defiantly and found a brown straw hat with a wide brim that almost hid my hair—a hat I had been ready to discard. My back was turned to my mirror as I finished dressing, for I did not want to see my reflection. I felt a little angry with myself as I pinned on my hat. Angry because I knew perfectly well that I was letting a small bit of green fluff spoil my afternoon. Why should I care what my mother wore? I winced as I pricked my scalp with the hatpin. I had been about to banish that green hat from my life and there was no point in feeling upset because Mama meant, innocently enough, to wear it. Not for a moment did she dream of how I had felt for a little while about the hat. Nor did I intend to tell her.

She shook her head, mother-fashion, when she saw me.

"Oh, not that brown, Skye! You could at least wear the white muslin."

"It's rumpled," I told her firmly. It was as if, having started off on the wrong foot, I had to keep going in this chosen direction.

Mama looked glowingly lovely and the hat might well have been made to flatter her particular beauty. I saw Courtney's quick look of astonishment when he saw her, and though he was as attentive to me as before on the drive out to the Garden District, I was well aware of the impression she had made. Nor did she settle back in the carriage and behave in a way that was at all matronly. All the little tricks of flirtation that I knew so well were brought into play: the tilting of her parasol, the ruffling of her little fan. But Courtney, to my surprise, addressed himself to me and paid her no more than courteous attention.

It was a pleasant drive. The horses turned off the wide avenue we had followed and our carriage moved into a section of handsome homes and spacious gardens. Everywhere grew the stately royal palms, shaggy-headed and lofty. Glossy-leaved magnolias and mysterious live oaks abounded and there were sweet olive and sour orange trees, crepe myrtles, hedges of Creole box. Creeping over everything was the ubiquitous rosa montana. Courtney set himself to identifying many of the trees and plants for me and I could not help but be pleased by his continued attention.

The houses were gracious indeed, some with the graceful white columns of the Greek revival which had swept the South before the war, many with a tracery of iron lacework threading the balconies in Creole fashion, and with intricate iron fences around the property.

The Law house was painted white, with white pillars and marble steps, a wide gallery above and below. Over the great door was a handsome fanlight. Whatever the American Harry Law had been, he had built well, with an eye for handsome living in his New Orleans home. I felt sorry to think that he had been forced to spend his life in probable discomfort on western frontiers, instead of in this lovely home he had built for himself and his wife. Why, I wondered, had he not returned after the war, when old scandals might have died down?

A Negro maid invited us into a wide hall, carpeted in faded yellow roses, and said we were to come right upstairs.

"I hoped Maman would come down today," Courtney apologized. "Since my brother's coming, she has chosen to avoid him as much as possible by shutting herself up in her own rooms. But there was no need today."

We followed the maid up the stairway, past a great gilded sunburst of a clock on the wall, and around the curve of wedged steps to the second floor.

Aurore Law, clad completely in black, and lying upon a chaise longue, extended both hands to us in greeting. She was a pale woman, nervous and thin, though obviously she had once been pretty. Widow's black did not become her and she did not look at all well. Nevertheless, I recognized at once that she had been the original of the youthful portrait in Uncle Robert's study. How odd, I thought again, that he had kept that picture of a young girl who had jilted him on the wall where he would see it every day. But how generous he had been to stand by her in her need and behave as a relative, rather than a rejected suitor, even to the point of keeping her husband out of prison. I was curious to know more of that story.

Mama went at once to take her hands and kiss her on either cheek, and Aurore looked at her wistfully. "You have changed so little, Louise, *chérie*. But then, robust good health was always yours. I have been delicate all my life. So this is Skye—the little one who was born in the country of the Yankees." And she gave me her frail, dry hand.

"It would do you good, Maman," Courtney said, "if you would come downstairs when Justin is out of the house."

She sighed. "It becomes too great an effort. And how is Robert, Louise? And your poor husband?"

As Mama murmured politely, I had a chance to look about this upstairs bedroom. Shutters were closed against the brilliant warmth outside and the room was dim and cool. Again there was an elaborate bed and by now I was beginning to recognize the work of famous Creole cabinet-makers. This bed bore the touch of Prudent Mallard—graceful carving, an armoire so large it occupied most of one wall, and a *duchesse* dressing table of rosewood, marble-topped, bearing an imposing array of pillboxes, philters and jars.

Courtney brought small quilted chairs for us and the maid scurried off for the inevitable coffee. Aurore Law settled down to an enjoyable hour of talking about her miseries, both physical and emotional. It was, I gathered, mainly the presence of Justin in the house that was causing both.

72

Mama, perhaps allying herself against Uncle Robert, began to defend Justin.

"After all," she told Aurore reasonably, "he was only a small boy at the time he went away. You can hardly hold such long-ago matters against him."

"He was raised by his father," Aurore said, as if that were explanation enough. "His father left New Orleans in disgrace. He even tried to force me to go with him. Pleaded with me, threatened to take my son, in order to make me come!"

So it had not been entirely desertion as I had thought. Harry Law had at least wanted his wife and sons to go with him when he fled. But Courtney took another view.

"That was unreasonable. Of course you could not leave your home and go into exile."

"But if he abducted the boy, then it was not the child's fault," Mama insisted, frowning prettily.

Aurore raised a haggard face and stared at her. "Justin went by choice. He always belonged more to his father than he did to me. He fought me, struck out at me when I tried to hold him."

"But a child!" my mother repeated. "Come, Aurore, you must not let his presence devastate you so. This is his home—surely he has a right to return to it."

Aurore continued as if she had not heard. "He is a gambler like his father, wasteful of money. Scarcely a picayune did Harry Law leave me when he fled New Orleans. If it had not been for the kindness of Robert Tourneau in supplementing my small income, we might have perished."

Our tray of coffee arrived just then, interrupting what had turned into a pointless argument, and my mother set herself to charming Courtney. She was all pert gestures and *moues*, all melting looks that both promised and withheld. Yet it seemed to me that Courtney was made uneasy by her little play and was not altogether entranced. I could not help a small feeling of gratification. The time must eventually come when Mama would realize that she was no longer a bewitching young girl.

Courtney drew me into the talk by asking me how I liked New Orleans, now that I had been here a little while. We chatted for a suitable length of time over our coffee, leaving my mother to gossip with Tante Aurore. When we rose to go, Aurore suggested that I first be shown the house.

"At one time, *chérie*, it was a show place," she told me. "Of course many of the rooms are closed now, since my

73

son and I live modestly. But I am sure you will enjoy seeing it. If you please, Courtney—"

Courtney rose obligingly. "I shall be glad to show Skye the house, Maman." He turned to my mother courteously, though I thought with no special emphasis. "You have seen the place, I know, but if you care to come, madame—?"

"Naturally I shall come," said Mama quickly.

We bade Tante Aurore good-by and Courtney led us through the upper floor, opening doors to darkened rooms, showing us some of the treasures with which his father had furnished the house.

"Had it not been for M'sieu Robert," he told us, "my mother must have sold many of these things."

This viewing of the house had been suggested for my benefit, but it was my mother who most exclaimed and commented. She looked so youthful and appealing in the little green hat, and she moved with such grace that I did not see how Courtney could resist her. Yet he continued to be attentive to me and I knew this piqued my mother.

When we went downstairs Courtney took us first to the library and I was entranced by the room. His father, Courtney said, had been a great reader and the shelves were stocked with hundreds of volumes. Here someone had opened a pair of shutters and a warm bar of sunlight cut through the gloom. The light fell upon a long library table with books and papers strewn upon it.

"My brother has been working here," Courtney said. "He has taken it for his office."

Mama shivered daintily. "A dull and gloomy place. I never liked this room. Do come along. I must see the wonderful double parlor again. Surely it's the most exquisite in New Orleans!"

But this room drew me and I did not wish to pull myself away. The long rows of books invited, tantalized. I wanted to run my hands along the bindings, pull the volumes out and dip into their pages. No library was a room to glance into and leave.

Courtney had not followed my mother to the door. He hesitated, waiting for me. But I knew what I wanted to do.

"Show her the parlor," I said, smiling at him, "and whatever else she wants to see. Let me stay here for a little while."

"If you prefer," Courtney said, but I think he too was puzzled by my desire to stay in this great dark room of books.

Mama drew Courtney quickly away, but I did not mind their going. I ran to a second pair of shutters and flung them wide so that the gloom retreated still more before bright shafts of sunlight. This, I thought, was the room in which Justin Law liked to work, and I looked about me with interest.

High bookshelves ran along one side and across the end. The fireplace was not tiny like those in the Vieux Carré, but wide and generous, with a mantel of fine black African marble. There were deep leather chairs that had no Creole look about them and had probably been chosen for this room by the American, Harry Law.

I couldn't help but look curiously at the long table where Justin's papers lay. The books which strewed its surface were not all business tomes, though several concerned themselves with Mississippi shipping. There were novels as well. Two were by American authors whom I admired, Washington Irving and Nathaniel Hawthorne. There was *The Moonstone* by the English writer, Wilkie Collins—an exciting story which had run serially. And finally there was a volume by Sir Walter Scott—my favorite *Ivanhoe*. An interesting collection which seemed to indicate that the man they termed a barbarian liked to read.

So engrossed was I in turning pages, glancing at flyleaves, that I did not hear a step, or know that anyone stood in the doorway until he spoke and I looked up to scc Justin Law watching me.

"Ah?" he said. "The lady of Gallatin Street! Good afternoon, Miss Cameron."

The sunlight touched his hair to gold as it had done that other time, and though he stood quietly watching me, there was a vigorous lift to his head, and I knew with my senses the vital quality of any movement he might make. My pulses began a thick pounding and I could not take my eyes from his face. I reminded myself that Uncle Robert had warned me against this man and I must not linger here in his company.

I let the book I was holding drop from my hands and moved away from the table. But Justin blocked the door and I did not want to approach him.

"I thought I might find you in the house if I returned unexpectedly," he said, and there was laughter in his eyes. "I wanted to know if your hair was really as red as it seemed that morning on Gallatin Street."

He came toward me with his quick, lithe stride and at his coming, I took a backward step that made him laugh out loud.

"You've been hearing about me, haven't you?" he said. "And you don't know whether to run from the devil, or listen to his wiles. Whatever they've told you—it's probably true. Perhaps you'd better run while there's still time."

There was no help for it. I must walk past him to make my escape. I did not answer him, but moved with what I hoped was dignity to the door. He stepped out of my path and for a moment I thought he would let me go. But his eyes were dancing with the blue devils I had seen in them before, and he stopped me most ignominiously. He simply reached out and caught the wide brim of my hat. The pin that held it to my hair tugged at my scalp and I stopped indignantly.

"Don't run away, little brown wren," he said. And with never an apology he plucked the long hatpin out of the straw and lifted the hat from my head. "Why didn't you wear the one I sent you? I saw it in a milliner's window and it was clearly your hat. It was a sample and not for sale, but I persuaded the woman to let me have it. And now I find you wearing an abomination like this!" With a scornful gesture he sent the brown hat sailing across the room to the library table.

Never had I been so treated! I let him see the anger in my eyes at his insolence. For just an instant I told him, without speaking a word, how much I detested him, how low I held him in my estimation. But if I hoped to wilt him with my scorn, I might have known I would fail.

"That's better," he said. "Now you're looking at me bright as a mockingbird. So why must you pretend that you're a meek brown wren?"

I closed my eyes and reminded myself that this man was a murderer, that his reputation was evil beyond my understanding and that I must leave this room at once. Then I opened my eyes and faced him again.

"I am quite sure that all the things they say about you are true," I told him coldly. "I wish to have nothing to do with you. If you will permit me, sir—"

But still he blocked my path and now there was a scornful look in his eyes. "What a pity that you have so little courage. Once long ago there was a spectacular New Orleans lady whose hair was as red as yours. I wish I had known Micaela."

I remembered what Courtney had said about Micaela resembling me in some way.

"The Baroness de Pontalba? What has she to do with me?"

"Nothing at all. Her hair was a flaming red and she was

never ashamed of it. She liked to display it with elaborate coiffures and put jewels in it when she gave a ball. They say she used to ride about on a horse and shout orders to the workmen when the Pontalba buildings were being built. She must have made her own rules, and she was never without courage. But then, she was no stiff-necked Yankee girl who must find New Orleans downright disturbing."

I found that I was trembling with anger so that I could not speak, could not find words to answer him. And all the while he stood there, laughing at me. I felt only relief when Courtney and my mother appeared in the doorway. Courtney was plainly disconcerted at the sight of Justin.

"I thought you were staying in the Vieux Carré for the weekend," he said to his brother.

Justin shrugged. "I chose to return."

Mama came into the room and the green hat was tilted saucily over her nose as she went toward Justin Law. I saw the lift of his eyebrows, caught the sardonic glance he flung me when he saw the hat, and I flushed to my very ears.

"So this is the wicked brother everyone is chattering about?" Mama said. "You may introduce him to me, Courtney."

Courtney spoke stiffly. "Madame Cameron, may I present Monsieur Justin Law."

Mama held out her hand and gave Justin an entrancing look from beneath the slanted bit of green. Justin played up to her with a natural grace that surprised me. Such a courtly bowing over her hand as he managed, such admiration as he put into his look! Apparently he had not forgotten the Creole training he must have received as a small boy in this house.

"An unexpected delight, madame," he told her. "It is hard to believe that you are this young lady's mother."

Mama twinkled at him and I saw that Courtney watched her in some disapproval.

"What flattery!" Mama said. "You have not lost your Creole manners, m'sieu. From what I've heard I'd thought you would never fit into a New Orleans parlor!"

Justin's laughter rang through the room. "To prove the rumors wrong I'm planning to give a party here in this house and invite New Orleans to come—friend and enemy alike."

Mama clapped her hands. "A party in the summertime?— lovely! But will anyone come, m'sieu? This is not the season for *soirées* in New Orleans."

"They'll come all right," said Justin with confidence. "I'll persuade my mother to send out the invitations to give the affair the proper tone, and their curiosity will bring them."

Courtney spoke between tight lips. "There will be no party here. This is not your house to do with as you please."

"Do you mean to say that my mother will begrudge a party to welcome home her long-lost son?"

"My mother can scarcely afford the expense of such an affair," Courtney said coldly.

Justin stared at him. "Scarcely afford? When you have lived in such style all these years? When you have kept up this house as my father left it and—"

"It is time you knew the truth," Courtney cut in and I saw a flush creep over his face. "M'sieu Tourneau has kept up the house. While you were making great wealth for yourself in Colorado, we had nothing. Yet now you come here and expect—"

Justin crossed the room in two long strides and took his brother by the arm. Anger blazed in his eyes. "What are you saying? Surely my father left our mother well cared for! Why should Robert Tourneau—"

Courtney twisted his arm out of his brother's grasp. "Perhaps you will recall there was a war which destroyed most fortunes in the South. Had you shown interest in our affairs, you would have understood before this how we live. All our gratitude is given to M'sieu Robert. Not, sir, to you!"

There was such tension in the room that I felt a real quarrel was about to burst into flame. But Mama stepped provocatively between the two, shook a reproachful finger at Courtney, and tapped Justin with the little fan she carried.

"What a pity!" she cried. "A summertime party to break the monotony would have been an elegant idea. And you are right, M'sieu Justin—if the invitations were sent by your mother, they would come. To see you!"

Justin recovered himself smoothly, though I think he was still angry. "Then we'll have the party. I shall take over the expense myself, naturally, and it will be a party New Orleans will remember."

"And I am to be invited?" Mama asked him sweetly.

"It would scarcely be complete without you," Justin told her. "And of course we will invite the little wren—your daughter."

He threw me a look in which mockery flashed again, but I did not speak to him at all as I picked up the hateful brown hat and went past Courtney out the door. My mother might plan as she pleased, but there would be no party for us, I knew very well. Uncle Robert would undoubtedly be furious at the very idea. Certainly he would never permit the ladies of his household to attend. And that, I told myself as we went out to the carriage, suited me very well indeed.

Nine ☙

I had already discovered that rain was a common portion of the weather in New Orleans. One moment there would be a bright blue sky overhead, and in the next, wind would send thunderheads piling toward us, blocking out the sun. Sudden showers were taken for granted and I could see why banquettes were built beneath sheltering galleries, or under the overslope of cottage roofs.

This morning, however, a week after our visit to the Garden District, no mere shower sprinkled the streets, to leave the day bright and steamy-hot afterwards. The rain came down resoundingly, setting up a great murmur against shutters and galleries. It clattered on shaggy banana leaves, pounded upon rosy courtyard bricks.

Aunt Natalie had set me to work at a special task in the dining room, and even young Caro, who had stayed home this morning because of the storm, was helping in an inattentive, hummingbird fashion.

The myriad crystal teardrops of the elaborate chandeliers were, I discovered, to be washed only by the hands of Aunt Natalie herself. Each crystal piece unhooked from the whole and she cleansed it carefully in sudsy water, rinsed and laid it aside to be dried. A sheet had been spread over the dining-room table, and we were working there. Caro and I dried each piece and polished it until it sparkled. Mama had escaped on the pretext that she must read aloud to Papa.

My mind was scarcely on the task before me. Once more, hatefully, I was going over what had happened in the library of Aurore's house. My cheeks still grew warm when I remembered Justin's mockery and my own helpless inability to answer him. These days I found myself too often inclined toward fantasies in which I appeared wearing the little hat he had sent me, and all between us was vastly different. Such futile imaginings could never erase the shameful reality, and all that was practical in me condemned them.

Caro, too, scarcely had her mind on what she was doing. In spite of reproof from her mother for a lack of attention, her concern lay in the courtyard, and every few minutes she must run to the gallery to look down at the fountain, whose basin brimmed to overflowing in the downpour. Her worry was for the goldfish.

"There are only five left," she told me sadly. "Rex and Comus and Momus all got washed out of the fountain during a storm last September. That's when it really rains. Now just the flower fish are left—Magnolia, Jasmine, Crepe Myrtle, Wisteria, and Camellia."

"Such foolish names for fish!" Aunt Natalie said. "Why not let goldfish be goldfish and stop counting them? If we lose them we'll get more."

Caro looked outraged at such callousness and her mother reached over to take a bit of crystal from her perilously waving fingers.

"If you are to grow up to be a good Creole wife," Aunt Natalie said, "you must learn to take care of fine crystal and china with your own hands. If you do not learn this well as a child, you will never receive the *demand : en mariage* when you grow up."

Caro danced a polka step to the gallery and back before she answered. "But, Maman, when I grow up I shall live in a house that has no chandeliers at all. Not one! I shall take them all out and give them to the Bottle Man. Then I'll never have to scrub and polish as you do."

She skipped lightly about the table singing, "Any bottles, any bones, any rags today?" until her mother clapped her hands sharply and told the child to sit down and be still. It was obvious that she would grow up in ignorance of what it took to manage a house, and no gentleman would ever consider her as a wife.

I could sympathize with Caro. The task of polishing these crystal dangles seemed to go monotonously on forever. As Aunt Natalie calmly continued to wash and rinse, her plump fingers twinkling in and out of sudsy rainbow bubbles, she spoke of coming plans.

"We are having a small supper a week from Saturday night," she told us. "Though this is not the *saison des visites* it is M'sieu Robert's wish to invite a few relatives to the house."

I listened to her and polished my bits of crystal till they shone, but my thoughts were building fantasies again. I could see myself dressed in a gown more beautiful than any my mother had ever worn. A gown of a pale fern-colored green silk that would set off my hair. And upon my head, of course, was the fern-green hat. I was not sure about my hair, except that its style was different and it had been dressed in a fashion that did not hide its thickness or its color.

Dressed thus, of course, I had Justin Law at my feet. Ah, what a humble tune he played then, seeking my favor, pleading for a kind glance, a word from me that would ease his sickness of heart. But I was a lady without forgiveness for his former rude ways. I listened remotely to his suit and smiled upon him coolly. No, indeed, I had no intention of—

"Skye!" Aunt Natalie's exclamation made me relinquish my childish game. "I have spoken to you twice, Skye. Your thoughts are as wondering as Caro's."

"I'm sorry," I said. "I wasn't paying attention."

"Just like me," Caro whispered impishly.

Aunt Natalie smiled equably upon me. "It is natural for the young to dream. As Robert says, we must soon set about finding you a suitable husband." She dried her hands on a towel and drew a slip of paper from the pocket of her apron. "I've made up my list of guests for the supper. Perhaps you will do me the favor to take it downstairs to your uncle. Ask him if he approves my choice."

"I'll take it, Maman," Caro offered quickly, holding out her hand.

But Aunt Natalie withdrew the paper from her reach. "*Pas du tout.* You would stop to visit your goldfish and forget what you were about. And you pester Courtney, take his mind from his work. So Skye shall take it, if she will. But don't interrupt, my dear, if my husband is busy with a client."

She handed me the paper, while Caro pretended to pout. I was glad enough to be released, both from the crystal polishing and my make-believe conquests that could never be real. Quickly I went down the curving stairway, to stand for a moment sheltered in the arched passageway where I could watch the curtain of rain shrouding the courtyard beyond. Caro darted after me and stood at the very edge of the rain, staring mournfully at the brimming fountain.

"It's growing lighter," I told her hopefully. "The rain isn't as heavy as it was. Perhaps it will stop before any harm is done to your goldfish."

I left her there and crossed the passageway to mount

the few steps to my uncle's office. The door stood open and I went in. It was my first opportunity to visit these downstairs rooms and I found in this anteroom none of the upstairs luxury. The floor was uncarpeted, the furniture plain. A straight brass rod hung from the ceiling, the brass hoop around it supporting bulging globes which shed pale gaslight on the room.

Near a window open on the rain-beaten street, Courtney sat on a stool at a high desk, a clerk's green eyeshade fastened over his forehead. The door of the room on the courtyard side was closed and I could hear voices beyond the panel.

Courtney came down from his stool with alacrity, plainly glad to see me.

"Why must a man leave so complicated a will?" He sighed. "You've come on a lengthy mission, I hope?"

He was an engaging young man and I liked him increasingly.

"I'm sorry," I said, "but it's a very brief mission. Only to show Uncle Robert a list of guests Aunt Natalie would like to have approved for her supper a week from Saturday night. You and your mother are to be invited."

Courtney's face brightened at the prospect of a social affair. "*Bien.* I shall look forward to the occasion. My mother wanted me to apologize for the unfortunate meeting with Justin at our house. Had we known—"

"Don't worry about it," I said. "There was no harm done. How is the situation at home?"

"Worse," he said, shaking his head. "Now that Justin knows we are indebted to M'sieu Robert for so much, he inquires into every expenditure. He has even had the audacity to speak of taking me into business with him. Like our father, he is interested in shipping. But of course I will have nothing to do with any of his plans."

"Do you like the law so much?" I asked.

It seemed to me that he winced faintly, but his voluble assurance followed. "This is gentleman's work, at least, Skye. And M'sieu Robert has made many plans for me. It would be ungrateful to disappoint him."

"Of course," I said. "Is there someone with Uncle Robert now?"

"A valued client," said Courtney, with a flaring of aristocratic nostrils which told me his opinion of the client was far from high. "But the conference should be over shortly. The lady who consults him is Madame Lobelia Pollock, the

82

proprietress of L'Oiseau d'Or. They should be through shortly."

I had heard the name of this "palace of chance" before and remembered it as the place where Justin Law had made considerable winnings.

"I'll return in a little while," I said, and went out of the office.

In the passageway I stood for a moment feeling cozy and dry in the tunnel it made, with rain still drizzling beyond. The downpour had lessened, however, and as I went toward the courtyard I saw that Caro had run into the wet to stand beside the fountain.

I called to her softly, hoping her mother wouldn't hear. She came back to me with raindrops ashine in her dark hair and streaming down her face.

"I counted every one of the flower fish!" she cried happily. "For once, they seem to have gone sensibly to the bottom."

"Then run upstairs quickly," I told her, "and dry off before someone scolds you."

She flew up the stairs and I stood for a moment longer watching the drenched courtyard, with every leaf dripping, every blossom brimming with raindrops. Behind me I heard the opening of a downstairs door and Uncle Robert's voice bidding someone good day. His client was about to leave, so I could now return to his office with Aunt Natalie's list.

As I watched, a woman billowed through the door to an accompanying undulation of purple silks and feathery plumes. She came down the steps and saw me standing near the courtyard. I thought she stared at me rather boldly before she turned toward the street. The woman Courtney had referred to as Madame Pollock came from another world than mine and my interest was caught. Even the name of her gambling house—L'Oiseau d'Or—had an exotic ring. The Creoles, Mama had said, were great gamblers, so hers must be a profitable establishment.

But I could not stand there being idly curious. I returned to my uncle's office and was at once invited through the inner door. I found him fanning the air vigorously with a palm-leaf fan to dispel the overwhelming scent of the lady's perfume.

He greeted me pleasantly and asked me to take the chair beside his desk. He did not look at Aunt Natalie's list at once, but went to close the door to the outer office. His thoughts, clearly, were not upon the coming supper.

"Tell me, Skye, what you think of Courtney Law," he said, returning to his chair.

"He seems very pleasant," I admitted readily. "And he certainly has great admiration and respect for you."

Uncle Robert nodded in satisfaction. "He has been like a son to me. I lost my own boy some years ago."

"I know," I said in sympathy.

"I myself," he went on, "find Courtney a most admirable and worthy young man. He has excellent Creole blood from his mother's side, and apparently his father's blood does not predominate in his character. He is intelligent and while he will not make a brilliant lawyer, I believe he will do well."

I waited, saying nothing.

"It is possible that Courtney Law might make a sound choice for you as a husband, my dear," he said.

My mother had warned me in the beginning that Uncle Robert was thinking of Courtney as a husband for me. Perhaps I had misjudged her in dismissing her words. However, coming directly from my uncle, I could regard the suggestion with more tolerance than when it came from my mother. From his viewpoint this must seem something which should make me happy and get me safely married. I had still not made it clear to him my feelings about marriage—so different from those of the Creole.

He smiled at my thoughtful silence, perhaps thinking it the natural hesitation of a girl. "I had hoped my suggestion would meet with greater pleasure," he admitted. "However, it is natural for a young girl to regard marriage with some trepidation and uncertainty, even though it is of course her chief aim in life."

"I'm sorry, Uncle Robert," I told him, "but truly it is not my chief aim in life. Not just now at any rate. I like Courtney very much. And I believe he likes me. But I am not yet ready to think of marriage."

"Then we have said enough for the present," he said kindly. "I find in you a certain spirit and strength that would be excellent for Courtney. You would complement each other. And of course, my dear, he will be delighted when he knows that this is my wish for his future. The boy is deeply loyal in his feeling of indebtedness to me. It would be a fine thing to ally our two families more closely."

I nodded. "I can understand all that. But, Uncle Robert, I must love a man before I marry."

I had put a hand on his desk and he reached out and covered it gently with his own. "The young seldom realize

84

that the truest love comes after marriage. But I shall be patient, my dear, and hope that you will come to see this in a different light. That is why I suggested to my wife that we plan a small supper. It will be an opportunity for you and Courtney to be thrown together. That will not displease you?"

"No, of course not," I said and smiled at him warmly. It was good to feel that he had my well-being at heart, and I knew he would never push me into something against my own desire.

He tapped the list he held in his hand. "This is not what I had in mind. Will you please return it to my wife with my respects and suggest that we merely invite Courtney and Madame Law for this occasion."

I took the list and rose, but before I could walk out of the room he stopped me.

"One moment, Skye." He reached among the papers on his desk and drew out a square envelope. "This very strange invitation came to me this morning. Perhaps you would like to see it and take it upstairs to my wife."

I took the folded sheet of paper from the envelope and looked at it. Justin had lost no time. It was an invitation from Aurore to an informal *soirée* to be held at her home in the Garden District the end of this week. Uncle Robert and his family were invited. I looked at him questioningly.

"The audacity!" he murmured. "The enormous audacity of the fellow! This is not, of course, poor Aurore's doing. Courtney says she was bullied into it."

"You will refuse?" I said.

There was a hint of fire in my uncle's eyes as he looked at me. "Kindly take this to your aunt and ask that she accept for the family. I wish you all to attend this affair."

I regarded him in astonishment. "But I thought—"

"We cannot embarrass poor Aurore," he said. "You will be in Courtney's care and you need speak to the man as little as possible. But I wish you to attend. I shall be there myself, naturally."

In my own confusion, I did not know whether or not I wanted to attend. I was not entirely convinced by Uncle Robert's solicitous thought of Aurore. There was something here I did not understand. Some purpose of his own. But my uncle's tone rang with finality and I could not question him.

Courtney knocked on the door to say that someone wanted to speak to M'sieu Robert, and I took the list and invitation upstairs to Aunt Natalie. She shrugged over one and stared at the other. Caro had dried herself somewhat sketchily and she came dancing along the gallery after me, to regard the invitation with equal interest.

"Do you mean that my husband actually wishes us to attend an affair given while this barbarian is in Aurore's house?" Aunt Natalie asked.

"Probably it will be easier for Tante Aurore if we do," I suggested.

"May I also attend, Maman?" Caro pleaded. "Never have I seen a murderer. It would be very exciting."

"But certainly you will not attend," said Aunt Natalie firmly. "And you may go to your room now and stay there until you have learned not to speak of this man as a murderer. Whether he is, or is not, is hardly your concern. These are matters beyond your comprehension, *ma petite*. Go now—at once."

Caro went skipping off as gaily as though she did not know she was being banished by way of punishment. Aunt Natalie had finished her rinsing and was polishing the last of the crystal drops. Since there was nothing more to do, I went out on the gallery toward Papa's room. I wanted to tell him what Uncle Robert had said about Courtney.

Mama stood outside his door, staring absently into the courtyard. She did not see me at once, and in that unguarded moment she looked so completely lost and lonely that my heart went out to her. As long as I could remember, my mother had been gay and irresponsible, leaning entirely upon my father for guidance and good judgment. And now there was no one on whom she could lean. But even as I walked toward her, I thrust back this unexpected sympathy. Too well I remembered how gaily she had flirted with Courtney, how carefree she had seemed that day in the Garden District, with never a thought for my father here at home. I must not forget. I did not dare to trust her.

As I reached her, my mother saw me and spoke softly. "I couldn't stay in there with him any longer. Bruce doesn't care what becomes of me. I think he would die, if he could."

"Hush!" I said, fearful lest Papa hear her through the gallery window. "You mustn't say that—you mustn't think it!"

I gave up my futile notion of talking to Papa and went to my own room. Mama followed me and sat in the small rosewood rocker that seemed to suit her dainty person so well. In her hands she held a magazine, which I supposed she had been reading to Papa. She opened it now on her knees and held it out to me.

"Today this came by post. I took it to your father's room and read it to him. I thought it might strike some echo, might make him want to take his pen in hand again."

I looked at the magazine and saw that it contained the last piece my father had written before his accident. It was called "A Scotsman Looks at Boston." Glancing at the words, I could remember the evening when Papa himself had read the piece aloud to us in its first draft. We had laughed at his kindly humor and loved the affectionate picture of the city which his words evoked. The piece had been the result of a holiday trip he and Mama had taken together earlier.

"Perhaps I shouldn't have read it to him," Mama said, dabbing at her eyes with a scrap of handkerchief. "But I thought it might bring back a happy time to him, and perhaps make him want to write something more. He could write about New Orleans if he wanted to, and I told him so. He knows the city well enough from the days when he first came here, before we were married. You and I could be eyes for him and bring him new material, if only he were willing to take hold."

Her solution would have been fine, had Papa taken any real interest in living. But he no longer wanted to write and how could we urge him to what he had lost interest in?

Ten ☀

The days before Justin's party became suddenly filled with preparation. Aunt Natalie, having consulted with her husband, approached me gently on the subject of a new dress.

"For New Orleans one needs light, summery things," she told me. "It's quite natural that your New England wardrobe is not entirely suitable."

I didn't explain that its lack of suitability was due mainly to my lack of interest in clothes. A lack which grew from my desire to avoid any sense of comparison with my mother.

"It is your uncle's desire that you dress well on this occasion," Aunt Natalie went on. "The modiste is coming to consult with us this afternoon and to take your measurements. After all, we wish you to look charming for Courtney that night."

A certain resistance began to stiffen within me. If others would only let us alone, Courtney and I might develop a friendship between us—and who knew where it might lead? But I did not like to feel that I was being thrust upon him from every quarter. I did not like to be dressed like a doll and held up for him to admire. Courtney had been nice to me when I wore my brown foulard. He had never called me a wren.

Anger flashed through me as I remembered. A brown wren! Oh, if only I could show his brother! But I knew how beautiful my mother would look and as always I feared what I so often glimpsed in the eyes of those who saw us together.

Mama and Aunt Natalie were both present when the dressmaker came for my fittings. Mama, of course, was delighted at the prospect of attending Justin's party. Away from my father's room and the unhappiness there, she seemed like a bird escaped from its cage. She took pleasure in dressing me up, though she had ceased to prattle about Courtney as an eligible young man.

On the morning of the party Delphine took a hand. She washed my hair and afterwards I sat with my back to the sun on the second-floor gallery, while she dried it with fluffy towels, scented as always with vetiver, that pleasant root used so often in New Orleans. She had washed my mother's hair first, and Mama sat near me, her heavy tresses shining darkly in the sun.

Delphine pressed the towel about my shoulders and fluffed my red hair over it. Then she touched a strand and let the drying tendrils cling to her fingers.

"The color is perhaps not *comme il faut*, mam'zelle, but it would be better to display it in a style more elegant. If mam'zelle will permit me—"

"But of course!" Mama cried. "Let Delphine dress your hair for you tonight. Why not try a new coiffure as soon as her hair is dry enough, Delphine? We can make a beautiful lady of her tonight, not only with the charming new dress, but with a lovely hair style as well. You will never find a husband, Skye, if you always dress like a wren."

There was the detestable word thrown at me again. I was

tempted to let them see what they could do with me so that no one would ever again call me a wren.

Delphine's dark eyes betrayed nothing except the veiled scorn that seemed so often to be in them.

"Perhaps mam'zelle is afraid to let herself be beautiful?" she said softly, and then went on before I could speak. "Soon the sun will make the hair dry enough. In Madame Natalie's room there is a great mirror and the light is excellent. Come soon, mam'zelle. I will go now to prepare."

She did not listen for my consent or refusal, but went quickly away, her head held high in its blue tignon. I had the strange feeling that while I might stand against Aunt Natalie and my mother, and even oppose Uncle Robert at times, I would be powerless in Delphine's hands. Her assurance compelled obedience. I did not like the thing she had hinted—that I was afraid to be beautiful. What if I picked up her challenge? What if I showed them all I was not afraid?

"You will be a *succès fou* when Delphine is through with you, Skye," Mama assured me. "As a girl she learned to be an expert *coiffeuse* from a hairdresser in Paris."

Paris? So that was why Delphine's accent was so markedly that of an educated Frenchwoman.

"How did a Negro slave happen to study in Paris?" I asked.

Mama rolled her eyes heavenward. *"Ma foi!* Delphine was never a slave, nor her mother before her. They are of the *gens de couleur libres,* a free people of color. Indeed" —she lowered her voice—"her mother was one of those on Rampart Street. A *placée.* The custom, most fortunately, is no more. Her father sent his daughter to France for an education. But since he would not have her follow in the mother's steps she was also taught a suitable way to earn a living. However, she came at length to this house and has worked here ever since."

"What is a *placée?"* I asked, fluffing my hair again with the towels to encourage its drying.

"This is not a subject which ladies discuss," Mama told me, suddenly prim.

"If you've never discussed it, then how do you know anything about it?" I demanded.

She had the grace to laugh a little. "Very well. You are, after all, of more than marriageable age and old enough to learn of these matters. Of course these wicked, old-fashioned ways are now dead. But up to the time of the war when Creoles were nearly all wealthy, a young man would often take a colored mistress and keep her in a house on Rampart Street. The girls were all quadroons, or perhaps even lighter than that, and they were well educated and carefully chaperoned by their mothers."

"I've heard of the quadroon balls," I said.

Mama nodded. "These girls were presented at such balls, where a gentleman could meet them and perhaps become the 'protector' of the girl of his choice."

"All this was done openly?" I asked.

Mama looked shocked. "Not so far as ladies were concerned. Wives and mothers and sweethearts were supposed to know nothing of such matters. And of course, when a gentleman married, he must never see his quadroon sweetheart again. At least his wife hoped that he would not. Though of course he was obliged to make a settlement that would take care of her for her lifetime, and of any children there might be. A girl who was so chosen was known as a *placée*."

"And was Delphine's mother one?" I asked.

Again my mother nodded. "You understand, however, one does not inquire into such matters, Skye." She reached out and touched my hair. "It is dry now. You'd better not keep Delphine waiting. I shall sit here for a while, since my hair is not a problem."

I hesitated a moment longer, still undecided. Then I went to Aunt Natalie's handsome bedroom.

Here the furnishings were more elaborate than in any other bedroom in the house. There was a little *prie-dieu* with a velvet kneeling cushion. The great bed had an embroidered canopy of pale blue satin beneath the tester. A *"ciel de lit,"* Delphine told me it was called, and said it had been given to Madame Natalie as a bridal canopy when she married Robert Tourneau. Through the door to an adjoining room I could see a white cradle with a curving swan neck, where Tina lay rosily asleep. My uncle chose to have a room of his own across the hall.

I sat like a doll before the dressing table and let Delphine do what she liked with my hair. I found myself watching as if I watched a stranger about whom I was not at all sure. Who was the girl with red hair who looked back at me in the mirror? Was she truly afraid to be more than herself? Was she the sort who did not dare to be anything that was not easy and safe? I did not like to think that. I watched, interested, but uncertain.

Delphine stroked scented pomade along strands of my

hair and then decided by experiment just how she would comb it for tonight. Finally she wound it in *papillotes*, so that it would fall into the style she wished when she came to dress it for dinner. Then she found me a lace cap to wear over the paper curlers.

Once Aunt Natalie looked in on us approvingly.

"Delphine is right. If you must have such hair, Skye, then it is better to display it modishly. I trust your uncle will approve. It was only the dress he spoke of."

Later in the morning the modiste arrived for the final fitting and Mama too came up to Aunt Natalie's room. I let them pinch me and push me about. The dressmaker was most distressed at the hurry with which this gown was being finished, and I gathered that it was only the Tourneau name which kept her from throwing up her hands in despair.

The frock was a simple one of white mull, since this was an informal summer occasion. But it was cunningly cut and draped, with touches here and there of pale gold ribbon. The dress, it seemed to me, was for a very young and pretty girl and I was neither. There were times when I felt older than my mother.

After an early supper that night Delphine brought the dress to my room and closed the door firmly upon any possible intruder. For the last time I made myself passive under her hands, while she dressed my hair and helped me into the frock, hooking the tight bodice up the back over my stays. As always her face was expressionless, yet I sensed in her an air of satisfaction in what she had accomplished.

"Voilà!" she said at length, and turned me toward a mirror. "Behold yourself, mam'zelle." She propelled me across the room with strong hands, as if I had been a child, and stood me before my mirror.

"You will look, mam'zelle," she said. "Then you will not desire to return to the old way."

I gazed into the mirror and saw with some surprise the girl who stared back at me. The white gown was soft with French lace about the throat, giving a gentler, more feminine look than the dark, plain things I so often wore. My hair, clustered in small curls across my forehead, was drawn back in loose waves and pinned high with silver combs. The mass of it fell in a sheer, wavy cascade to just below my shoulders. Delphine held a hand mirror for me and turned me this way, then that.

"I don't want to look like a child."

"When you appear in a box in the Opera in November,"

Delphine said complacently, "this will become the mode. Every eye in the house will be upon you. No lady in New Orleans will have so *splendide* a *coiffure rouge*."

"And what will Uncle Robert think of that?" I said. "No Creole woman is supposed to make herself conspicuous."

"You can be nothing less, Mam'zelle Skye," said Delphine. "You must resign yourself." She thrust a few combings into the china hair receiver on my dressing table, and picked up her brushes. "You are yourself, mam'zelle. You do not need to be like your maman."

I stole a second look at the mirror and saw that bright color had come into my cheeks and that my gray-blue eyes had in them a shine of excitement. My breathing quickened and I had the queer sense of being both attracted and frightened as I looked at this unfamiliar self in the mirror.

"You begin to see, do you not, mam'zelle?" Delphine said knowingly. She reached into the pocket of her apron and drew out several crumpled rose petals which she dropped on the dressing table before me. "For your lips, mam'zelle. It is also wise to bite the lips strongly under the cover of one's handkerchief. Have you earrings? Pearls, perhaps? Your ears are of delicate shape—you should not hide them. Pearls will set them off."

She did not wait for my answer, but opened the jewel case on my dresser and found a pair of tiny drop earrings of creamy pearl that Papa had given me long ago. Again without permission, she removed the plain gold rings I wore to keep the piercing in my ears open, and replaced them with the drops of pearl. Then she stood back to view her handiwork.

"Tonight," she said, your maman will be as nothing. Every man will look at you."

I turned from the spell the mirror put upon me. "Why do you say that? You don't like my mother, do you, Delphine?"

She walked to the door without a word. "I must go to help Madame Natalie now." And out she went, drawing the door softly closed behind her.

What a strange woman she was. The others in this household took her so entirely for granted, yet I suspected that strong emotions could blaze behind the still mask of her face. What did she think about as she served us, and why should she care how I looked tonight? I could understand that she might like to dress me up and show me off as an example of her own handiwork. But why should she say that tonight my mother would be nothing? Why should she care?

The mirror drew me again like a magnet. My window shutters had been closed against the warmth of the afternoon, but now I pushed them ajar so that more light could fall upon me. With the light came the heady scent of the garden, and I felt again the strangeness I had experienced on my first night in New Orleans. But now I no longer wanted to guard myself against this tropical beauty; as if all of me that belonged to New Orleans were ready to surge up with frightening force, to possess me entirely.

The girl in the white dress, with the soft waves of bright hair, belonged to New Orleans as surely as did the scent of roses and jasmine, and I knew she could revel in such a belonging. The Creole might lie submerged, but it could come to the fore and have its day.

Very well, let it come! For this one night I would belong to New Orleans. I would dare what I had never had the courage to dare before. And I'd see to it that Justin Law would never again think of me as a wren.

I caught up the crumpled petals and rubbed them into my lips where a little of their pinkness remained and the scent clung to my fingers. Then I went quickly out upon the gallery to my father's room.

His door stood open, and I went in with only a tap and stood before him, both eager and hesitant. Perhaps Papa had been dozing, for he opened his eyes and looked at me as if I were something out of his dreams.

" 'Tis your grandmother you look like, lassie. Your hair, your eyes, the lift of your head. These are hers as I remember them."

His words reassured me. For a moment I had forgotten that I was a Scotswoman as much as I was a Creole. I pulled a chair over beside his bed and sat down. There was time to talk to him before we had to leave, and for once he did not seem lost in apathy.

"Tell me about Scotland," I said. "So I'll remember who I am tonight. Tell me about your Isle of Skye."

He smiled as he used to when I was a child begging for stories and he told me once again of that day when my grandmother had stood at the bridge below the glen at Sligachan and waved her eldest son off to Portree. From Portree a boat would take him to the mainland, and finally his way would lead across the seas to distant America.

Near the bridge was the place where the crossroads met and parted—to Dunvegan and Portree and Kyleakin.

"The gray mists were coming down upon the glen that

day," he said. "Old Sgurr nan Gillian had lost its jagged head in the clouds and mists hung low over the hump of Marsco. The black Cuillin had vanished beyond, but the spell of those dark mountains lies forever upon that glen, and their voices are heard in the burn that tumbles down its length. I remember how black and wet the boulders looked that day, strewn across the moor. And I remember your grandmother's bright red hair with mist drops shining on every strand. That was the last time I saw her, lassie."

I felt a little ashamed, as though I had forgotten something important.

"I am *her* granddaughter too," I said softly. "I belong to a race that does not lose its head or go giddy with frivolity like the Creole."

He reached his hand to me, smiling a little. "The Scotsman who cannot on occasion lose his head to his heart isn't worthy of wearing the plaid. If you recall, there have been French and Scottish mixtures like yours in history, and they've as often as not run into trouble about the losing of heads."

Before I could answer, Mama came lightly into the room and gave me a quick, astonished look.

"So here you are. Robert wishes to see how you look. Stand up, daughter, and turn around. Let me see how the dress hangs."

My earlier confidence faded a little before her scrutiny.

After a moment she nodded. "The gown looks well— quite suitable and *jeune fille*. But the hair—about that I'm not so sure. Delphine inclines toward the overly dramatic. For you it is not—"

"Let the child be," Papa said, and my mother glanced at him in surprise. It had been a long while since he had shown interest enough to intervene in our affairs. "There'll not be a woman at the party tonight," he went on, "more eye-taking than your daughter."

Mama pouted a little and moved toward the door, and I knew he had said the wrong thing. He knew it too, though he had not intended to hurt her.

"For me, Louise," he said as she paused in the doorway, "you are the most beautiful. Always."

But she was not mollified. I think she had not expected to find me looking as I did, and she had an impulse to punish us both. So she glanced at him indifferently, as though his words did not matter, and went out of the room. I saw the dark blood rise in his face and knew how deeply she had cut him.

I could have shaken my mother in bitter anger at that moment, but she had gone on toward the parlor, where the shutters upon the courtyard gallery stood open and Uncle Robert waited to judge my appearance.

Eleven ✼

I stood before my uncle in my new gown, with my hair upon my shoulders, and he studied me so gravely that my heart began to thump beneath the tightly fitted bodice of the dress. What Uncle Robert thought meant everything at that moment. Papa, after all, was prejudiced from the start in my favor. But to some extent I could test myself in my uncle's eyes.

At length he nodded in approval. "I am pleased, indeed, Skye. The evening should go well. I shall be proud to present my niece to this gathering tonight."

A heady sense of confidence possessed me. Surely if I could pass this severe scrutiny, I would meet no disapproval anywhere.

My mother fluttered her blue silk fan and coughed gently for attention, but he scarcely noticed her, though she was breath-taking in pale blue silk. I thought she looked very young and lovely tonight, but for once I knew I could hold my own beside her.

When Courtney called for us I saw his startled look of astonishment when he saw me, and then a dawning pleasure in his eyes. I caught him staring at me oddly once or twice, and certainly he was attentive during our drive to the Garden District.

Mama was far from pleased. I could sense the pique in her faintly pouting look and in the lack of vivacity she showed while we were in the carriage. For the third time tonight a man had remarked on my appearance and ignored hers, and I had a feeling that someone would be made to pay for this. But for now it was my evening and I could not worry about her. There was a new sense of joyousness in me, an eagerness to embrace all the color and warmth of a gay and brilliant New Orleans evening. I was ready to love everyone and to believe everyone would love me.

When we reached the Law house and Courtney helped me from the carriage, pressed my arm and whispered that he could not wait to dance with me, all my tingling anticipation increased a thousandfold. Yet it was not of Courtney I was thinking, but of Justin. How would he like me now that I was no longer a wren? And would he too be eager to dance with me?

The house was brilliantly lighted in all its windows and we heard the sound of gay laughter as we went up the steps. In the parlor someone was playing the piano and a Chopin waltz drifted pleasantly into the scented night.

Justin himself came to the door to greet us. He bowed to Aunt Natalie, to Mama, to me, but his eyes skimmed over us as if he were barely aware of our presence. The unexpected fires I had found in myself blazed up in bright anger, and I might have spoken to him deliberately, forced his attention, had I not suddenly realized that all his concentration was on my uncle.

A curious moment of silence fell upon us there in the bright hallway as the two men faced each other. It was as if Justin and my uncle were caught together in a strange isolation through which hostility crackled like a living thing. No one else existed in that instant for either of them. The antagonism that sprang between them was so sharp and frightening, so wrought with suppressed violence, that it was shocking to see. What lay between these two that they were so ready to hate each other? And how could my uncle and his family possibly step into this house when such antagonism lay between him and his host?

Then Justin moved and held out his hand. "Good evening, sir," he said quietly and the hint of violence I had glimpsed was hidden. Uncle Robert took his hand and returned his greeting with equal calm. Whatever had flared between them had been submerged, concealed, but it was alarming to know it was there.

Justin led the way into the great lighted parlor, and Mama, Aunt Natalie, and Uncle Robert followed him. Courtney offered me his arm, but an unexpected panic seized me. The real test was now upon me. I must step into that room and be the woman I wanted to be, without doubt or faltering. I must face Justin Law and make him aware of me, make

96

him recognize me as he had not yet done because of my uncle.

Then, before Courtney could lead me after the others, Tante Aurore's little maid came running up to him.

"If you please, m'sieu, Madame Aurore refuses to come downstairs. She says she cannot attend the party, and I do not know what to do."

Courtney sighed and turned to me. "This is a difficult thing. All day, Skye, she has been saying she will not attend Justin's party. She will not see him, will not take part in anything he plans. But for the sake of propriety she must put in an appearance."

I grasped at this opportunity for a reprieve. Somehow I must recover the sense of joyous confidence I had felt in the carriage, before Justin's look had slipped over me without seeing my transformation and doubt had beset me.

"Let me go upstairs and talk to your mother," I offered. "It may be that she will listen best to someone outside the close family."

Courtney was grateful for my suggestion and I went quickly upstairs to Aurore's room. I found her lying upon the bed, fully dressed, but plainly in a state of limp collapse. She pressed a handkerchief dipped in violet water to her temples and greeted me almost tearfully.

"Is it true, *chérie,* that Robert has accepted this invitation? That he has come to this house tonight?"

"Of course," I said. "We are all here. Aunt Natalie, Mama and I. And naturally Uncle Robert. So you must find the strength to join your guests downstairs."

"They are not my guests!" she cried. "I agreed to invite them in a moment of weakness, but it is not my party."

I took the violet-scented handkerchief from her hands and sat beside the bed, stroking her forehead with the bit of cool, perfumed linen. Outside the dark garden stirred faintly in the evening breeze and the mingling of June scents drifted through the window, sweeter than the perfume in my hands. In the dusk the birds were chirping sleepily as they settled down for the night.

"Nevertheless, they are your guests too," I told her gently. "And they are all your friends. If you do not appear to greet them, Courtney feels there will be much gossip."

"There will be gossip anyway." Aurore turned on the bed, and put a hand upon my arm. But now she was not thinking of the problem downstairs. "When he first came here," she said, and I knew she meant Justin, "he told me

97

I should have gone to Colorado with his father when he left New Orleans. But how could I have gone with Harry when he wanted me to? How could I have endured disgrace and exile and hardship? *Chérie.* I had been gently bred and sheltered all my life. How could he wish this of me?"

"You mustn't worry about that now," I said as I touched her frail wrists with the handkerchief, pitying this woman who seemed to feel so guilty about a long-distant past. "Tell me one thing, Tante Aurore. If your husband was really a spy, why didn't he join the Union Army?"

"I think he was never a spy. He said to me often that the South was his second mother. He would never betray her, or take up arms against her. But it was thought at the time that he was against us because in open argument he opposed our fighting the North. Robert Tourneau himself believed he was dangerous to the South. Feeling was very strong against him and so it was necessary to escape, lest they hang him first and inquire afterwards. But Harry should not have taken the boy." She put a hand to her heart as if it were beating painfully. "Justin has grown to look like his father. I came near to fainting the day he walked into this house."

"You loved your husband, didn't you?" I said softly.

She closed her eyes. "What is love? Of what practical use is it? I'd have been far better off if I had married Robert Tourneau, as my family wished me to do."

It seemed a release for her to talk, so I drew her on. "Do you really mean that?"

"Yes, yes!" She pounded one thin hand into the pillow beside her head. "None of this suffering would have been mine had I married him. I would have been cherished, loved. I would not have had to take charity from a man who once cared for me."

"But all these things are done and past," I said. "We have to deal with what exists in the present. So now you must be brave and go downstairs."

She sat up and pushed back a strand of hair nervously from her forehead. "I suppose it is necessary to make the effort. If I do not, Robert will be displeased, and I cannot afford to anger him."

I helped her straighten her black silk dress and tidy her graying hair. Then we went together to the door. Downstairs someone played the piano again and the sound of a lively polka came to us. Now I knew that I could postpone the test of stepping into that room no longer.

Aurore hesitated at the top of the stairs. "I think Justin

has not come here out of an idle wish to reacquaint himself with his old home. He has come for some wicked purpose of his own."

Then rigorous Creole training came to her aid. She raised her head, tightened her lips to still their trembling, and walked quite steadily downstairs, her hand resting lightly on my arm.

As Creoles loved music, so they loved dancing, and already chairs had been pushed back against the wall and in spite of the warmth of the summer evening, couples were circling the floor. I saw my mother go by in Courtney's arms, smiling up at him captivatingly that he did not notice us there in the doorway.

In the North the combination of these enormous double parlor rooms would have been called a drawing room. The two rooms stretched from the front of the house to the back, with tall windows along one side, opening onto a veranda, and high ceilings which kept them airy and cool. The Empire touch was evident in carvings over the high doors and in the cornices, marking a division of the rooms. Handsome mantels set off twin fireplaces, and two great mirrors at either end of the long expanse, reaching from floor to ceiling, gave back all the movement and color that glowed in the room.

But my eyes, even as they noted details, were searching for Justin Law, and at first I did not see him. Uncle Robert came toward us across the room, looking so handsome, so assured and distinguished, that I wondered how Aurore had ever managed to leave him for Harry Law.

He greeted her pleasantly and told her the party was charming. By his manner he seemed to set her in her proper place as hostess, as if it were she who had planned this *soirée*, and not Justin. She responded gratefully and as she moved away from us to meet her guests, I saw that she was fully in control of herself once more.

Uncle Robert regarded me with approval and offered his arm. His wife, he said, was chatting happily with her women friends, and he would be honored to show me about. And as I moved through that gay gathering at his side all my confidence and courage came sweeping back full force. For now I was no wren to be left neglected and overlooked. I moved at the side of a handsome and distinguished man of some consequence in New Orleans, and he paid me affectionate homage.

On every hand I saw interest come to life in the eyes of

the young men to whom my uncle introduced me. In no time at all I was dancing as I had never danced before, and loving every moment of it. This new exhilaration was like champagne bubbling in my veins, so that my head felt as light as my feet. Courtney came to dance with me too, and then I saw him again with my mother. But I did not care. There were so many attentive young men, and I was riding on the giddy crest of such a wave as I had never risen to before. Yet all the while, dancing now with this one, now with that, I was aware of one man I had glimpsed at the far end of the room. Justin was not dancing, but he was the center of a constantly shifting group who engaged him in conversation.

I sensed the whispering that went on all around him, especially among the ladies. What chatter there would be in the Vieux Carré tomorrow, what lively gossip! They would whisper that the fellow was recently out of prison. A murderer in their midst! "Naturally," I heard one lady murmur, he will not be received in any good home. We are here only for dear Aurore's sake."

But if scandal buzzed about him, Justin ignored it and seemed completely at ease. Of course I took care that my eyes should not meet his as my partners whirled me by, but just as I was aware of him, I hoped he was aware of me, aware of my triumph. How that brown little word he had named me with ate at my being, so that I could never rest until I heard him retract it.

At last there was a lull in the dancing and Uncle Robert came to my side again, and once more we moved from group to group, stopping to chat here and there. This time our course took us ever nearer to the place where Justin stood. I had the opportunity now for an occasional careless glance in his direction and I could not help but be impressed and a little surprised by the way he conducted himself. His manner, perhaps, was a bit more hearty than that of the Creole, but the polish of good breeding was there when he chose to assume it. He had the air of a gentleman, no matter what his past.

My uncle, I realized, was moving deliberately toward him, and taking me along. This time Justin must certainly look at me, must reveal whatever he thought of my appearance tonight. But when we reached him, there was nothing about his look or manner to show that he saw the slightest change in me. His eyes recognized me, he smiled politely, but at once his attention went past me to Uncle

Robert, and again that sinister hostility leaped like a spark between the two men.

There was no escape for me. I was drawn into the circle of their meeting, my hand upon Uncle Robert's arm.

"You are planning to take up residence again in the city of your birth, m'sieu?" Uncle Robert asked him.

Justin's look rested steadily on my uncle's face, and I saw his mouth tighten.

"Perhaps," he said. "I've grown tired of mountains made ugly by the men who mine them. The river has called me ever since I was a boy. Perhaps I'll take it for a partner."

Beneath my hand I felt the stiffening that ran through my uncle. "Your meaning, m'sieu?"

"To make it clear," Justin said, and there was an ominous note in his voice, "my intention is to recover my father's shipping business."

"As you know," Uncle Robert told him coldly, "that business is being well managed for me and it is not for sale."

"Perhaps purchase is not what I had in mind." Justin's tone was even, but I sensed the suppressed anger beneath his words.

Uncle Robert turned abruptly from him and led me away. His face was tight with a fury he could not conceal, and I did not dare to question him about Justin's meaning.

The dancing had started again and Courtney came once more to dance with me. Uncle Robert seemed to be glad enough to be released from his duty for the moment and I went whirling away in Courtney's arms.

"Why has Justin come to New Orleans?" I asked his brother. "What does he hold against my uncle?"

But Courtney would not speak of serious matters. "You are beautiful tonight, Skye. You should always dress like this and wear your hair upon your shoulders. And you must not trouble your lovely head about the affairs of men."

I did not want to be put off like that. "I'm quite capable of understanding that one plus one makes two," I said a little tartly. "And I'm interested in knowing why such enmity exists between Uncle Robert and your brother Justin."

Courtney waltzed me gently down the room. "Ah well, if you insist, I'll try to explain. Before the war my father was the owner of a large and profitable shipping business which ran boats upon the Mississippi River. Of course all this was lost during the war. Later your uncle was able to salvage something of the business and build up the company again. My brother's notion that he somehow has a right to this business as my father's heir is nonsense of course. If Justin wants to get into shipping, let him start a company of his own. However, M'sieu Robert will deal with him properly when the time comes, I am sure. I am willing to trust his judgment in this matter."

Again I sensed in Courtney his deep respect for my uncle, and I liked him for it. Yet I found myself wondering how strong this feeling was and how far Courtney would go to please Uncle Robert. I wondered what my partner would say if he knew that my uncle had plans to marry him to me. I didn't believe Uncle Robert had said anything to Courtney as yet, and I thought I would test him a little.

"I do believe," I said lightly, "that you would do almost anything Uncle Robert asked you to do."

"I would die for him, mam'zelle," said Courtney simply.

"Would you even—marry for him?" I asked. "I mean, suppose he should pick out a young lady whom he wished you to marry. Suppose it was someone whom you didn't care for seriously. Would you obey him then?"

The music had stopped and the dancers paused in couples around the room, talking and laughing. The buzz of sound covered our odd conversation.

Courtney seemed mildly surprised by my question, though not in the way I might have expected. "But this is not unusual—that one's elders arrange a marriage. When that time comes I shall certainly seek M'sieu Robert's advice."

"That would be different," I pointed out. "If you picked the girl yourself and asked his advice, then you would undoubtedly be in love with her. I was referring to an arranged marriage where there might be no love on either side. How do you Creoles feel about that?"

Courtney's shrug dismissed the matter. "It is a romantic notion that one marries for love. When our elders choose for us wisely, a more lasting affection is certain to follow."

He was parroting what had been taught him, but for the moment at least, he believed his own words.

"The whole idea seems barbaric to me," I said lightly. "When I marry, it shall be for love and nothing else. And I would never have a man who was not in love with me."

Courtney laughed. "Ah, but you would be most easy to love, Skye."

A hand touched my arm just then and I looked up to see Justin beside us. Courtney stiffened at the appearance of his brother.

102

"What's all this about love?" Justin asked, and his glance rested curiously on my partner.

Courtney's eyes were bright with challenge. "What else is there to speak of more important than love? Naturally I was confessing my undying adoration of this young lady with the red hair."

The music started again and Courtney moved to draw me away, but Justin's hand clasped about my wrist and held me where I was.

"It's my turn to dance with Skye," he told his brother.

Courtney might have objected, but I wanted no disturbance that would give rise to more gossip. "It's all right," I said quickly to Courtney. He bowed to me stiffly and walked away.

There was nothing of gallantry about Justin. His fingers were clasped firmly about my wrist, and under cover of dancers sweeping past us, he drew me toward a tall window that opened upon the veranda.

"We can dance later," he said. "Right now I want a breath of air and space enough to turn around in. Drawing rooms cramp me. Come along."

I tried to draw back, angry at his calm assumption that I would go with him, when he had ignored me until now. And anxious as well not to displease my uncle by slipping away from the dance with this man. But I had little choice. He pulled me quickly along the veranda to a flight of wooden steps. Long patches of light from the windows cut across the lawn, but beyond the garden lay dark and sweet and quiet. Fireflies danced above shrubbery and twining rosa montana, their light more beautiful than the brilliance behind us. There was nothing I could do. I stopped resisting and went with him.

Twelve ※

As we walked, circling the wide garden that lay between the Law house and its neighbors, Justin spoke absently, as if he thought aloud.

"My brother would make no husband for you," he said.

All the annoyance this man so often aroused in me surged again to the fore. Everything that he did was wrong, as far as I was concerned. After criticizing me earlier, he had not noticed my hair or my dress, and now he had high-handedly plucked me out of that Creole gathering, assuring me of Uncle Robert's displeasure, when he discovered my absence. He even had the temerity to state that his brother was not for me.

"Oh, I don't know," I said, trying to sound casual. "Courtney is a most charming and amiable young man."

"I'm sure of that," Justin admitted. "But he'd be no match for you. You'll need a man with a strong hand on the reins."

I whirled to face him, though light from the house shone in my eyes and I could not see his expression.

"What do you know of me? How dare you say a thing like that!"

"I was fond of Courtney as a little boy," he went on, ignoring my indignation as if it were of no consequence. "He used to follow me around and admire me as a big brother when he was hardly more than a baby. I hated to leave him when I went with my father. But his mother has done a thorough job of turning him away from any resemblance to his father. He is owned by your uncle now. Still, I'd like to do something for him, if I could. Perhaps take him into business with me."

The indignation within me began to quiet a little. For the first time I wondered about Justin's motives in returning to New Orleans. Had he come back, not to make trouble after all, as everyone said, but because he was driven by a longing to retrace boyhood steps, to re-establish family ties?

"Don't sentimentalize over me," he said, as if he read my mind, and I realized that he could see my face in the reflected light and that my expression must have softened. "At least I'm glad you wore your hair loose tonight, as you should always wear it. But the dress doesn't suit you. It's better than that brown thing you wear, but it's too childish for you. I'd like to see you in colors that match your spirit and give you dignity."

All the softness went out of me. "I didn't realize you had noticed me, let alone that you'd observed what I was wearing," I snapped, and hated my own words because they sounded like absurd feminine pique.

He laughed out loud at me. "I grew up in a country where a man sees what has to be seen in the twinkling of an eye. But if you expected me to be overwhelmed by the change in you, thunderstruck by your beauty, then I'm sorry —that wasn't the effect."

He was mocking me now, and I turned away from the revealing light. Somehow he had stripped all the sham of beauty from me and made me once more so much less than my mother. I felt ridiculous tears sting my eyes and I would have fled back to the house if he had not put a hand on my arm again.

"What a goose you are!" He shook me lightly. "Don't you think I can recognize what a woman looks like when I see her, regardless of furbelows? I've seen you before—that day on Gallatin Street, and again in the library here in this house. I hope I've the good sense to recognize more than a brown dress that doesn't become you. Your spirit was evident and your intelligence, even if you weren't doing justice to the woman you are. Tonight you've done a better job— but that doesn't change my first recognition of you, Skye Cameron."

Now it was he who faced the light in the shadowy garden. I could see the planes of his face clearly, catch the radiance glinting on his fair hair. There was a strange mingling of emotions in me as I looked at him. There was violence in this man, and rebellion and anger. Everything he stood for revolted me and went against all my father's sane and gentle teachings, against all that Uncle Robert wanted for me. Yet no one had ever seen me before as this man had seen me. No one had ever spoken to me like this. I was a woman spellbound and only a disturbing wonder filled me. How would it seem to be loved by such a man? Would his hands be hard and cruel upon a woman's shoulders? Could that grim mouth ever soften to the tenderness of a kiss?

My face was burning hot and I pressed my hands over it, bent my head in confusion and shame. But Justin drew my hands away and held them in his and I could look nowhere except into his eyes. I saw the change in his face, in the hard muscles of his jaw. The grim lines of his mouth relaxed and he put his hands upon my arms. Once more I sensed the strength that flowed through him. I do not know whether he pulled me to him, or whether I went of my own accord into his arms, but I felt them close about me. His mouth was so very close to my own—I need only turn my head a little.

There was somehow a sense of surprise in his kiss, as if he, no more than I, had meant this to happen. He put his

mouth roughly upon my own, bruising my lips. Yet I did
not want to pull away. When he raised his head I stood on
tiptoe and put my cheek for an instant against the roughness
of his own cheek. I did not want him to let me go. I wanted
no words, but only sensation. His hand lost itself in the
thick fall of hair upon my shoulders and I felt his fingers
tighten until there was a tugging at the roots of my scalp.
Then he thrust me away from him and there was a look
in his eyes that startled me. In it there was no kindness, but
something I could not read.

"So you're not, after all, the prim Yankee I thought you,"
he said. "I should have known no Puritan could have hair
like yours. Shall we go back to the dancing now?"

I did not know how to face him, or what to say to him.
His words were like a slap across my face and my cheeks
stung with scarlet. I turned quickly away and started toward
the house. But once more he halted me.

"Wait, Skye. I've a damnable tongue. You took me by
surprise, but still the fault is mine."

"You needn't apologize," I said. "That is more insulting
than the act."

He laughed wryly. "You needn't trouble to tell me that
I'm not a gentleman. I know that. But before we return to
the house, I must say one thing to you."

I shook my head angrily, wanting only to get away from
him. "There's nothing you can say I want to hear."

But he would not let me go. "You may not want to hear
me, but I'll have my say just the same. Be as angry with me
as you like, but one thing must be made clear. There's no
place in my life for women." His voice hardened. "I've
never known one who could be trusted. Neither my mother
nor any other. When I play at love I don't play for marriage.
And regardless of your red hair and the way you kissed
me just now, I fancy you're for marrying."

I choked with anger and something more. Something that
was sharp and hurtful. But there was nothing I could say to
him, no answer I could make. He came with me back to the
house and I flew up the steps ahead of him, wanting only
to escape. But we slipped through the open window together
when no one was looking our way and there was nothing
I could do but dance with him.

I know that I can dance well. My mother had sent me to
dancing school early and she had taken a hand in training
me herself. But always when I danced the picture of myself
as tall and awkward beside her lightness and dainty grace

was in my mind. Tonight for the first time, I had been able to forget myself in dancing.

Now, however, I was too angry and wounded to relax and I followed Justin automatically, rigidly. His arm was tight about me so that I could not falter.

"Miss Cameron," he murmured and I hated the sound of laughter in his voice, "you would be an excellent dancer if you did not hold yourself as stiffly as a poker. Relax a little and you will find the movement not unpleasant."

I let my eyes blaze up at him as they had done once before, and I saw to my surprise that the smile twisting his mouth was not unkind.

"You're angry with me," he said, close to my ear. "Stay that way, Skye. Hate me with all your heart. I'm not a man any woman should want."

"As if I did!" I answered heatedly. "Your—your conceit—!"

"I know," he said. And somehow he looked as if he wanted to kiss me again right in the midst of that gay New Orleans party.

At least my anger stood me in good stead through the rest of the evening. It stiffened my spine and kept up my chin. It contributed to the pretense I made at having a good time, when all the while I was sick with angry humiliation.

I did not have to dance with Justin again. My uncle, busy watching Courtney, had not noticed my disappearance. There was reason now to watch Courtney, I saw, for it appeared that my mother had at last succeeded in charming him. I knew he had danced with her several times, but somehow I'd begun to think he would resist her. I should have known that Mama could not bear defeat. Of course her little flirtation was decorous, with glances and words so skillfully veiled that only one who knew her well would see what she was up to. My uncle was her brother and he knew her as well as I.

When I stood beside Uncle Robert he nodded to me gravely. "I shall have to take this matter in hand. Tomorrow I will speak to Courtney and tell him my wishes as far as you are concerned. Otherwise he will do what many another young fool has done before him. He will fancy himself in love with a married woman."

I did not answer. This was my mother's fault. I could see that clearly and I wondered how far this flirtation was likely to go, with my father in no position to take her in hand. Always before I had been sure that her love for him had never wavered. But how long could he hold her in that cage of a room where he lay? Especially when he had given up all pretense of trying.

"I shall speak to your mother, too," said Uncle Robert softly. "It is hardly fitting that she flirt with her future son-in-law."

At any other time I might have spoken up. I'd have reminded him of my objection to a planned marriage of any sort—to Courtney or anyone else. But my senses were still in a turmoil over what had happened between me and Justin Law. I had brought upon myself exactly what I deserved. Uncle Robert had done his best to warn me against the man, to make me realize that he was not to be trusted. What would my uncle think now if he knew that Justin had held me in his arms and kissed me only a little while before, and that I had kissed him back? No, this was not the moment to voice objections to anything Uncle Robert suggested. Perhaps he took my silence at that moment for acquiescence. I do not know.

The party ran very late, as New Orleans affairs were wont to do. Two or three guests sang for us, there were piano solos and always more dancing. Tante Aurore had recovered herself enough to supervise the serving of the lavish supper, and the *soirée* was not over until well past midnight.

Uncle Robert's carriage came for us and after a fond parting with Tante Aurore, we drove back to the Vieux Carré. Such a lovely night it was, with the moon riding high and June scents from all the gardens perfuming the air. Such a beautifully sad night, I thought, and against all reason my spirits began to rise in the very face of this wistful mood.

At home, when I was ready for bed, I stood for a little while at my windows, looking down into the courtyard where silver light touched the water in the fountain. Strangely enough I was no longer angry and my moments of self-recrimination were forgotten. I could remember only that Justin Law had held me in his arms and kissed me. He had not wanted to, but he had done so. True, he had mocked me, humiliated me later, but more in the manner of a man trying to flee from his own emotions.

How many times Mama had said that men were seldom for marriage in the beginning. Every one of them tried to escape the silken noose as long as possible. And Justin, perhaps, would struggle more fiercely than some, being more fiercely independent.

By the time I climbed into bed I was almost happy. All

that really mattered was Justin's sharp awareness of me as a woman. In the end he could not turn away from that. I did not wholly dismiss my uncle's judgment of him, but told myself this was a matter of misunderstanding between the two men. In the end each would come to recognize the other's worth. How could it happen otherwise when both were fundamentally worthy? As for that matter of prison—no one had clarified that, and there were undoubtedly circumstances of which I knew nothing, or he would not now be free. This I must believe.

Of course I would see Justin again—and again. Next time I would be sweet and submissive, never angry or sharp. And in the end I would have him. For I knew now quite surely that I wanted him as I had never wanted any other. Justin Law was the man I would love all my life.

How rosy my dreams were that night, how childishly buoyant!

Thirteen ☀

On the following Saturday I made my first bid for freedom since I had come to New Orleans. At home I was accustomed to long brisk walks in the open air and I ached to get out of this tight domestic world that revolved about a small courtyard, ached to push aside the walls that shut me in. I wanted to think about many things, and my mind always worked better out beneath an open sky with plenty of breathing space. I remembered the way Justin had said he wanted space in which to breathe and turn around. We were alike in that respect.

Since I did not want to disappear and worry my mother, I told her what I planned. She tried to persuade me that it was out of the question in this house. A well-brought-up young Creole lady who was still unmarried did not, in my uncle's opinion, wander the streets of the town alone. Perhaps it would be possible for Delphine to go with me.

But the last person whose company I wanted was Delphine. She would only chain me as the house chained me.

So in the end Mama gave up and said that the responsibility was, after all, my own.

I dressed myself in plain dark green and borrowed a little round-topped straw hat of my mother's. I'd thought a moment of wearing the fern-colored hat, but somehow the occasion did not seem right.

When I was ready I descended the circular staircase and stood for a moment in the shadows of the arched recess at its foot. The maids were busy upstairs and I had seen Delphine talking to Aunt Natalie in the parlor. Jasper had taken Caro out to her music lesson an hour before. The yard boy was raking up the court and had his back to me, and the stone passageway stretched empty to the street. I suppressed a desire to run and walked toward the iron gate without a glance toward the door of my uncle's office. I could only hope that he would not be in a position to glance out and see me.

Nothing happened, no one called me back, and I reached the gate unhindered. It stood unlatched, for my uncle's clients came and went by this entrance all day, and I slipped through and turned onto Chartres Street.

The busy life of a New Orleans morning engulfed me and I walked briskly now, with a sense of release and freedom. The narrow streets teemed with vehicles, from pushcarts to elegant carriages, and vendors were abroad as usual. The odd figure of a chimney sweep ducked past me at a crossing. He wore a frock coat too big for him and two top hats, one above the other, both the worse for wear. His long-drawn-out cry of *"Ramonez la cheminée . . ."* rang out above other calls.

I walked past the ancient building of the Ursuline Convent that Courtney had identified for me, and looked through the gate at a peaceful garden. But my goal lay farther on and I quickened my steps. Jackson Square had invited me before. I would find a place on one of its benches and be utterly alone.

My plans, however, were unexpectedly interrupted. A square away from my destination, I saw Caro and big Jasper approaching me. The little girl was coming home from her music lesson and when she saw me she ran toward me eagerly.

"Cousin Skye! You are out alone! Did they permit you? Does my papa—"

"It's perfectly all right," I told her hastily as Jasper hurried to catch up with his charge.

"Where are you going?" Caro demanded. And then,

110

without waiting to be told, let her words run on. "Take me with you, Cousin Skye! If I go home now I must study lessons and practice and embroider. And oh, the morning is so beautiful! Please let me come with you."

She was such an eager, dancing little thing that I could not resist her. Perhaps if we stayed together there would be less trouble at home because of my escape. We could chaperone each other.

"Very well," I told her and tried to make my nod to Jasper casual. "I will take charge of Miss Caro. We will go for a little walk through the Square and come home shortly."

Jasper looked doubtful, but Caro entreated him. "Do go home and let us be," she pleaded. "I'll be perfectly safe with Cousin Skye, and you needn't tell them right away at home. Need you, Jasper?"

Quite clearly, Caro was a favorite with Jasper, and he gave her a sympathetic smile. "You'll catch it for sure, li'l missy," he said. His glance in my direction told me that I would probably catch it too. But Jasper's heart was kind and he went off, leaving us to continue toward the Square.

Caro giggled as she watched him go. "He'll be slow," she told me. "He'll give us lots of time on purpose. And we can take our punishment bravely later. We Creoles are most courageous people. Did you know that, cousin? Come now, let's hurry."

When we reached the high iron fence that enclosed the Square we found a colored woman in starched white apron and bright tignon selling pralines nearby. Feeling like a child on holiday, I bought one for Caro and one for me. The woman thanked me in the strange patois I had heard on all sides in Creole New Orleans.

"That's Gombo," Caro explained. "It's a mixture the Negroes began to use when they came here in the early days."

We moved on, nibbling at our delicacies, but in spite of Caro's urging, I did not seek the nearest gate of the Square at once. For a few minutes I stood admiring the grace of the structures across the street. Here towered the triple steeples of the St. Louis Cathedral, flanked on either side by arcaded Spanish buildings.

"How beautiful they are," I murmured, and Caro tugged at my hand.

"You can see them better from the Square. Do come along, before someone is sent after us!"

We moved on, but just as we reached the gate, with its iron lampposts towering on either side, my eyes were caught

111

by the appearance of a woman in the doorway of the Cathedral. She wore a brilliant gown of purple satin, swathed very tight in front and swirling about her feet in tiny multiple pleats. On her head was a large hat, its ostrich plumes waving in agitation.

I recognized her as the proprietress of the gambling place, L'Oiseau d'Or. "Madame Pollock," Courtney had called her, though there was nothing in the least French about her.

At the moment the woman was plainly disturbed. She looked frantically in either direction up and down the street. Anxiously she questioned two or three people who went by. All shook their heads and she twisted her hands together in anxiety. Then she saw us, frankly watching by the gate. Picking up her purple skirts to keep them free of dirt, she sprang across the gutter and fairly ran toward us, her plumes heaving as she came. By the time she reached us her large bosom was panting heavily beneath its purple encasing.

"Have you seen a little boy of about ten?" she gasped. "The child has run away and I don't know which way to look."

We could only shake our heads, having noticed no small boy.

"I thought he might have gone into the church, but I can't find him there. I must catch him before he gets too far away!"

"If he wanted to run away," Caro said, "he'd surely stay out in the sun."

The woman looked at her quickly, as if noting the child for the first time. Now that she was close I could see the face beneath the tossing plumes. Her papery-white skin was plainly touched with rouge and so were the lips of her full and generous mouth, twisted now in anxiety. Between mascaraed eyelashes, her eyes were a lively blue. Her hair, piled high in coils of metallic gold beneath the overwhelming hat, had an oddly greenish tinge. She bent toward Caro eagerly.

"Well, then, where do you think he has gone?" she demanded.

"I know where I'd go," Caro said. "I'd run straight into the Square. And if I went into the Square, I'd most certainly go to look at the statue of General Jackson."

"Come help me find him, there's a good girl," the woman beseeched. "He's a slippery one and I can't move as fast as he can."

Caro went with her readily as she hurried through the gate. I had no choice but to follow. Along the outer rim of the Square trees and bushes grew in profusion—palms of various kinds, banana trees, oleanders and many others. But around the central enclosure were open walks and lawns. The statue, high on its pedestal in the center, was visible at once.

The bronze figure of the man who had once saved New Orleans from the British sat astride a great horse prancing on its hind legs. The General held his hat aloft and wind from the river seemed to lift the hair on his head. Time had turned the statue to the greenish hue of weathered bronze and there were lacings of soot in every sculptured fold.

Our strange companion, however, had no time for the admiring of statues. She followed one of the broad paths the circled the enclosure like the strands of a spider web, and turned onto one that rayed toward the center. Caro, not troubling with paths, darted ahead across the grass. Thus it was she who reached the far side of the statue first and turned back to us in triumph.

"I was right! Your little boy is here looking at General Jackson."

Lobelia Pollock billowed plumply along ahead of me, puffing with mingled relief and annoyance. Even before she rounded the statue and could see the child, she began to scold.

"You're a naughty boy, Lanny! To worry your Aunty Lobelia like this. You know you are never to leave the apartment alone. Never to—" At that moment the other side of the statue must have come into view, for she broke off and halted in astonishment.

A second later I saw what had startled her and I too stopped in surprise. Her Lanny was not alone. He was a thin boy, rather tall for his age, and he stood planted on the walk with legs astride, his hands behind his back as he stared up, not at the statue, but into the face of the man beside him. The stranger with whom he discussed the statue was Justin Law.

Justin stood as the boy who imitated him, with legs apart and hands behind his back, head tilted as he studied the equestrian figure above him. I had schooled myself to patience and a mild, friendly manner when I saw him again. But I couldn't help the hurried thumping of my heart. Since I stood almost behind him, some distance back on the path, he did not discover me at once.

Not one of the three paid any attention to "Aunty Lobelia," who now bore down upon them in a purple cloud of alarm.

She would have snatched at the boy's thin shoulder to whirl him about, had Justin not turned and fixed her with an abrupt, cold look.

"Ah?" he said. "Madame Pollock. We have met in your establishment, if I'm not mistaken."

Mrs. Pollock gaped at him for a moment as though she could not recover her wits. Then she snatched at the boy again. But Lanny wriggled out of her grasp and retreated behind Justin. I saw that the boy was straightly built, a handsome child, for all his fragile bones. His hair and eyes were dark, and his skin rather too white for health. He had a bit of the Creole look about him and I wondered about his connection with the far from Creole Mrs. Pollock.

Now, from his sheltered post behind Justin, he spoke to her courteously. "This gentleman has been telling me about the statue. Do you see how the horse balances without other support on the hind legs? This is an amazing feat of the sculptor. Do you see—"

"Never mind that!" Mrs. Pollock snapped. "Come here to me this minute. We must go home at once."

The boy did not move, and Justin was plainly laughing at the irate and frantic lady. There seemed to be an impasse. Until now Justin had not seen me, but Caro turned to draw me into the circle.

"Do come over here, Cousin Skye," she entreated. "Then you can see better. All the times I've looked at General Jackson before, I've never noticed how he was balanced."

Justin turned also and for a moment his eyes rested on me, cool and remote. There was in them no recognition of a woman he had held in his arms. He swept his broad-brimmed hat from his head and made me an elaborate bow.

"Good morning, Miss Cameron," he said formally.

Mrs. Pollock gave me a quick, sharp look in which there was tardy recognition of me as someone she had seen at the Tourneau house. And with recognition her anxiety seemed to increase. She did not wait for my "Good morning," but stamped her foot and shouted at the boy.

"If you don't come here at once, you'll get a good beating when I have you home, sir!"

"A poor way to encourage cooperation," Justin said. "Why not let the boy stay for a while and play in the Square?"

Caro jumped up and down and clapped her hands. "Oh, yes, yes! Please let him stay and play with me!"

This was too much for Mrs. Pollock. She made a sudden swoop around Justin and caught the boy by the arm—firmly

114

this time, so that he could not wriggle free.

"We'll go *now* and that's all there is to it. I'll swear, no lock and key ever seems to hold you. You're a real bad boy, Lanny."

He gave up struggling and went with her dejectedly. But before she took off, Mrs. Pollock stopped beside me and spoke in a low, anxious voice.

"Would you mind, dearie—I mean, I'll be in your debt if you'll just say nothing to your uncle about seeing me today."

"Why should I say anything to him?" I asked in surprise.

Her gaze shifted from mine. She gave Lanny a little shake and pulled him away without answering. As he went with her he called back to Caro pleadingly.

"Please come visit me! I live right over there in the upper Pontalba building." He waved one hand toward the rows of buildings that lay uptown from the Square.

Mrs. Pollock hurried him off toward a gate and out of our sight. I glanced at Justin and he raised an eyebrow mockingly.

"Another lady who thinks me the devil, apparently. I suppose she can't forgive me for clipping the wings of her Golden Bird the other night."

Caro's attention swung back to the big blond man before us. "What does that mean—clipping its wings? That is a place where gentlemen play games of chance. I have heard my father speak of it."

"And I was there, taking my chances," Justin told her smiling. "My name is Law, mademoiselle, if I may present myself. At your service, Miss Tourneau."

Caro's mouth shaped itself into an "O" of astonishment. I grasped her hand nervously, but she was not to be stopped.

"Then you must be the wicked brother of whom they speak! But you were very kind to that boy Lanny, monsieur, and I do not think you can be as wicked as they say."

I flushed, but Justin's laughter rang out in enjoyment.

"I wish all young ladies had your perception, mademoiselle," he told Caro.

She twirled about in self-conscious delight, and then stopped with a squeal of dismay. "Oh, dear! There's Delphine looking for us."

I followed the direction of Caro's pointing finger and saw Delphine as she moved beyond the iron fence, approaching the gate on Chartres Street. I might have known they would send her after us. She reach the gate and entered the Square, approaching regally down one of the rayed walks, her head high and her hands crossed before her.

There was nothing hurried about her advance, but she came toward us as implacably as fate.

I glanced again toward the monument of horse and rider, expecting to see Justin watching my predicament in amusement. But he had disappeared, and I felt both relieved and disappointed. He must have taken himself off when Caro called out that Delphine was coming. At least it would not be reported to Uncle Robert that I had again been in the company of this man he did not like. But how tantalizing it had been to see him like this, in public, and never exchange a direct word with him.

"Come along, Caro," I said and we walked slowly to meet our guardian.

On the way Caro whispered that Delphine wasn't a bit like Jasper. She would run to Papa with everything. Now we would be scolded for lingering in the Square.

Delphine, however, made only one remark. A young lady who was *bien élevée,* she said, did not leave her home unescorted. It was not clear which young lady she addressed, but I'm afraid we both looked guilty and chastened. At least she had not seen us in the company of either Justin Law or Mrs. Pollock. I was sure no young lady who was *"bien élevée"* would associate with Lanny's odd protector.

As we went home with Delphine I wondered about Lobelia Pollock. She had seemed almost frantic there in the Square. And why had she asked me to say nothing to Uncle Robert about seeing her? There was something here that I did not in the least understand.

Fourteen ❀

When we reached home Aunt Natalie greeted me with sad reproach.

"I realize, my child, that you are unaccustomed to our ways, and not to be held entirely accountable until you learn. But among *les bonnes familles* Creole ways are to be respected. Your uncle feels that it is necessary to live our lives according to a *gentil* pattern of which he approves. You understand, *chérie*—it is the only way."

I felt that it could never be the only way for me, but I did not want to distress her further. My Aunt Natalie's one function as a good Creole wife was to please her husband and keep him contented. My father, however, had taught me to think for myself and it was not in me to conform so meekly to the unreasonable.

Aunt Natalie saw my rebellious expression and tried to cheer me. "We will forget this now. Tonight we have a little party among ourselves, you remember. That handsome young man, Courtney Law, is coming to supper. And you will be gay, you will enjoy yourself."

I had forgotten about the invitation to Courtney and his mother, and I could not look forward to it with anything but concern. By now Uncle Robert had undoubtedly made his wishes known to Courtney. And Courtney had already told me that for him my uncle's wishes were law. This might be an evening of grave embarrassment for me.

When I saw Courtney I would know his reaction at once, I thought, and braced myself against the first sign of too affectionate attention.

But Courtney surprised me that night. He took my hand with his usual gallant air when we met, but his eyes were grave and seemed to probe my own. Beneath the gallantry was someone I did not know. He conversed readily with my uncle, but he did not banter with the ladies as he usually did, or flatter us outrageously. There was a subdued quality about him tonight that I could not decipher. One thing in particular I noted. He paid little attention to my mother, seeming not to see her small efforts to gain his interest. No longer was he an entranced young man who could not take his eyes from the charming Louise Cameron.

This in itself told me that my uncle had spoken to him, yet I could not read Courtney's reaction. His attention to me was so grave and quiet that perhaps it signified resistance. I began to wonder if I might, after all, find an ally in Courtney. Together we could surely convince Uncle Robert that marriage should not be thrust upon us by the wishes of others.

The meal was especially delicious that night and I was able to enjoy my pompano as I had not expected to in Courtney's company. I wondered if there would be any opportunity to talk to him frankly, so that we might both lay our cards on the table and perhaps decide how best to meet Uncle Robert's desire for us.

But it was never the Creole custom to leave two of the opposite sex together when both were young and unmarried. When we rose from the table, Aunt Natalie came with us into the parlor and sat there cheerfully with her embroidery work. Mama would have joined us gaily, trying to coax Courtney into laughter and fun, but Uncle Robert asked her into his study for a talk and she went with him regretfully.

I wondered if Uncle Robert meant to chide her for her irresponsible flirtation with Courtney, and perhaps tell her of his hopes for me. I sat on the small sofa beside Justin's brother and could find nothing at all to say that I would want Aunt Natalie to hear.

Courtney did his best. He spoke of the weather, of the fine meal we had eaten, of an odd case that had come up in court, but his usual animation was lacking. Uncle Robert's wishes lay between us like a barrier across which we looked at each other with reserve and self-consciousness.

Nearby was a china vase filled with sand, in which several palm-leaf fans had been stuck. I reached for one and began to fan myself nervously. At once Courtney took the fan from my hand and moved it gently back and forth, stirring the air against my hot face.

Aunt Natalie looked at us fondly. "Perhaps you will find it cooler on the street gallery," she suggested, and I could have blessed her. She thought, of course, in her innocent way, that she was aiding young love. On the street gallery we would still be well chaperoned, yet perhaps we could talk.

Courtney rose with alacrity and helped me up. We walked the length of the two parlors, past portraits of Creole ancestors who watched with varying degrees of approval from the walls. Courtney opened the shutters and we stepped onto a narrow gallery that reached the entire width of the building. The gallery was separated into sections by wood and ironwork guards which gave privacy to the individual houses that shared the stretch of gallery. Below us Chartres Street lay dim and quiet in the dusk. The busier traffic uptown seemed far away. Behind shuttered windows few lights were visible.

I stepped to the gallery rail and leaned upon it, tracing the iron lacework with absent fingers. In the heart of the filigree the letter "T" had been woven into an oak leaf design.

Courtney stood close beside me, yet not touching so much as my sleeve. He watched my fingers follow the iron tracery.

" 'T' for Tourneau," he said softly. "This house was built

by the Tourneaus long ago. That design was made especially for it."

I looked out upon the Old Square of New Orleans—the Vieux Carré—and found it a foreign-seeming town, its houses far removed from the buildings of New England. Most of the structures about us were two or three stories high, with gently sloping roofs of slate, and the straight Spanish façade of the Creole house. In the dusk, all soft, light colors had vanished and everything was a shadowy gray.

" 'T' for Tourneau," I repeated. "Sometimes I don't know whether I can ever truly belong to my uncle's family, or fit into the place he wants me to make for me."

Courtney was silent and I had the feeling that thoughts I could not guess were going on behind the mask he wore tonight. I began to feel that I did not know him at all, that there might be more depth, more thoughtful sensitivity in him than I had dreamed.

"I know what you mean," he said at last. "I too have at times the sense of not belonging to the place in which I find myself. Or perhaps it is not this time to which I belong."

I glanced at him curiously and saw that in profile he bore a faint resemblance to Justin. But Justin's nose and chin were stronger, more aggressive.

"What time and place would you have chosen?" I asked.

Courtney's hands were graceful, long-fingered. He gestured affectionately toward the town about us. "I would always choose to live here, Skye. But I'd prefer the old days early in the century, when Creole life was at its best. How brilliant and gay New Orleans must have been then. That was the day of the aristocrats."

There was a lift to his voice now and I nodded in understanding. Yes, Courtney would have done well in the *ancien régime* before the democratic Americans came in and began a leveling of all classes. I could well imagine him in the company of other gay young men with wealth to spend and little to do with their time. No wonder there had been duels and dancing till dawn and love-making in more quarters than one. Courtney seated on a high stool in an office, with a green shade over his eyes, was an anachronism.

He shrugged, made a sudden gesture of dismissal. *"Alors!* It is necessary that I find a place for myself in my own generation and time. The way has not yet opened."

I wondered what he thought of Uncle Robert's current effort to open it, wondered if I dared speak. If I waited, when would there be another chance?

"Has Uncle Robert mentioned his wishes to you?" I ventured.

Courtney looked faintly shocked, so I suppose he considered such bold acknowledgment unmaidenly.

"M'sieu Robert has mentioned them," he admitted gravely. But he said nothing more, gave me no clue.

Time was slipping away and I had a fear of being caught in its tide. My voice when I spoke was more tense than I intended, but I made no effort to halt my words once they had started.

"Don't listen to him, Courtney! We mustn't be swayed into a course that might be disastrous. Surely there's a pretty Creole girl whom you could love and marry for love. You mustn't let Uncle Robert pick the wrong wife for you."

"I am, then, so abhorrent to you, mam'zelle?" Courtney asked quietly.

"Of course not," I told him. "I've never liked you better"—and that was true—"but we're not for each other. No matter how well-intentioned his plans, I'll never let Uncle Robert persuade me into a marriage I'm not ready for."

Courtney took my hands in his. "How concerned you are! All I ask is an opportunity to know you better, Skye, to have you know me better. There is nothing more your uncle wishes for the moment."

I was not reassured. I did not want Courtney to play this waiting game. Once I had been willing to wait and see where he was concerned. But that was before my thoughts had settled so strongly upon Justin. Now I knew my love and there was nothing for Courtney to wait for.

"I suppose Uncle Robert expects young love to take its course," I said more tartly than I intended.

"Why not?" said Courtney, laughing a little. He bent his head and kissed my hands. The grave stranger who had looked out of his eyes for a little while was hidden again.

I drew my hands away and went indoors, looking, I suppose, as disturbed as I felt. Aunt Natalie glanced at me knowingly, seeing what she wanted to see—a shy young girl embarrassed by the attentions of an attractive man.

"I—I've a headache," I said to Courtney. "You'll excuse me, please."

I did not wait to hear his murmured regrets, but went somewhat precipitously out of the room and ran along the gallery to my father's door. It stood open and I looked in.

My mother's interview with Uncle Robert must have been a short one, for she was here, pacing rapidly up and down the small expanse, her bosom heaving with indignation. When I appeared she whirled upon me as if I were to blame. I gave my father an apologetic look for this emotional upheaval and stepped into the room.

"The very idea!" Mama cried. "What can Robert be thinking of to desire such a marriage? This young man has not a sou to his name, Bruce. He owes everything to Robert. Oh, I can see the whole plan clearly enough. If Robert marries Skye to Courtney he will have us all under his thumb forever. And this is what he wants more than anything else—power, always power. He must forever be manipulating lives, moving us upon his chessboard!"

While I might wish that Uncle Robert had not taken this course, I did not believe he had chosen it for any reason but what he considered my own good. My mother, as usual, was mistaking generosity for something ignoble and uncharacteristic of my uncle. But I knew she was too angry to argue with and I kept silent. Though I could not help thinking that her own motives were not above suspicion. She might well be nettled at having an admiring young man removed from her reach.

From his bed my father held out a hand to Mama. "Don't excite yourself so, my lass."

Now she whirled upon him. "Why shouldn't I excite myself? Someone must think of our future. What hope is there for us unless Skye can make a good marriage and get us out of this house? I can't live here forever! I can't bear it!"

She burst into tears and ran out of the room. I watched her go in miserable silence. Whatever happened, my father should not be subjected to such words, or such storms. I went to sit beside him and held his hand in mine. He lay with his eyes closed, but I felt his fingers clasp themselves about my own.

"She behaves like a child!" I said. "You'd think to hear her that only her comfort matters, that your life and mine mean nothing at all."

"Hush, lassie," my father said and looked at me with eyes in which pain lay deep. "Your mother feels herself caught in a trap. She is reacting like any small caged thing. And I, who would do anything for her, am helpless to raise her bars."

I could not help wondering again how much of her anger had to do with the loss of a young man who had shown her some attention, but I said no more.

Papa's clasp on my hand tightened. "Never must you

marry without love, Skye lassie. You are strong enough to stand for what you believe in. Let no one tell you otherwise, my girl, or move you against your own convictions of what is good for you."

I bent and put my cheek against his hand. It was good to have him talk to me like this. Without his care, I had begun to feel too much alone, too vulnerable.

"What manner of man is this elder brother of whom your mother has told me?" he asked me. "The man who gave the party."

What manner of man was Justin Law? Since my father was ready to listen, I tried to tell him that night. I went back to my first meeting with Justin and retraced my steps. There were some things I left out, but it was satisfying to speak from my heart, and to put into words something of my confusion and the contrary way I so often felt toward Justin.

Papa heard me through in sympathetic silence. He offered me no advice, uttered no warnings. But when at last I rose to go to my own room, he said gently that I must one day bring this man to see him.

That night I went to bed feeling more at peace than I had for some time. Now at least I need not hold all my strange turmoil secretly in my heart. There was relief in being able to speak the name of my love aloud, even though I could not fully confess my feelings for him, even to my father.

During the hot July days that followed, my mother was contrite and very sweet to me. And because she grieved over her outburst in Papa's room and regretted it, I tried to forgive her. When she asked me one afternoon to come for a walk with her, I went willingly enough.

We were both glad to get out for a little while. Mama flung off her weight of despair, as she always managed to do when escape was possible, and as we walked along Chartres Street, she told me gaily of the good times she had known as a girl in this Creole city.

There had been great wealth among the Creoles before the war, and she had danced at magnificent balls, gone visiting in sumptuous plantation houses, made trips across Lake Pontchartrain in the summertime. Particularly she remembered an elaborate ball the year of her coming out.

"It was given in the lobby of the French Opera House itself," she told me. "Ah, but it is dull here now, compared with those gay times."

122

"Yet you married Papa and left New Orleans," I reminded her.

She put a hand on my arm to draw me against a wall, lest I be spattered by an arc of mud thrown by wagon wheels. The elation had left her when she spoke again.

"Your father was—different. Not like the young men of my acquaintance. I believed that he would love me forever." An unusual candor was in her voice. "It is necessary for me to be loved," she said.

I felt closer to her than I had since before that day when I'd found her in the orchard with Tom Gilman. Gently I slipped a hand through her arm in sympathy.

"He hasn't stopped loving you," I said. "It *is* forever."

Her dark eyes brimmed with tears and she turned away from me. "No! He has forgotten that he ever loved me. Now he is in love only with death."

Chilling words, to which I could find no answer.

After that we walked for a while in silence past the pale pink and cream and gray-green houses, often with their plaster cracking, their shingles loose, a gentle air of decay upon them. There was evidence of crumbling everywhere, evidence of a need for loving hands to repair and rebuild. Still, the very weathering of colors in this tropical climate gave a patina of beauty that was more appealing perhaps than that of fresh, clean paint.

As we neared Jackson Square and crossed the little flagstone bridge laid across a gutter, my mother gestured. "Look —here is the Cathedral. Let me show you where Creole gentlemen used to fight duels."

We turned down St. Anthony's Alley toward Royal Street and she showed me the garden behind the Cathedral, almost hidden from the street by tall evergreens.

"They could leave a ball quietly with smiles on their lips as if nothing was wrong," she said. "And in a quarter of an hour they'd be here with their seconds, darting at each other with those evil *colichemards*. Many a young man met his death in St. Anthony's garden."

I could almost see them there in the dawnlight, or by bright moonlight perhaps, with steel flashing and ringing.

"Do you think Uncle Robert ever fought a duel here?" I asked.

"That one! He was deadly with a rapier, and a sure shot with the pistol when dueling moved out to the parks. I had great fear that he would challenge my Bruce when he wanted to marry me and take me North. To the Creole, all who are not of our blood are of the *gens du commun* and not to be accepted by a Creole woman in marriage."

"What happened?" I urged. "Why did Uncle Robert let you marry Papa?"

"There were two reasons," Mama said with an effort to keep her tone light. "Your father always had a reasonable way with those who were ruled by their emotions. I think Robert suspected that Bruce might not accept a challenge. And there is great disgrace incurred by both parties in that case. Only of course Bruce was going North. He wouldn't have cared."

The *Code Duello*, as I was beginning to learn, must have been a complicated affair.

"What was the second reason?" I asked.

Mama made no further effort to keep her tone light. She answered levelly as we retraced our steps to Chartres Street. "My brother hated me. He was glad to see me go."

I doubted her then. Always she had been prejudiced against Uncle Robert, unfair in her judgment of him. I suspected that if she had incurred any disapproval on his part, it had probably been her own fault.

Under the old arches of the Cabildo, which had once been the Spanish government house, vendors were showing their wares and Mama, her mood changing again, stopped in delight near an old Negro woman who was cooking some sort of concoction in a pan. The woman, noting her interest, called to her at once.

"Hot *calas*, madame! *Toutes chaudes! Belles calas, toutes chaudes*, madame!"

"Rice cakes in the New Orleans fashion," Mama said. "Of course we must have some!"

Pennies and *calas* changed hands and we bit into the thin delicious fritters as we went on. Mama seemed as gay as Caro now, and nearly as young.

At St. Peter Street we crossed to the upper Pontalba building. Remembering my meeting with Mrs. Pollock and the boy Lanny, I noted the place where they lived with a special interest. Then too, I remembered what Justin had said about Micaela de Pontalba—the red-haired baroness who had built these apartments. The structure stretched the entire width of the Square, as did its twin on the other side. Wide galleries overhung the banquettes for the full length of the second and third floors, with handsome cast-iron work at both levels.

"Do you see the entwined 'AP' in the iron grillwork?" Mama asked. "The monogram stands of course for Almonaster and Pontalba."

The street level had been arranged for shops, but here and there a door stood blank and empty. Some sections of these fine Creole apartments were falling into neglect and disrepair.

When we reached the corner we turned back through Jackson Square, skirting once more the statue of the General on his horse. But today no blond giant of a man was to be seen in the vicinity and my heart ached a little with longing. How was I ever to win my love if I could never see him?

Then, as we approached the Chartres Street entrance to the Square, I heard my name called entreatingly and turned to see Mrs. Pollock's young charge dashing across the grass toward us.

"Mam'zelle!" Lanny called. "If you please, wait for me!"

Fifteen ❀

This looked like another runaway, I thought, as Lanny hurried toward us. But I was already committed in my heart in his favor. He was a winsome, manly little boy, with charming manners that set him off in contrast to Mrs. Pollock.

He came to a breathless halt before us, bowed to me and glanced shyly at my mother. Today he wore a slightly outgrown gray suit, with tight, short breeches, long blue stockings and high boots. His little bowler hat had a dent in it, but it had been neatly brushed, and there was a certain elegance in the black bow tied at his round stiff collar. Again I was struck by the Creole look of the boy. Already he was dandy enough to snatch up his hat, even when running away.

"I'd like to present you to my mother," I told him, while he caught his breath. "But I'm afraid I don't know your last name."

"My name is Fontaine," he said. "Lanny Fontaine."

I completed the introduction while Mama watched in amused surprise.

"You've run away from Mrs. Pollock again, haven't you?" I asked him directly.

He made no attempt to dissemble. "They locked me into the apartment and left me there alone. But there is a window which I am able to open. It is possible to walk along the gallery and get out through vacant rooms. From the gallery I saw you here in the Square. I may walk with you for a while, mam'zelle? You will not send me back at once? No one will know, since no one is home."

I couldn't resist him, and besides I was indignant at the thought of adults shutting a little boy up in that place and then going off to leave him alone and locked in.

"Of course you may come with us," I said and signaled my mother with a look to ask no questions until we were alone.

Mama, however, had already taken to Lanny Fontaine and she too disliked the thought that he had been shut in and left alone. Always she had a soft place in her heart for children. Sometimes I've thought that she might have been a different woman if she could have had a large family of her own.

"You did not bring the little girl, Caro, to see me," Lanny said reproachfully as we left the Square.

"I'm sorry," I said. "It was not possible. But she must be home from school by now. Perhaps you could come to our house and visit her for a little while. Then someone will take you home later and explain to Mrs. Pollock if she has returned."

Lanny was delighted and there was a skip to his walk as he moved along between us. I felt sure that only his notion of what a gentleman's conduct should be when out with ladies, kept him from turning a cartwheel or two in glee. He was further delighted when Mama suggested that we return home along Royal Street, where we could have the fun of looking into shop windows as we passed.

Already I loved the old Rue Royale, with its bustle of carriages and carts, its tiny shops elbowing each other from square to square, always with the lacy iron balconies above, and the blue-green shutters closed against daytime warmth.

There were grocers' stores, and the tiny *rabais* shops that carried pins and needles, threads and other notions. But there were also what I termed to myself the heartbreak shops. Here the great Creole families, impoverished by the

126

war and years of carpetbag government, had brought one and another of their treasures of furniture, French china and *objets d'art* to dispose of for whatever they would bring. Mama was fascinated by a great sunburst of a garnet pin in one small window, but it was the blue cat in another that caught Lanny's eye.

"Look, mam'zelle!" he cried to me. "What a most proud fellow this one is. He is unhappy, don't you think, to stay in a shop window?"

The cat was a weighted china doorstop of Delft blue, and never had I seen so complacent a feline face. Its eyes had a superior, rather scornful look, and its blue little tongue licked wisely over its upper lip. It seemed so entirely pleased with itself, so indifferent to the opinion of any other creature, that it made me laugh out loud. Once my father would have loved the whimsy of this china figure. Perhaps even now it might cause him to smile.

"Lanny's right," I said. "Such a proud fellow should never have to reside in a shop window where all and sundry can stare at him. Let's take him home to Papa."

My mother did not think the gift either beautiful or suitable, but she consented to the small purchase and we went into the shop.

"He doesn't need a doorstop," she protested as the clerk wrapped the cat in brown paper. "He always wants his door closed. Your gift is not sensible."

"Then perhaps this will coax him into leaving the door open," I said as we left the shop. "If he doesn't like it, I'll take it for myself. The creature reminds me of something, though I can't think what."

I gave it to Lanny to carry and the boy was touchingly pleased with the trust. What a lonely child he seemed. I wished I dared ask questions about why he lived with Lobelia Pollock. But there was a certain reserve about him that held one off. For all that he had taken a liking to me, I did not quite dare question him.

When we reached the Tourneau house I left Lanny in the parlor, suggesting that he wait until I found Caro. He seemed content enough, looking about the room with great interest. There was a set of sea shells on the corner whatnot, and since he was obviously a careful child, I said he might play with them if he liked. Then I went to my room to leave the china cat and remove my hat, meaning to search out Caro in the next few minutes.

It was Caro, however, who searched for me. I heard her

calling my name in high excitement and stepped out on the gallery. She ran toward me at once, her eyes wide with alarm, all her eager, dancing quality vanished.

"Oh, it is terrible, terrible! You didn't tell me the little boy was here, Cousin Skye. And now he has gone into Papa's study—and—oh, it is most terrible!"

I took her by the hand and we hurried toward the upper hall together. As we ran, I asked questions breathlessly.

"What is it, Caro? What has happened? I left him in the parlor and I thought he would stay there until you came."

She clung to me tearfully, pulling me back for a moment. "I came downstairs just now and heard Papa's voice from the study, speaking angry words to someone. He has come home early from the courthouse. So I peeped between the dining-room doorway curtains and saw that Lanny was in there with him. Come quickly, Skye, we must save him!"

The door to the study was open and we entered without knocking. Lanny stood with his back to us, his legs astride, and his hands behind his back, much as he had stood that day looking up at the statue of General Jackson. Uncle Robert faced us and I was shocked by his appearance. His skin had gone a blotchy, furious red. Between the two, chessmen lay scattered upon the carpet, and the silver cover had rolled upon its side on the floor.

Lanny looked white and shaken, but he was trying valiantly to explain. "I'm very sorry, monsieur. I did not know when I lifted the cover to see what was beneath, that I would knock the chessmen from the board. If any harm has been done, I will find a way to repay you, monsieur. If any are broken—"

Uncle Robert had seen us and he made an effort to recover himself. "Stop your chatter, boy. You may leave us, Caroline. This is none of your affair."

I had never heard him speak so harshly and I was dismayed.

Caro stood her ground bravely. "Oh, but it is, Papa. Lanny has come to visit me."

The boy looked around at us and I saw that for all his brave apology he was close to tears. I drew him back from the scattered figures of ebony and ivory, put an arm about his shoulders.

"The whole thing is my fault," I told my uncle. "I'm terribly sorry, but no harm was intended and I don't believe any real damage has been done. Mama and I met Lanny this afternoon while we were out for a walk, and—"

128

Uncle Robert broke in on my words with less than his usual courtesy. "Lanny? Lanny? What is your name, boy?"

"My name is Lance Fontaine," said Lanny quietly.

Uncle Robert stared at him for a long moment.

Once more I tried to explain. "There is a woman named Pollock—I believe she is a client of yours. The boy seems to be in her charge."

The look my uncle turned upon me startled me. It was bright and dark, almost malevolent.

"What do you know of this Mrs. Pollock?"

"Why—nothing very much, really. The day I saw her come out of your office Courtney said she was the proprietress of a gambling house." There seemed no reason now to suppress the fact of our meeting in Jackson Square and I told him of that too. "Mrs. Pollock was looking for the boy that day," I concluded, "and we helped her find him."

Again Uncle Robert made an obvious effort to control his indignation. "Under no circumstances, Skye, are you ever to speak to this woman, or have anything to do with her. It is not fitting for a young lady of your birth, and what I hope is breeding, to consort with such women." He fixed his attention once more upon his daughter. "What is this? You no longer obey when I make a request? Go downstairs at once and tell Delphine I wish to see her."

"Yes, Papa," said Caro, suddenly meek. She went without daring a backward glance at Lanny. My hand on the boy's shoulder tightened consolingly, but he moved away from me and knelt to pick up the scattered chessmen. I suspected that he wanted to hide the tears that filled his eyes and my heart went out to him.

"Please sit down, Skye," said my uncle more calmly, and drew a chair for me beside his desk.

When I was seated, he took the other chair and for a few moments seemed lost in thought, his fingers drumming absently on the desk. Lanny replaced the chessmen one by one upon the board, not attempting to set them up for a game. Uncle Robert thanked him courteously enough, and when Delphine tapped on the door he spoke to her as evenly as though he had never lost his temper.

"You will take this boy back to the Pontalba apartments at once, Delphine. It seems that he has run away from his home."

Delphine nodded without expression and held out her hand. "Come," she said to Lanny.

The boy turned and made me a grave little bow. It was

clear that he no longer expected help from me. I longed to pull him into my arms and somehow console him for what had happened, but under my uncle's stare I could not manage it. He bade Uncle Robert a polite "Good day, monsieur," before he left the room, disdaining Delphine's hand, and went downstairs with her.

My uncle and I were left alone. I felt like running after the others, but he had told me to sit here and I was experiencing more than ever before, the compelling quality of his will. After a moment of toying with a carved ivory paper knife, he turned his dark gaze upon me. But now he seemed more unhappy than angry.

"I'm afraid we must have a talk, Skye," he said.

I waited in silence. I had not wanted to offend and distress him, but I did not see how I could have conducted myself in any other way.

"I have not been altogether happy about your behavior on various occasions since you have come to this house."

"I'm truly sorry I've disappointed you," I said. Tears stung behind my eyes. Always before I had been confident of his understanding and sympathy. It hurt me to see him distant and critical.

A slight smile moved his lips. "It is not altogether a disappointment, my dear. As I've told you before, I like your spirit. However, I feel that your energy and vitality can be turned to better use than by this idle stepping off down indiscreet roads."

I stirred in my chair. "Uncle Robert, I had to befriend that child. I could do nothing less."

"Knowing nothing about him, you brought him here to play with my daughter Caroline." The smile had vanished.

"He seems a well-brought-up child. She liked him and I think they would not have harmed each other." I hated to be forced into defending my actions to him, but I did not know how else to regain the ground I had lost in his estimation.

"I do not ask you to think about these matters," Uncle Robert said coldly. "I ask you to listen to me and do exactly what I ask you to do."

"I can't help thinking," I told him unhappily. "My father has always taught me to think for myself."

"This is not your father's house. At present you are entirely my charge, not his. Under no circumstances are you to have anything to do with the Pollock woman or with this child who is in her care. Do I make myself clear?"

130

I no longer felt like crying. In spite of the dismaying turn our affairs had taken, I grew a little indignant.

"You make yourself very clear," I said. "But I can't promise such a thing. I don't know what situation might arise in the future and I can't promise something that would force me to be unkind to that little boy."

My voice had risen and my defiant words seemed to echo in the room, frightening me a little. I didn't want to anger him further.

The mottled flush had come into his cheeks again and he did not look at all well. I wondered if I should call Aunt Natalie, but I feared that might disturb him all the more. He flung out his hands, as if in repudiation of me and everything I had said. Hoping that the gesture was a dismissal, I half rose from my chair. But he waved me back and spoke with something of an effort.

"You leave me no choice. I have done my best to move gently with you, Skye, to give you every chance to come willingly to the point of taking sensible action. But you are too unruly, too undisciplined. We can wait no longer. You must marry in the near future."

I stared at him in disbelief. How could he possibly say such a thing? How could he believe that I might be forced into marriage just because he wished it?

He nodded gravely. "Yes, this is the only solution. I have spoken to Courtney Law and he is most grateful to me for wishing to take him into my own family. He admires you greatly, feels that you would make him a fine wife. He advised giving you time, however, not attempting to rush you into anything. It was his feeling that you should get to know and like him, as is apparently the foolish custom in the North before marriage. But now I realize we cannot wait. I shall speak to my wife so that preparations may be started. I shall, of course, give you a suitable wedding and dowry. The date can be set a month ahead. You leave me no other choice, my dear."

He reached for the pen on his desk and began to write on a sheet of paper. This time I knew I had been dismissed. For a moment I was too shocked by his words to answer him. I felt as if a blow had knocked the breath completely out of me. Then the power of thought and motion returned, and I stood up in order to answer him all the more forcefully.

"I'm sorry to oppose you in any way, Uncle Robert," I said. "I am very grateful for all you've done for us. But I cannot marry Courtney Law. Not now or later on. I cannot marry anyone except a man I love."

The hand with the pen moved smoothly on. He did not even turn his head to look at me.

"My dear," he said casually, "you have no other choice. Your father's well-being depends upon me. Let us speak no more about it for the moment, Skye."

I stared at him in utter disbelief. What I had heard was too cruel a thing to be true. He could not possibly mean—! But watching him as he wrote on, indifferent to my presence, I knew exactly what he meant. And I knew he would not retract it. If I did not choose to marry Courtney Law, he would put us all out of his house and he would not turn a hair in so doing.

I turned and ran out of the room, lest I say or do something rash before I had time to control myself. Along the gallery I ran, past my father's door and into my own room. I locked the door after me and flung myself on the bed. Across the room the blue cat stared at me disdainfully from the bureau. It wore an expression as superior as that of my uncle and I was tempted to pick up a slipper and fling it at the china doorstop.

But that would be a childish release for the shattering emotion that shook me. How could my uncle, whom I had loved and respected, whom I had trusted so completely, change to something monstrous before my very eyes? And how was I to deal with what had happened? How was I to find the means of resisting him?

Torn by a mingling of fear for the future and misery because my belief in him had been destroyed, I turned my face to my pillow and wept like the child I could no longer be. Yet in my depths of unhappiness I thought of Justin, reached out to him despairingly.

"Justin, Justin, help me!" I whispered. "You are my love. Don't let this happen to me!" But Justin Law was far away from this house and how could he know or care?

Yet he would know, I thought, thrusting back my sobs. If my uncle forced this action upon me, Justin would know that I was going to marry his brother. And what would he think then of the girl who had kissed him with all her heart one night in a garden?

Sixteen ✽

I could not lie there on my bed for long because the supper hour was approaching. I'd have preferred to avoid the table, avoid seeing my uncle again until I had rallied my courage, had come to some decision. But I did not want anyone fussing over me and I didn't want word of Uncle Robert's threat to get back to my father. If Mama dreamed of what he'd said, she would run tearfully to Papa—and that was the one thing that must not happen.

Reluctantly I left the bed and the luxury of a despair I could not afford and bathed my face in cool water. Then I sat at the dressing table to tidy my hair. Had my mother, when she was younger than I, sat at this very table and gazed with anguish into this same mirror? She too had lived under Uncle Robert's domination and I remembered her dread of returning here, of being in the same house with her brother again. I had always dismissed as exaggeration the things she said about Robert Tourneau. I had been eager to admire and respect and love my uncle. But this after-noon I had seen behind the sympathetic mask he had shown me, and the glimpse terrified me.

What was I to do? What could I do?

The marble top of the little dressing table was cool to my warm hands and for just an instant I bent and pressed my hot cheek against the soothing chill. Then I sat up and combed my hair, faced the girl in the glass. Not since the day of the party had I worn my hair loose, and it was drawn back tightly now in the old way. I looked pale, and my eyes were dull with unhappiness, the lids reddened.

A tap sounded at my door and Caro called to me softly. I forced myself to smile and went to let her in. She entered tiptoeing like a conspirator and closed the door behind her.

"Did Papa scold you very much, Cousin Skye?"

"A little," I said. "It doesn't matter."

She shook her head wisely. "It always matters when Papa scolds. But I am sad that I could not play with Lanny."

133

She might have pursued the subject further, but her eyes rested just then upon the blue cat, sitting proudly high, with his tail curled about blue toes. I was glad to have her attention distracted.

"Oh, but he is wonderful!" she cried and flitted across the room to make the cat a dancing little bow. "What are you going to do with him, Cousin Skye?"

"He's a gift for my father," I said. "Lanny saw him in a shop on Royal Street this afternoon."

Caro smiled her delight. "He is most distinguished. What are you going to name him?"

I told her she might think of a good name, if she liked, and suggest it to my father.

"But no one will let me trouble your papa by visiting him," she said, and I realized for the first time that my father had not met this most interesting member of the family.

"Let's do something about that right now," I said. "Let's take the cat to him."

I was glad to have her company on this visit to my father. With the cat to give him and Caro to present, everything could be kept cheerful and light and my own troubled state of mind more easily concealed.

There was at once a friendly acceptance between Papa and Caro. The man who could hardly move and the child who was never still, understood each other by the exchange of a look and a clasp of their hands.

I set the cat upon Papa's bureau where he could see it plainly and he smiled as he looked at it.

"It is a Creole cat," he said. "And most perfectly in character."

He was right, of course. No wonder the cat's expression had seemed familiar. It would never have occurred to cat or Creole that anyone else on earth but another cat or Creole was truly worthy of his attention.

"When you get irritated you can sit up and throw things at him," I told Papa. "And perhaps sometimes I'll come in and help you."

Caro whirled suddenly about the small room. "I know the cat's name! I know just what we must call him!"

Caro's gaiety pleased my father and it seemed to me that he was looking better than I had seen him look in a long while. The realization stabbed through me. Nothing must happen to halt this improvement.

"Tell us the name you've chosen," he said to Caro, "and I promise to use it."

"It must be Beauregard, of course!" Caro cried. "And we can call him Beau for short."

Thus it was that a new member was introduced to the household that day. And Beauregard, whether he liked it or not, had helped me through the first difficult moments with my father. Now that I had faced him without betraying the thing that must remain hidden from his knowledge, I was that much stronger, that much more ready to take the next step.

It was in just that way—one careful step at a time—that I managed to get through the supper hour and through all the hours of the long week that followed. Outwardly I managed to listen, to smile, to speak when I was spoken to. Inwardly my thoughts darted this way and that like cornered mice and I could find no escape from the trap, no answer to my searching.

In the North I might have overruled my mother's wishes and become a teacher. But here in the South a northern teacher was not wanted. Nor would the pittance earned have cared for the three of us, even if we had been able to leave Uncle Robert's house.

From Aunt Natalie's gentle, happy manner toward me, I knew that Uncle Robert had told her the marriage was settled. But he must have asked her to say nothing as yet to the others—which indicated that he still awaited my agreement. I knew, however, that he would not wait for long. Each morning at breakfast his eyes questioned me coldly, and each morning I looked away from him without giving my answer.

On Sunday afternoon Courtney called to take me for a drive along the lake and I wondered if there would be any chance to speak with him alone. But Mama announced gaily that she needed an outing too and it would be her pleasure to chaperone us. I believe Courtney truly did not want her to go. He was behaving in the most decorous way possible and I had to give him credit for treating me as a young man who was courting a lady should.

Later I remembered that drive chiefly for the sense of discomfort and unhappiness it gave me. The afternoon was sunny, but our parasols shielded us from the hot rays and there was a pleasant breeze blowing in over the water. We drove through the park and along a road that rimmed a section of the lake. The water stretched away, seeming as vast an expanse as the ocean, but I paid little attention to the drive or to my surroundings.

Mama was tantalizing and provocative. She teased Courtney for his sober manner, flirted with him outrageously, until I began to feel that I was the chaperone and she the girl who was being wooed. Courtney did his best to hold out against her. He addressed most of his remarks to me, he tried to keep his eyes away from her face, from her smiling, tempting lips, but her light voice kept up a rain of patter all about us. The fragrance of her lilac scent, her beauty—all were an invitation too close for Courtney to escape.

I saw his eyes stray more than once, and though he was no longer the feckless young man I had first met, who played easy court to every lady, it was plain which of these two ladies attracted him. I had nothing to offer. No gay conversation came lightly to my lips. I sat in moody silence and felt myself plain and dowdy and dull. Nor did I mind being these things. No longer did they matter. But I was angry with my mother and sorry for Courtney, yet helpless to deal with either of them.

By the time we had turned toward home, I had come to one conclusion. My time of grace, I knew, was up. And I had found no solution. Somehow I had hoped against hope that Justin might come unexpectedly into the picture and save me in some unforeseen way. I'd even woven a little fantasy in which he invited himself along on this drive and found a way to settle matters between us. But I'd had no sight, no word of Justin all that week, and now, slowly, relentlessly, I brought myself to an acceptance of what he himself had told me.

There was no place for marrying in Justin's life. Because I had not wanted to believe that, I had fooled myself for a while, promised myself the moon. But now I must face the fact that Justin had really meant what he said. Perhaps I had interested him briefly, but he had taken care to escape any serious entanglement. Now there was just one door left for me to walk through, and only one. The door my uncle had chosen. If I could not have my love, what did it matter, so long as I saved my father?

But first I must somehow have a private talk with Courtney. I wanted no one else to dream of the threat that had been made against my father. But Courtney must know. If, in the end, I had to marry him, I would not do so without telling him all the truth save one thing—that I loved his brother.

It was something of a relief to choose a course of action. There was still the faint hope that if Courtney and I got together in this matter, we might between us find some means of making Uncle Robert change his mind.

With these thoughts to sustain me, I endured that endless drive and pretended that I did not see my mother's flirtatious efforts. I knew it would do no good to reproach her, for she would have met any accusation on my part with wide-eyed innocence and astonishment. So I let the game go on and simply endured.

Two days later, when Uncle Robert spoke at breakfast of a visit he must make that afternoon to a bedridden client in the Garden District, I knew I would have my chance.

I waited until my uncle had been gone for a half hour and then slipped downstairs quietly and went to the office door. It stood open, but Courtney was not in sight. I ran up the steps and looked about the anteroom. His pen lay upon a paper on the desk and it had splattered ink that was not yet dry. He could not be far away. A sound reached me from the inner office that was my uncle's and I stepped to the door and looked in.

The fragrance of my mother's perfume warned me even before I saw them. They parted just as I stepped into the room. My mother's eyes were bright and her cheeks flushed. She had the look upon her of a woman who had just been rapturously kissed. Yet it was my mother who showed the most presence of mind. She smiled at me as if there were nothing unusual about this meeting, told Courtney a polite *"Merci,"* as if she had come down for no more than to borrow an envelope, and went unconcernedly past me and out of the office.

Courtney looked at me with dark, unhappy eyes and he, at least, made no attempt to dissemble.

"I'm sorry, Skye," he said miserably. "I am truly sorry."

Here was the opportunity I had wanted to talk to him. But now that I had it, I could not speak. Anger against my mother left me shaken and with no heart for a quiet talk with Courtney Law. I said nothing at all, but turned and followed my mother upstairs.

The time had come when I must open the dam I had held against the words I longed to say to her. Somehow she must be halted on this foolish course she was taking with Courtney. For one thing, I had to know if she fancied herself in love with him, if she had turned away from my father. Or was this a repetition of past behavior and no more than a game to her?

I found her in her room sorting through a heap of dresses

137

she had flung across her bed. There too, tossed carelessly to the floor, was the fern-green hat, of which she had grown tired by now. Her lower lip was caught prettily between white teeth as she studied the garments with an air of concentration. I tapped at the open door and she bade me enter without troubling to look up.

"Natalie's seamstress is to see what can be done to bring these things up to date, Skye. Which frock do you think becomes me best? When the *saison des visites* commences I must look presentable."

Her audacity took my breath away. A moment ago she had been in Courtney's arms. Yet now she spoke of her wardrobe as though the matter of how she dressed this fall was all she had to concern her. Did she think me blind, stupid? I was neither!

"Mama," I said, "I want to talk to you, but not about dresses."

She flicked my words aside with a wave of her fingers. "Not now, *chérie,* if you please. The woman is coming this afternoon. I must have these things ready for her."

The impetus of my purpose carried me along. "We'll talk now," I said. "You must let Courtney alone!"

She looked at me questioningly. "That poor boy! He is sweet, but rather foolish, I'm afraid."

As always she made judgment difficult with her air of innocence. But the time had come to be blunt and direct.

"You've made him fall in love with you," I told her. "Or at least you've bewitched him into thinking he is in love with you. You're injuring not only Courtney, but Papa too. Do you no longer love my father?"

Her eyes widened in astonishment and she looked convincingly shocked. *"Chérie,* what are you saying? What madness has overcome you?"

I was far more shaken by this interview than she.

"I'm not mad. I know very well what I'm saying. You were always ready to charm away the young men who came to see me. How can you have forgotten that day in the orchard when—when Tom—" I broke off because I knew my lips would tremble if I tried to go on.

She came to me sweetly and put her hands upon my arms, looking up at me from her diminutive height. "How you must have suffered believing such wicked thoughts. I was no more than an older woman with whom your Tom found comfort in talking. Your father was wrong to send him away. How foolish that you should think—"

138

I moved from the touch of her hands. "It's you who must see the truth before it's too late. You never rest until you have every young man at your feet. You took Tom away from me. Now you're trying to charm Courtney. Do you think I don't know that he was kissing you just now?"

All the color had drained from her face and she looked at me with displeasure. "I see. It is jealousy that moves you to say such things. This foolish notion of Robert's that you and Courtney are to marry has apparently gone to your head. Please leave my room, Skye. I will not listen to these evil words."

I blocked her doorway, but I did not step through it. "You might as well know that I have decided to marry Courtney. And I will not have you making love to him."

She gasped softly and I knew that I had reached her.

"Have you stopped loving my father?" I repeated. "Have you forgotten how much he needs you?"

"Needs me!" She laughed in my face and the sound had a bitter, unhappy ring. "He needs me not at all. He will not talk to me, or listen to me. He no longer wants me in his room. And I am lonely, lonely, lonely! In this house where my brother hates me and my daughter is jealous of me, I have no friends. It is as it was when I was a child after my parents died."

She covered her face with her hands. I heard her small, broken sobs, but I remained unmoved, waiting in silence. After a moment she looked at me, her cheeks flushed and tear-stained.

"Courtney has been no more than kind and sympathetic. He has given me a little brotherly affection and I am starved for affection. But the rest of what you say is false. What could I hope for with Courtney? I am a married woman and far older than he. I am tied and there is no escape possible. But I can have this little thing he gives me, this small affection to comfort me in my loneliness."

A trembling had begun within me and I knew it grew from my helplessness to deal with her. My mother saw only what she chose to see, so how could she be made to accept the truth of her actions? She would not face that truth. The "little" affection she would take from Courtney could easily turn into a blaze that would ruin him and crush my father, but Louise Cameron would stand safe in her own cool innocence, untouched by the flames she had lighted, protected by the defenses she put up in her own mind. It was possible to deal with one who would look honestly at herself. But how could I deal with a woman who did not know the truth from the lie? And she had not answered my question as to whether she loved my father.

"This evening," I said quietly, "I shall tell Uncle Robert that I am willing to marry Courtney."

Then I bent and picked up the little green hat, took it away with me to my room. I would have that to keep, at least. One bright small memory of my love for Justin Law.

Seventeen

Uncle Robert accepted my agreement to his wishes as calmly as though he had known all along that I must capitulate. He was very charming and kind to me that evening in his study, but I could not ever again feel toward him as I had in the beginning.

His mood was so excellent that he decided we must celebrate with a small dinner away from the house. At Antoine's perhaps. Of course Creole ladies did not as a rule dine in public restaurants, but he would take a private room and secure us proper seclusion.

"Just ourselves, my dear, and Courtney's family. It is a pity your father cannot join us. But we will invite Courtney's mother, and perhaps even the brother."

I looked at him, startled, but he was paying no attention to me. The ivory paper knife was in his long fingers and he studied the carving with concentrated interest.

"Yes—I believe we shall invite the brother to our little party. It will be most appropriate."

"Please, Uncle Robert," I said, "don't ask Justin Law."

"And why should I not invite him?" he asked, giving me a sharp, keen look.

I knew I had gone too far. Opposition was sure to strengthen my uncle's determination. But I could imagine nothing worse than a supposedly gay engagement party, with Justin looking sardonically on and my heart breaking within me.

"You have said yourself that he is a criminal," I pointed

out. "Why should you wish the ladies in your family to associate with such a man?"

"Your association with him, I assure you," said Uncle Robert, tapping the bit of ivory against a fingernail, "will be inconsequential. This is not altogether a personal matter. It is also a business matter. Until I am ready to settle with this fellow, it is best to remain on amiable terms."

They had not been on amiable terms the other times I had seen them together. Indeed, I had sensed an almost sinister hostility between them. So it seemed all the more strange that my uncle should make this gesture now.

There was no use in arguing with him, however. My one hope was that Justin would refuse to come.

"If that's all, may I go?" I asked my uncle in the dutiful manner he approved.

"One moment, Skye." With a sudden gesture he reached out and took the silver warming cover from the grooved table, revealing the chessboard beneath. I saw that once more the ebony and ivory men had been set up for a game. But this time with a difference. The white king had been replaced on the board.

"I thought you played with only one king," I said dryly.

If he heard the faint gibe in my voice, he did not show it. "That was before the boy knocked the chessmen from the board," he said. "Perhaps he did me a favor. In re-establishing the game, I thought my gambit through again and this time my attack is far stronger than before. You say you know the game of chess? Tell me then what you see, *ma petite*."

Reluctantly, I studied the board and found that the position of Black was very strong. The white queen stood helpless and of little use. The enemy advanced upon the white king and he would soon be in check. I could see no countermoves for White. In a few plays he would be done.

"Black should win in four moves," I said, studying the board. "Unless White is a very clever player."

"What do you mean?" Uncle Robert asked curtly. "There is no way out for him."

"There's no way out that I can see," I agreed. "But one should never underestimate an opponent."

Uncle Robert replaced the silver cover and that sharp bright look I had learned to know as a prelude to anger came into his eyes.

"What does it matter?" I said. "It's only a game."

He stared at me for a moment longer and then shrugged.

"But of course," he admitted, and the look of danger went out of his face. "I am more than pleased, Skye, at your wise decision to marry Courtney. I think you will never regret it."

I rose to leave and he showed me to the door courteously. I went, enormously glad to escape from his presence.

I had begun to suspect why a king was back in the game. If the king who was dead was Harry Law, and the poor helpless little white queen was Aurore, then the new king was Justin. But the thing I could not perceive was why he should indulge in this fanciful warfare.

Justin could probably take care of himself, but I did not like this secret plotting, this confidence with which my uncle behaved. It seemed to bode well for none of us, and least of all for Justin.

For several days I could not bring myself to tell my father that Courtney and I were to be married. Nor did Mama tell him. To a great extent she avoided Papa's room these days and left most of his care to Delphine, who nursed him faithfully. When I finally gathered my courage, I took Courtney with me to meet my father, and we did our best to present the outward appearance of a happily engaged couple.

My father took Courtney's hand, looking up at the man beside his bed for a long, puzzled moment.

"I hope you will both be very happy," he said gravely.

He was kind to Courtney and I hoped that he liked him. But I did not believe my father was really fooled. He looked at me with a question in his eyes and I knew he wondered about Justin. However, the next time I went to his room he seemed sunk in apathy again and I did not talk about Courtney or my marriage at all.

I dreaded the coming dinner party and still hoped that Justin would refuse the invitation. Once I asked Courtney if his brother planned to attend, but he had no answer for me.

"I have no knowledge of what that one plans. He has been invited, but he says nothing. These days he is involved in buying boats to carry cargoes on the river. Nothing else seems of importance to him."

"He knows the occasion for the dinner?" I asked.

"I have not told him," Courtney said. "I see him as little as possible. There is no friendship between us."

I had to leave it at that. After all, what difference did it make whether Justin had heard of our engagement or not? It was not a public matter as yet and I fancied it would make no difference to him, one way or another.

Whether I cared or not, I had a new dress to wear for the

occasion. Aunt Natalie said Robert had insisted upon that. She wanted to dress me in girlish white again and I would never have opposed her. But this time Delphine interfered. In her quiet way she could be a force when she chose and Aunt Natalie respected her opinion. So it was settled that for once I was to be dressed in rich dark colors that would complement my hair. The gown was of changeable golden-brown taffeta, shot with an orange flame. There was a diagonal trimming of dark green velvet. Folds of rich dark green showed in the bustle and I wore a green taffeta petticoat with a frilly hem.

Once more Delphine dressed my hair so that it fell over my shoulders, but all through her ministrations I was apathetic and did not care. If Justin was to be there, I did not want to be a wren. But how I dressed was only a shield I wore. I had begun to learn that, for a woman, to dress bravely is to meet life with greater courage.

Delphine tried to prod me into interest by assuring me of my good fortune in marrying Courtney. He was a Le-Maitre on his mother's side—a fine Creole family. And a most excellent young man. Already he showed himself able to approach marriage soberly, and avoid foolish entanglement.

I looked at her sharply in the mirror and her gaze met mine without pretense.

"The nose of your maman," she said quietly, "is, as the Americans say, out of joint."

I was not going to discuss Mama with her and I told her rather curtly to pay attention to what she was doing.

My mother, at least, took an interest in her appearance that night, and I suspected that she meant to extract the last drop of suffering possible from Courtney by showing him how desirable she could be. Aunt Natalie's seamstress had remade an old dress of white lace that had something of a Spanish look to it. In it my mother was breathlessly lovely—a sad, romantic lady who broke your heart a little because you were almost taken in by the illusion that her own was broken.

Under other circumstances I might have looked forward to dining at this restaurant whose history dated back before the war. It had been a favorite spot of Papa's when he had first visited New Orleans in the days before he'd married my mother. He had told me something of the Alciatoire family, who had built a tradition for fine foods over these forty years. But as it was, I could only regard the evening as an ordeal and hope that it would be over quickly.

Tante Aurore, Courtney and Justin joined us first in Uncle Robert's parlor, where we sat chatting for a little while before going to the restaurant. I could not keep my eyes from Justin's face as he came into the room. He looked, I thought, rather like a man who was on guard among enemies. His manner was courteous, but not overly friendly, and I had no way of telling whether or not he knew why this dinner was being given. My uncle was completely in control of himself, and he allowed none of his antagonism toward Justin to reveal itself. Yet I sensed it there beneath the surface. In both men no more than a veneer concealed the hostility which so easily flared between them.

When we rose to go downstairs, Justin walked beside me for a moment, and spoke to me softly. "Tonight you do yourself justice," he said and his smile was warm.

Such words came too late and led nowhere. I would have turned away from him without speaking, but he was close to me on the curving stairway.

"I've not seen you in Jackson Square lately," he went on, "but I've seen Lanny again. The boy told me that you brought him home and there'd been a to-do at the house."

I could only nod. The stairway was no place to tell him of what had happened.

"We had quite a talk before the Pollock woman came out to snatch him again as if I were the devil himself. I wonder what she has against me. I like the boy and I'll not harm him."

We had reached the passageway and now Courtney was at my side, drawing me away from his brother.

My wish for the evening to be over quickly was a futile one. At Antoine's they did not rush so important a matter as eating. We went through the modest entrance on St. Louis Street and were led through a large, rather bare dining room. Hardly a table in the big room stood empty and one sensed that this room was given over nightly to laughter, gay conversation and the appreciation of good food.

Uncle Robert had taken a small private dining room and we were a family party. I was placed on my uncle's right, with Courtney on the other side of me. Since my mother and Justin were across the table I was in a position to see Justin's face clearly when Uncle Robert raised his wineglass and proposed a toast to the "young couple so recently affianced." I could not look anywhere else—I had to look at him to see how he reacted. For once he did not manage a poker expression. He looked plainly astonished and he was the last to raise his glass to the toast. Over the rim, as he sipped, his eyes met mine, with the old, sardonic amusement in them.

Then the moment had passed and Uncle Robert was examining the vast expanse of the French menu and commenting expansively on the excellence of certain dishes.

Like the others, I ordered the *huitres* that were a specialty of the house, but when the oysters came I could hardly swallow them. Nor could I manage to join in the conversation that Uncle Robert set flowing around the table. It seemed that everyone was attempting to do justice to the occasion but me. Courtney, plainly, wanted to please Uncle Robert and if his glance strayed across the table toward my mother more often than was wise, I think only Mama and I were aware of it.

She had roused herself from her role of a lady of sorrow and was bending her efforts upon Justin, ignoring Courtney completely. Justin seemed to play her little game, but I think his thoughts were elsewhere.

When Uncle Robert asked him, somewhat too pointedly, I thought, about his life in Leadville, Justin took no offense. We ate our *pompano en papillote* and he told us of his life in the West—a subject I had never heard him mention before. I listened to all he said, storing away every crumb of information that might be added to my knowledge of Justin Law.

Justin's father had bought for a paltry sum a mine which gold seekers had abandoned. He and a friend had believed there was silver in that shaft in the ground and had thrown themselves eagerly into developing it.

"My father and his partner held onto the mine, no matter how things went," Justin said. "Father always thought he would make a fortune and someday return to New Orleans. But the fortune came too late. My father was dead."

Uncle Robert's deceptively melodious voice broke the moment of awkward silence that followed. "But what of your schooling in that wild place? Your education?"

"I was not sent abroad for a year or so like many a Creole boy in the old days, if that is what you mean," Justin told him wryly. "Our shack had only a single room, but even one room can hold shelves for books. As you know, my father was a well-read man and he taught me himself."

A challenge seemed to ring beneath his words, but Uncle Robert let it pass, and brought the conversation back to New

145

Orleans, as if the local scene clearly interested him more.

I saw Aurore's gaze rest upon her older son in momentary pain, and then turn sadly away.

Never have I sat through a longer, more uncomfortable meal. It was the custom to serve fish, flesh and fowl at a Creole dinner, and before the *meringue glacée* arrived I had lost all taste for food. Mama was deliberately tormenting Courtney by flirting with his brother and I think it made no difference to her whether Justin responded or not. She wanted only to punish Courtney.

I tried to talk to him about anything that came to mind, to distract him from what was going on across the table, but I could sense the growing anger in him. Not against my mother, who deserved it, but against Justin.

It was not until the meal was nearly over that Uncle Robert astonished me. Always in considering marriage to Courtney Law I thought in terms of an escape to that spacious house in the Garden District. There Papa would be more comfortable than he could ever be in the narrow confines of the house in the Quarter. Even my mother would be happier there, away from Uncle Robert. And Tante Aurore would probably welcome company in her empty house. As for Courtney—if I married him, I would try to make him a good wife. I was doing this to save my father and Courtney must understand that fact. But I would also do my best to carry the responsibilities of a wife and if possible make Courtney happy. I did not think true happiness for me would ever be possible. I could only hope that Justin would have the consideration and the desire to move elsewhere. I gave him no part in the picture I was building. Perhaps he would want to move to another part of New Orleans, and since there was no love lost between him and Courtney, I would seldom see him after that.

But while we ate our dessert, Uncle Robert spoke the words that caused my make-believe to vanish like a pricked bubble.

"I want you to know, Courtney," my uncle said, his affability increasing with the good food and wine, "that I shall be proud to have you for a nephew-in-law and to encourage your career as a coming young lawyer in this town."

He glanced at his wife and Aunt Natalie dutifully added her own words of agreement. I sat frozen in my place.

"We have spoken of giving you and Skye a bedroom on the third floor larger than the one she now occupies."

Mama looked as startled as I felt and I knew that she too

146

must have been thinking in terms of leaving the Tourneau house.

Nervously Aurore crumbled bread in her plate. "But, Robert—" she faltered, "I should be lonely in my big house. I had thought—"

He patted her hand benevolently. "Of course, my dear. That would not do at all. There will no longer be any point in keeping the house. It can be sold and you will then be able to move into a small cottage I own on St. Ann Street. You will be most comfortable there and not far from your son."

Thus carelessly, casually, he disposed of our lives, giving us no opportunity to speak our own wishes. Or if we had spoken them, I am sure he would have dismissed them lightly. It was only the wish of Robert Tourneau that mattered. How, I wondered, had I ever thought him kind and understanding? It seemed to me now that even the pointing of his small black beard had a cruel look.

I was afraid Tante Aurore would crumple into her plate after her bread crumbs, but once more Creole training— and the fear of Uncle Robert—kept her upright. If she did not trust her voice, her hands, her eyes, at least she did not burst into tears or topple over in a faint.

To my own surprise, I found myself speaking. "The house in the Garden District is Tante Aurore's home," I reminded Uncle Robert. "There is room for us all there, without crowding you in the Chartres Street house. Perhaps Courtney and I would like to live there."

Uncle Robert shook his head as if I'd been a stupid child. "You do not understand these matters, Skye. The house will not be available. It must be sold. Aurore will do as I advise."

Tante Aurore's lips trembled and at last her control dissolved. She put a handkerchief to her eyes and wept uncontrollably.

"It is not possible!" she wailed. "I—I no longer own the house!"

"What are you saying?" Uncle Robert demanded, the affability falling away from him. "It has been in your name from the first. I have never had any taste for the place."

Courtney tried to comfort his mother, at the same time throwing an angry look at Justin. "You had better tell M'sieu Robert the truth," he said. "I have not yet had the opportunity to do so."

Justin seemed faintly amused. "My brother means that I have just purchased the house from my mother, sir. I wanted it to fall into no hands but my own. The transaction was completed only yesterday."

Uncle Robert half rose from his place, the mottled red surging into his cheeks. Then he remembered where he was and sank back in his chair. By an effort he managed to speak levelly to Justin, while the rest of us watched aghast.

"By what right did you take such a step, monsieur? Do you not know that money had been poured into the up-keep of that house? With never a penny contributed by those closest to Aurore! Meaning yourself, monsieur. Of course it would be easy to confuse, to take advantage of Aurore. Easy to persuade her to give up her property. She has never had a head for business—"

Where his tirade might have led, I don't know. But it was broken off at that moment because our waiter appeared, prepared for the customary serving of New Orleans' famous *café brulôt.*

We sat in rigid silence watching, each one thinking his own thoughts. The waiter brought in the silver bowls and ladle with a flourish. The ignited cognac was poured over the contents of a bowl. In our dining room the lights were extinguished and the blue flame leaped high. Our strained faces seemed to brood in the blue light as the waiter ceremoniously ladled the mixture over and over again, raising the ladle and allowing the flaming blue liquid to stream back into the bowl. Once for good measure, he strewed a few flaming drops across the table near me, and so tense were my nerves that I nearly screamed. But the drops burned harmlessly for a moment and then went out, with apparently no more than a stain left on the cloth.

Then the lights came on again and the coffee was served to us in tiny cups. No one spoke until the waiter went away.

By that time Uncle Robert had apparently remembered that he was host and Justin his guest.

"We will continue this discussion another time, monsieur," he said stiffly. "Do not consider that the subject has been closed."

Justin nodded. "At your service. But let's have it clear that my mother and I will continue to live in my father's house. And if Courtney wishes to bring his bride there, he will be welcome."

Uncle Robert restrained himself, but the hand with which he raised his coffee cup shook so that the liquid lapped brown against the rim. The moment of danger when there might
148

have been an open conflagration between the two men had once more passed. The unhappy meal was over.

Now I felt trapped whichever way I turned. I could not bear to continue living in my uncle's house when I married. Yet neither could I endure existence under the same roof with Justin.

As we left the table Tante Aurore came to me, still a little tearful, and took my hands. "I am happy for Courtney," she said. "You will make him a good wife, *chérie*. You must come to visit me again soon."

I promised that I would, feeling sorry for her. Of us all, she, perhaps, had been the most helpless in Uncle Robert's hands. It must disturb her greatly to have gone against his wishes. I wondered if all his seeming kindness to her had been a form of cruelty by which he revenged himself for her long-ago insult to him. My mother had once said that he never forgave anyone for anything and my mother had been right more often than I had admitted.

As we walked out of the restaurant to our carriage there was once more a moment in which I found myself beside Justin Law. So near to me he was, and so dear, yet I must not feel, I must not think.

"May I congratulate you on your coming marriage," he said so softly that only I caught the mockery in his voice.

I thanked him, outwardly cool, and turned away. What right had he to mock me when he did not want me for himself? Here was further unkindness. I saw that Courtney looked pale with strain and I went to him quickly, slipped my hand through his arm.

"I know how you feel," I whispered. "But don't let them see. We must have a talk together soon, you and I. Perhaps on the day I visit your mother."

He pressed a hand over mine, thanking me, but I knew he was sick at heart and growing a little desperate.

During the days that followed before my visit to the Garden District, I had long hours in which to think of this trap of my uncle's making in which we all seemed to be caught. I paced my cage from wall to wall, futilely seeking some way out.

What happened to me no longer seemed to matter. I wanted to do what I could for my father's sake and I meant to try with all the courage in me to do it without betraying my true feelings. But there was a limit to which the human spirit could be pushed, and the situation did not depend wholly on me. I could not believe that any chance existed

for this marriage if Courtney and I had to live in the Tourneau house. As long as we were here, Courtney would be
under my uncle's thumb, bound to him by long habits of
gratitude, admiration, affection. Robert Tourneau was Courtney's ideal of the Creole gentleman and any blame he might
place upon what was happening, I think he would place
upon himself, or upon Justin.

And how could he adjust to living in this house with my
mother so close at hand? I knew now that there could be no
making my mother recognize the harm or the guilt of her
own actions. She saw herself in an altogether different role
and would never believe the ugly reality. Yet neither could
we accept the strain of living beneath Justin's roof. Courtney
disliked his brother too much. And I—but my thoughts darted
quickly away from that futile path of longing and torment.

The only solution seemed escape from New Orleans altogether. But how could that be managed if Uncle Robert
would not help us? And I knew he would not. Around and
around, over and over, until my very spirit smarted at the
hopeless circuit. About Justin I would not think at all. Or
at least only in the quiet hours of the night when I could
not help myself. Then would come bittersweet memory and
dreams of what could not be, to weaken me in my resolve.
But always in the morning I would put the weakness aside
and the thought of Justin with it.

The answer I sought came to me suddenly one night
from some well of consciousness within me. How often it
seems that difficult problems are thus solved. There is no
answer anywhere that the mind awake can find. And then
from this inner source, without warning, fully fledged and
thought out, comes an answer. I lay wide awake until
morning broke knowing that I must postpone my painful
visit to Aurore Law no longer. Sunday afternoon I would
go out to the Garden District. And somehow, while I was
there, I would see Justin. If he was not home, I would wait
until he came.

For I knew now that Justin held the answer to my problem
and that he alone might be able to help us all.

Eighteen ✿

The fact which had come out during the dinner at Antoine's concerning the ownership of the Law house must have upset Uncle Robert mightily. In the days that followed he was preoccupied and had little to say to any of us. More than once I wondered wryly if the white king had, after all, managed to make an unexpected countermove, and if Uncle Robert had been forced to reconsider the game in a new light.

At least it was simple enough for me to arrange a visit to Aurore through Courtney. He seemed touchingly grateful that I wanted to call on her. Uncle Robert did not altogether approve. Justin had taken Aurore's care out of his hands, and he considered that she had betrayed him over the house. He could hardly refuse to allow me to visit Courtney's mother, yet his wrath against Justin was plainly smouldering. There would, I gathered, be no more entertaining or being entertained as far as Justin was concerned.

It was decided that Delphine should accompany me on the visit and I accepted her presence as inevitable, and at least better than having Mama go along.

The afternoon was steamy hot and sultry. Shade offered little relief, and even the passage of the carriage stirred only warm air. When we reached the Law house, Courtney, strangely enough, did not come to the door to greet me. The maid took me up to Tante Aurore, while Delphine remained downstairs. There was no sign of Justin. I could only hope that he was not staying in his quarters in town and that an opportunity to see him would arise.

Tante Aurore lay stretched upon a chaise longue in her airy, high-ceilinged bedroom, wearing a negligee of thin muslin against the heat of the day. When I entered the room she was taking from a spoon some green medicine that had the odor of licorice about it. There seemed to be even more bottles and jars in the array on her dressing table than I had last seen in this room.

She wrinkled her nose in distaste over the green stuff

151

and dropped the spoon into a glass. Then she managed a tremulous welcome.

"*Chérie*, it is good of you to come! How well you look, Skye. Ah, you young people—never appreciating your health while you have it! Would you believe it—when I was your age there was many a time that I danced all night at a different ball for four nights running, and never felt tired at all. But now I am old and ill, and life is over for me. I can live only for my children. Come, sit near me, Skye. We must have a good talk."

I brought a small quilted chair and sat beside her. She looked tired and ill and forlorn.

"I do not like to tell you this, *chérie*," she said, "but I am troubled about Courtney. What can you tell me of him? He is truly happy in his plans for this marriage?"

I had to be evasive. "I know he wants to do as Uncle Robert wishes," I said. "He has a great sense of indebtedness to my uncle."

"Yes, of course. That is natural. And once he is married to you, Skye, then I am sure all will be well. But now he feels that Robert blames him for the sale of this house to Justin. Though it was all taken out of my hands before Courtney knew. Many things are tearing at my son, and I do not know how to help him. Sometimes I fear that he will do something wild and impulsive."

Since I could not tell Tante Aurore the truth of Courtney's hopeless infatuation for my mother, I nodded sympathetically and was silent. She liked to talk and I knew she would carry the burden of the conversation if I let her. After a while I would inquire about Justin, find out if I might see him.

"I wonder sometimes," she went on sadly, "whether I chose the wise course of action with Courtney after all. Of course I was guided by Robert at every point. How could a poor foolish woman exist without a wise man to guide her? Always I showed Justin's letters to Robert and he took them away for safekeeping."

"There were letters from him then? And you never showed them to Courtney?"

"*Mais non*. It did not seem wise to build in the boy any liking, or even curiosity about his brother. My elder son had revealed a wild strain that did not come from my side of the family. Robert warned me that Courtney must never come under his influence. After a time, as the years passed and on Robert's advice I did not answer, there were no more letters. When I learned he had been imprisoned, I thought him safely gone from our lives."

For a moment I could think only of the boy Justin, writing home to his mother and never receiving an answer.

"How do you account for the fact that Uncle Robert now receives him, entertains him?" I asked.

"Robert has not confided in me. I see him so seldom. And now he is angry with me." She covered her face with her hands. "I know I have become distasteful to him. He never lets me forget that I am no longer the girl whose portrait hangs on the wall of his study."

"Nor is he the young man who wooed that girl," I said dryly. "What does Uncle Robert expect—that time will stand still?"

But it was not in her to blame him. All that she had, her very life and her son's future had depended for so long upon Robert Tourneau.

"He is terribly angry over what I have done with the house," she went on. "You do not blame me, Skye? My older son is so strong, so forceful. And truly, he has been far kinder than I expected since his return. And I thought Robert wanted me to welcome Justin. But there is bad blood between him and Robert. I do not know what the outcome will be. Often I am frightened, *chérie*."

At least she had softened a little in her attitude toward Justin. I was about to inquire for him, but she continued her wistful reminiscence.

"If only you could have known Robert as a young man. Ah, he was handsome, that one! Such flashing eyes and tall, erect carriage. But with less harshness in his face in those days. Though he always frightened me a little. In some ways he did not seem a true Creole."

Such a statement surprised me, since, of all things, Uncle Robert prided himself most on being everything that was Creole.

"What do you mean?" I asked.

She moved her hands despairingly. "It is difficult to explain. We Creoles are a thrifty people in many ways, though capable of spending lavishly for pleasure. Nevertheless, we do not as a rule set great store by wealth. We know that blood, a good family name, means more than money. But Robert was not like that. He liked money for itself and for the power it gave him. After the war he became even worse. In spite of great losses, he would not change his life in any way. He worked insanely hard to become wealthy again.

And there were other things that were strange in him."

She sighed, remembering, and I waited quietly until she was ready to go on.

"He did not laugh as easily as a true Creole laughs. Our men may have hot tempers and are given to reckless acts at times, but they are gay, as the women are gay. We have great hearts and we know how to live. You know our families came from Santo Domingo in 1791 when there was an insurrection of Negroes against their masters. Many *emigrés* escaped to New Orleans at that time."

She was wandering from the subject, but I gave her time to come back to it. I had a desire to understand Uncle Robert, perhaps even to find a key to his behavior in what she could tell me.

"What a difference the coming of those wealthy, gay, well-educated French people made to this city!" Tante Aurore said proudly. "They knew how to laugh and cry, how to be gay, how to feel. They were, as we say, all heart. And so are we who have descended from them. Perhaps that is all that is wrong with Courtney at the moment. Too much heart. It is natural that he should harbor certain resentments against Justin."

"But my uncle," I prompted her. "You were telling me of him."

"Ah, yes. Robert, even as a child, was a glowering one. He would demand his own way, instead of winning it as his sister could always win what she wanted. I speak of your mother, *chérie*. Of course Loulou was always the favorite of her parents. Her mother could have no more children and she had lost all but those two. Loulou was the loving, winning one upon whom the parents doted. Their death must have been doubly dreadful for her."

Always before I had received only my mother's views on her life in the Tourneau house. This interested me.

"What do you mean?" I asked. "How was it doubly dreadful?"

"Because she, who had been so surrounded by love, so tenderly raised and given her every desire, had all love removed from her life. I was older than she, but still a child, yet I remember the blight that was put upon her. There was an elderly aunt, but she was a stick, wholly obedient to Robert. And of course he had always been jealous of his sister and helpless to attract to himself the love his mother and father gave the little girl. When they died and he became head of the family, though still young, poor Loulou was cut off from all affection."

I listened gravely, asking no questions now. I had never seen my mother in this light before. Compassion stirred in me for the girl she had been, though it was hard to forgive the woman that girl had become.

"I can remember," Tante Aurore said, "how wild she was for affection. At home she was nothing after her parents died. Always at home her small gifts and talents were ridiculed, belittled. So at every party she must charm everyone to her. She had a compulsion to be loved, admired. Of course as she grew to marriageable age, that meant by men, more than by women. Perhaps she sought again the worshipping love her father had given her. She was a greater flirt than the rest of us, and more determined in her efforts. Yet somehow she was gay and innocent, strange as that may seem. Truly I do not know how she answered to herself for some of the things she did."

I knew exactly what Aurore meant, though hearing it from her lips did not comfort me.

"Why didn't you marry Uncle Robert?" I asked. "You must have admired him a great deal."

"Ah, if only I had! But I did what many another foolish girl has done—I lost my heart and married for love. And what has it ever given me but heartbreak?"

I was tempted to remark that her heart might have remained intact if she had been willing to follow her husband into the West. If she had found the courage to make that choice, perhaps much tragedy might have been averted.

The carpeting in the hallway hid the sound of Delphine's approaching steps. We were not aware of her until she tapped and then opened the door without waiting for a response. Her face seemed as expressionless as ever, but I knew by her quick-moving manner that something was wrong.

"Madame," she said to Tante Aurore, "it is necessary to come at once—they quarrel fiercely. It is to be feared they will come to blows."

Tante Aurore sat up with a cry. "Skye, go downstairs! I have not the strength to face those two. Hurry, chérie, before they kill each other. Ah, I have known this would come!"

As I ran through the hall and down the stairs, I could hear the sound of angry voices from the library. Delphine followed me swiftly. Just as we reached the library door I heard the ringing sound of a slap, followed in an instant by a blow and a fall. I pushed open the door and stepped into the room.

What had happened was clear. Courtney lay sprawled on the floor, while Justin's left cheek bore a red, splotched mark. Courtney had slapped his brother, and Justin had knocked him down.

Courtney stumbled to his feet rubbing his jaw, his eyes blazing with anger. For a moment I feared that he might hurl himself upon Justin again, and I rushed to him, put my hands upon his shoulders. He was furiously angry and I could feel his trembling beneath my fingers.

"What they say about you is true!" he cried to Justin. "That you are a criminal and a barbarian. Only a gentleman would recognize the significance of an insulting slap."

Justin rubbed his cheek where the mark of the blow showed scarlet. "If you mean that I'm supposed to play the Creole gentleman and challenge you to a duel because you're making a fool of yourself about Louise Cameron, you're talking nonsense. She's not worth your blood or mine."

My hands tightened on Courtney's shoulders, but he put me aside. "You refuse to fight?" he asked his brother. "You are afraid—a coward?"

Justin regarded him coolly. "I'm afraid of many things. This may be one of them." He looked at me standing beside Courtney and his mouth tightened. "I'm sorry this happened, Skye. But it was necessary for Courtney to know the truth about your mother."

I did not think Justin knew the truth about my mother, but my concern was wholly for Courtney at that moment.

"Don't mind what he says—don't listen to him," I pleaded.

Courtney looked at me blindly and I saw in his face all the anguish he must feel because a trap had closed about him. He believed Robert was angry with him because he had fallen in love with my fickle mother who only played at love-making, he hated his new dependency upon his brother in this house, and he was going to marry me, whom he did not love. Circumstances were pushing him too far and he looked as if a breaking point had been reached.

He turned away from us and went out of the room, though I called to him again in pleading. He did not stop and I heard him running up the stairs. The sound had in it the ring of desperation. I hesitated only a moment before I went after him, without so much as a glance at Justin.

Courtney had disappeared by the time I reached the second floor. A door stood ajar at the rear of the wide hall and I ran toward it, pushed it open quickly. Courtney was withdrawing a pistol from a bureau drawer.

For a shocked instant I thought he meant to kill his brother. Then he faced the mirror on the tall bureau and I realized what he intended. I flung myself across the room as he raised the gun and pulled down his arm with all my strength.

The crash of the shot deafened me, and for a shocked instant I did not know whether Courtney had shot himself or me. Then I saw the shattered window and the smoking gun still in Courtney's hand. He stared at the window, stunned, and let the gun drop from his fingers.

The unhappiness and shame in his eyes broke my heart and I went close to him, put my arms about his neck, pressed my cheek against his, as one might comfort a child. Far away I heard someone screaming and knew it was his mother. There was a sound of running on the stairs, but I could think only of this shamed and shattered young man.

"You must never, never attempt such a thing again," I whispered gently. "You're not alone, you know."

His arms came about me and he held me to him, but it was as if he clung to me for safety, for reassurance. Justin and Delphine rushed into the room and saw us thus. I raised my head from Courtney's shoulder and looked coolly into Justin's eyes.

"Please go away. It's all right now. And you've done enough harm for today."

He must have taken the scene in quickly enough—the window broken by the shot, the pistol on the floor, and me in his brother's arms. For once he had the grace to say nothing, but wheeled and went out of the room.

Courtney put me gently from him, but his eyes did not meet mine. "Forgive me, Skye. Madness seized me for a moment."

Delphine spoke briskly. "Mam'zelle, if you will attend Madame Aurore, all will be well. I will get warm water to bathe the bruise on M'sieu Courtney's cheek. It is best if you leave him now."

Courtney nooded. "Yes, Skye. Please go to my mother."

When I returned to Aurore's room, I found that Justin was already with her, administering smelling salts and calming words, while she lay stretched on the bed. She saw me and held out her hands.

"Skye! Tell me at once what has happened. Did my son—"

I took her fluttering hands in mine and held them quietly.

"It is nothing, Tante Aurore. An accident. Everything is quite all right now. But Courtney is upset from the quarrel with his brother. He will come to you later."

She looked uncertainly from Justin to me and then pushed away his hands and got up from the bed. "I will go to my son now. No, do not try to stop me. If he is in trouble he will need me."

Her strength had returned. I went with her to Courtney's room. She leaned over the bed on which he lay and took her son into her arms. When I turned quietly away, I found Justin waiting in the hall outside the room. And now I remembered tardily the plan that had brought me here today.

"I would like to speak with you," I said.

Justin rubbed the knuckles of his right hand—the hand with which he had struck his brother. For a moment I thought he might leave me there in the hall, without an answer. But he reconsidered and gestured toward the stairs.

"I am at your service," he said formally. "Shall we go down?"

He led me to the parlor where I had danced so gaily the night of Justin's party. Its shutters were closed today against the sultry heat. He seated me in a little gilt and satin chair, then went to stand with an arm against the nearby marble mantelpiece and waited to hear what I had to say. I pulled at the handkerchief I held in my fingers, not knowing how to begin, now that my opportunity was at hand.

What had happened between Justin and Courtney had changed the mood in which I'd come to this house. Now the fact of Justin's brutal act was uppermost in my mind and it made the words I was about to speak seem doubly futile. How could I ask aid for Courtney from this man who had just knocked down his own brother?

While I sought for words, Justin spoke curtly into the silence. "What about this marriage to my brother? Do you love him?"

I remembered the words Aurore had spoken to me once and I repeated them. "Of what practical use is love? It will be a good marriage. It is what I want."

"I see. With Robert Tourneau's blessing, you will of course have everything. Is that what you mean?"

I folded my hands together fiercely so they would not tremble. I must not lost my temper.

"Not with my uncle's blessing," I said. "With yours. That's what I've come to ask you, today."

This time I had startled him. "What are you talking about?"

"You've seen the state your brother is in," I said. "He cannot be forced into life in the Tourneau house where Uncle Robert wants him to live. Something terrible will happen if he is. He must get away where he can stand on his own feet. The only hope is for us to leave New Orleans. You spoke once of helping your brother into business. That's what I've come to ask of you now. Loan him the money to start in for himself, but away from New Orleans. He will pay you back every cent. I promise you that."

For a moment he stared his astonishment and then his mocking laughter rang through the room. "You mean you want me to finance your marriage to my brother?"

"I mean I want you to help him, to save him."

"You intend to marry him without love, knowing he would make a fool of himself with your mother?"

In the beginning I'd meant to tell him of Papa, to throw myself upon his mercy. But now I could not. I had the feeling that he would not lift a finger unless I convinced him of the strength of my intention.

"Please believe in my affection for Courtney," I said. "We both need your help."

He left the fireplace and came to stand before me. "I don't believe in it. I don't for one moment I believe that you're in love with Courtney. If you want help, you can find it elsewhere!"

This was the moment in which I knew that Justin Law could never be my friend, but only my enemy. I could expect nothing of him but violence and cruelty. I rose, not looking at him, feeling sickened and helpless.

"Will you please tell Delphine I am ready to leave," I said.

He bowed and went away.

Delphine and I drove home to the Vieux Carré in heavy silence. We spoke only once when she asked me a question.

"You will tell your maman what has occurred, mam'-zelle?"

"Yes," I said, "I will tell my mother." I knew that if I did not, she would.

Nineteen

I told my mother that very evening after supper. She had a headache and lay listlessly upon her bed, but I felt little sympathy for her pain. I stood beside the bed and told her without glossing over the details that this afternoon Courtney Law had been embroiled in a quarrel with his brother because of her. That he had slapped his brother for the insulting remarks Justin had made, and that Justin had knocked him down.

Mama pressed her fingers to aching temples. "Must you tell me this now, Skye? I cannot be responsible for the foolish quarrels of young men."

I continued my story. "Courtney went upstairs and tried to kill himself. If I had not come upon him with the pistol he might be dead by now. He tried to kill himself because you have tormented him, made him love you hopelessly. What manner of woman are you that you can do such things and then laugh and smile so innocently?"

She struggled up on her pillow and now there was shock in her eyes as she stared at me. This time I had reached her. This time I had cut through her guard, her pretense, her self-deception.

"Oh, no!" she whispered. "He would not do such a thing!"

"Because of you he tried to kill himself," I repeated. "What do you think it would do to my father, if he knew this?"

Her beauty seemed to crumple before my eyes. She looked what she was—a frightened, middle-aged woman who had been suddenly confronted with the result of her own foolish actions and was completely stricken. I hoped the lesson would do her some good, though I had little confidence in that.

The hand she reached toward me trembled pitifully, but I did not dare to weaken in my anger against her. I went out of the room and left her to face reality as she had never been willing to face it before.

The evening was long and I was restless and distraught. I could not trust myself to visit Papa until I found some peace within myself. And where in this pattern did peace exist? Justin had refused my appeal for help and I did not know whether I was wholly sorry. Desperately as I needed to find a solution, it would have tormented me to have him cheerfully ready to aid me in my marriage to his brother. I could not help but cling to the pallid comfort of his distaste for this marriage. That was better than having him indifferent.

The afternoon had been blazing hot and the sky had burned brilliant and blue above our courtyard, baking the very bricks. For the most part I had found the climate of New Orleans moderate and not so uncomfortably warm as I had expected. But this had been one of the bad days. The night was heavy and oppressive with heat. No breeze from the Gulf, no breath of air from the river blew in to stir the pall of heat-laden air.

I took off my clothes and bathed myself in water that stood in my pitcher. But even that was tepid, far from cool. When I slipped into a thin nightgown and cotton wrapper, I was just as warm as ever. It would not be a night for sleeping and I sought the escape and solace of books. To step into another world and other lives was to lose for a little while the urgent problems of my own world. And often I had found I could bring back from such a sojourn greater courage and wisdom to face my own problems.

Since insects hummed incessantly about my lamp, I put it on a table near the mosquito *barre* and then got into bed, plumped up the pillows behind me and read where the winged intruders could not reach me.

I don't know how long I read, but it must have been after midnight when I stopped, because my eyes were smarting and yawns had begun to interrupt my reading. Perhaps now at last my thoughts would be still and I could fall asleep. I tossed my book aside on the bed, wiped my damp hands and brow with my handkerchief and lay still for a moment, listening to the night.

The quiet was as oppressive as the heat. Only the fluttering wings of a moth, bent on self-destruction above my lamp, stirred the silence with a whisper of sound. A hard-shelled beetle flew in the window and dashed himself against the lamp chimney with a brittle crash. The moth miller singed its wings and died. The night was brooding and still.

In that stillness I heard the soft opening of a door somewhere near at hand. Then a long pause, while I waited and wondered, listening. As softly the door closed and there was a faint creak of the gallery floor. I threw back the mosquito *barre* and ran barefooted to my door, pulled it open. In the dim light I saw my mother turn the corner of the gallery and move like a shadow toward the stairs.

I was fairly caught. I dared not cry out and rouse the household. Nor could I rush after her without making more noise than I cared to. Already she was running lightly down the stairs and I could hardly pursue her into the street dressed as I was. Then, to my relief, I saw a tall figure move out of the courtyard toward the stairs. It was Delphine, fading into the shadows at the foot of the stairs. My mother, whatever her intention, would be stopped.

I leaned upon the rail, listening intently. A faint cry of distress reached me—too slight to rouse the house. Then there was the sound of a soft scuffle there in the shadows. But I knew Delphine's strength and that she would stop Mama forcibly if she must. A few seconds later I heard the rustle of petticoats as the two came upstairs and moved along the gallery. Delphine was bringing Mama back to her room.

On impulse I flung my own door wide and let lamplight flood out upon the gallery. My mother came into the radiance, drooping like a flower on its stem. She wore a heavy gray veil over her hat and I could not see her face, but she moved with the bent shoulders of a woman whom fate had crushed. Over her drooping head, Delphine looked at me without expression.

"In here," I whispered. "Bring her in here."

Delphine obeyed willingly, and Mama sank into my small rocker with a moan and covered her face with her hands. Moving with the softness of a cat, Delphine closed the door after her, went to the windows and closed them so that we were shut into the warm little box of a room. Yet the heat seemed no greater than that of the courtyard, where no air stirred. Now at least we could talk without waking the household. I saw that Delphine still wore her daytime clothes. Not even the tignon had been disturbed. She must have been waiting for my mother—on guard against whatever might happen.

"How did you know?" I whispered.

"Always as a child your maman was one to run away from this trouble into that one. At times she ran away

162

from this house. Often she does not use the wits the good God gave her."

Mama flung back her veil and stared at Delphine despairingly. "How can you speak to me like that? You forget your place."

"No, madame," Delphine said. "Never in this household do I forget my place—which is to serve M'sieu Robert. Once you were a child in my care in this house. If you behave like a child again, then so you must be treated. What will M'sieu Robert think of your behavior tonight, madame?"

At mention of my uncle's name, Mama wilted completely. She made no effort to answer, but began to cry softly, her hands pressed over her face.

"What did you mean to do?" I asked her. "Where would you go?"

She answered me between sobs. "I don't know. But away from this terrible house where there is only hate and never love. After what happened this afternoon, I do not care if I live or die. Nothing matters."

"Do you love Courtney that much?" I demanded. "Does he mean more to you than my father?"

She roused herself enough to flash me a look of outrage. "You are ridiculous! I have never loved anyone but Bruce—who needs me no longer."

There was no doubt in my mind that Delphine was the wisest person in the room. I turned to her without hesitation.

"What is to be done?"

She stood with her back to the door, on guard, as if my mother might try to escape, and her eyes met mine without wavering.

"If you ask my advice, Mam'zelle Skye, then I say we must go to your father."

Mama started up from her chair, her eyes wide with alarm. "No, no! I couldn't bear that."

"Yet," said Delphine, "you would go away in the night and leave others to tell him when the time came? Is it, madame, that you can bear only what you do not see?"

I broke in with my own objection. "Of course we can't go to Papa. He is the last one who must ever discover that his wife could take such action. Or the reason for it."

"Without doubt he is awake now," said Delphine, as if she had not heard. "Often he tells me how it is he does not sleep in the night. We will go to him now, Mam'zelle Skye. Madame will stay here in this room while we speak with him. The door will be locked, and I shall take with me the key."

My father's feelings *must* be spared. I tried to make a last stand against her. "I won't permit you to do such a thing. It's out of the question, Delphine." But as I spoke I knew there was a strength in this woman greater than mine. Only chance had cast us in these roles and it was hard to remember that she was the servant and I the mistress.

"Your father is a good man, mam'zelle, and a brave one," Delphine said softly. *"Un homme vaillant.* It is necessary that we cease to treat him as a sick child." She removed the key from the inside lock and opened the door. *"Venez,* mam'zelle, if you please."

Mama flung herself from her chair and caught Delphine by the arm. "You can't treat me like this! I won't stay in this room. I'll scream and rouse the house."

"As you wish, madame," said Delphine. "In that case we will not be able to keep this affair from M'sieu Robert— as I have kept certain other matters, not wishing to distress him."

Mama let her hand drop from Delphine's arm. I went out on the gallery, while Delphine locked the door softly behind us. No sound came from the bedroom.

"Your maman will be quiet," Delphine whispered. She went to my father's door and tapped on it lightly. We both heard his "Come in."

Delphine let me go first into the small, dim room. She begged my father's forgiveness for the intrusion and went to light a lamp near his bed.

"I was not asleep," he said. "I heard Louise leave her room, heard the sound of voices. Is anything wrong? Is she ill, perhaps?"

"She is ill, m'sieu," said Delphine, tapping her breast with her forefinger. "But it is an illness of the heart. You must cure it, m'sieu. There is no time to waste."

Papa looked at me. "Tell me what has happened, Skye."

I tried to speak, faltered, fell silent. I could not tell him. Helpless as my mother, I looked at Delphine, and she at least did not hesitate.

"Compose yourself, m'sieu. It is necessary to tell you the sad truth. This afternoon a young man tried to kill himself for love of Mam'zelle Loulou. The same young man who is affianced to your daughter. Foolishly your wife intended to leave this house tonight because the affair left her so distraught she did not know which way to turn. I stayed awake to watch,

164

and at this moment she is locked in the room of Mam'zelle Skye."

He did not move, or speak, or cry out. He closed his eyes and lay very still on the bed. I ran across the room and dropped to my knees beside him, leaned my head against his arm. But there were no words of comfort I could offer.

His hand reached across and stroked my cheek gently, as if I were the one to be comforted. "There is hurt to you in this also, Skye. But you mustn't lock her in. I knew it must come eventually. She must be released from her bondage as the wife of an invalid. I should have found a way to let her follow her heart before this. But it is hardly a wise course to flee in the night."

I raised my head and stared at him. "You mustn't talk like that! She's married to you—she loves you!"

"If I may speak, m'sieu?" Delphine stepped to the foot of the bed.

"Never have I seen a body stop you, Delphine," said my father wryly.

"M'sieu has only to be a husband to madame. He has only to speak with the force of a husband, to chastise her with the tongue of a husband. Mam'zelle Loulou was a child in this house. I knew her well and—"

"And you never liked her, Delphine," my father broke in.

The woman bowed her head. "That is not for me to say. She is what I am not. Believe only, m'sieu, that I knew her well. You know her well also. You know how to bring her to you. But you have forgotten this. You have forgotten to give her the safety of love which she must have."

My father stared at the tall woman with her light, sun-tinted skin and great dark eyes, then slowly, unexpectedly, he smiled.

"This is a true thing you say to me, Delphine. But I do not want to imprison her with my love."

"I think it is not too late. She has need of such a prison, m'sieu," said Delphine and moved toward the door. "I will go to fetch her here."

"Wait!" Papa said quickly and there was a note of panic in his voice. "You are a good friend, Delphine, but I'm not yet ready for this move. 'Tis not her pity I want."

Delphine looked at him almost haughtily. "What I do, I do for the good name of Tourneau—for M'sieu Robert," she told him. "There is no more time to make ready. You must speak with her now, m'sieu." She went out of the room without waiting for his answer.

I rose from my knees and stood beside Papa's bed. In a few moments Delphine thrust my mother ahead of her into the room. Mama had taken off her hat and veil, loosened her hair, so that strands of it hung untidily down her face. Tears had left stains on her cheeks and her dark eyes were wide with fright. She was wringing her hands nervously, more upset than I had ever before seen her. All her coquettish ways, her confidence in the power of her own charm were gone. She looked like a frightened little girl about to receive punishment. She was far from a beauty now, and never had I felt so sorry for her.

Papa held out his hand, and if he was uncertain, he hid the fact. "Come to me, lassie. Did you truly think you could leave me? Or that I would let you go?"

She uttered one wild little sob and ran to fling herself upon the bed beside him, with her face hidden in his shoulder. Across the room I met Delphine's eyes, saw the faint nod she made toward the door. I followed her quickly from the room, and once more that night a door was softly closed.

We stood together on the gallery and I sought words with which to thank her.

"You were right," I said. "You were wiser than the rest of us, Delphine."

She looked at me without emotion and I could not know what she was thinking. Gently she inclined her head and went away across the gallery, treading so lightly that never a board creaked. I stood where I was and watched her emerge from shadow at the foot of the stairs and cross the courtyard. She did not look up at me again and a moment later the darkness of the long-ago slave quarters swallowed her. Soberly I returned to my room.

Great tragedy and disgrace had been averted that night. And every one of us in the Tourneau house had Delphine to thank for it.

Twenty ❊

For the next few days I moved remotely, as if in a dream. I had been tossed by too many storms and I did not want to come to life and feel again. If I could just drift, perhaps nothing would matter.

But July melted into August and I could not be allowed to drift. The wedding date was set ahead to September at Aunt Natalie's plea, since she said a trousseau could not possibly be prepared in less time. Already there were fittings and shopping and I did numbly whatever I was told to do.

The long New Orleans summer that lasted from April to November would finally end. Then would come the *saison des visites* with all its social whirl. There would be the opera and balls and *soirées*. And later the Carnival. Even though the social life of the city was not so lavish as before the war, there would still be much to keep us busy. By that time I would be a young married woman in my uncle's house and I would be expected to take an active part in social affairs. At least I would be busy. There would be little time for thinking.

I heard no word of Justin. Courtney did not mention him at all when he came to visit me. Courtney looked thin and pale and he tried to avoid my mother about the house, as she also avoided him. But at least there had been no more emotional upheavals. Our feet were set inevitably on the path that led to marriage and neither of us tried to rebel.

Whether or not I saw Justin made little difference to me. My heart was a stone in my breast, but a stone that ached as stones should not. I longed for him—and hoped I would never see him again. Pain, I found, was something one must endure and live with. A man or woman might be tested sorely, but never more than could be borne. We said we could not endure, but endure we did and went on living. As my father had lived with pain, now I learned to live with mine and tried not to let it weigh too heavily upon others.

In my mother there was considerable change. Her restlessness, her air of hunting for something was gone. She hummed about the house, happy as a bird in the courtyard, her eyes bright, her lips smiling. Now that my father showed his love and his need of her, the sun shone brightly in her sky. My father was her sun and her sky, and while in many ways she would never change, she now had the walls of her prison safely about her and she was content. She would always flutter her eyelashes at every handsome man. She might never learn the dangerous consequences as she had so nearly come to learn them. And yet—I could not hate her as once I had done.

My one pleasure grew from the change in my father. It was as if he had lain, not lifeless as he seemed, but fallow all this time. The seeds of life were still within him and they had begun to grow again in the warmth of my mother's need for him. Indeed, he spoke of this to me one morning when I sat in his room, sewing lace on a wedding petticoat.

"It seems a queer thing, lassie, but 'tis as if I'd had time at last to know myself as never before. As if I'd been down to the edge of the last rocky shores of the reason, with black waters curling to my very feet. Yet I've turned my back upon the tide and walked away from it. And having done so, I know waters black as those can never touch me again."

Because he had walked away from the darkness, because he had vanquished his own demon, there was now a force of life and hope and energy that seemed to emanate from him. I had known him as a man of force in the past, but this new thing was somehow greater. Inert his body might be, but his spirit had fought free.

He talked to me now as he had used to do in the old days and I listened gladly, hopefully. Once more the urge to write his thoughts was upon him and sometimes I found him scribbling in an old copybook. It was the beginning of new life for him.

While I sat with him that morning, working without heart at my trousseau making, the maid came tapping at the door. Aunt Natalie and Delphine had gone to the market and the girl seemed at a loss.

"There is a gentleman to see mam'zelle," she told me and cast a nervous glance over her shoulder.

I looked out on the gallery and saw that Justin Law had followed her upstairs and around the gallery's turn.

"Good morning, Miss Cameron," he said as I stared at him in astonishment. "I wanted to see you, and I couldn't take the chance of being asked to leave before I found you."

168

I sent the maid off, too shaken by Justin's sudden appearance to know what to say to him. I glanced at my father and he smiled and nodded.

"Bring him in here, my lass."

"I—I'd like you to meet my father," I told Justin and led him into the room.

Somehow he looked larger than ever in that small space, and I had once more the impression of a man who could be angry and violent. A man with a dark and ugly past. I tried to remind myself of these things as I introduced him to Papa, but I saw his expression soften as he took my father's hand and my own resistance to him softened as well.

I knew the handclasp my father gave him would be strong and affirmative, not the handshake of an invalid, and I was proud that he could meet Justin equally as a man, even though he lay supine upon a bed.

"Sit down for a moment, sir," Papa said with a gesture toward the chair I had left. "I know you want to talk to Skye, but I am glad of this chance to meet you. I've heard about you from others in this house."

Justin seated himself in the chair beside the bed, a wry amusement in his eyes. "I'll wager you've had a varied account of me, in that case," he said.

"I make up my own mind about a man when I meet him," Papa said. "You look like your father. I knew Harry Law for a short time when I was in New Orleans before the war. I counted him a friend. And proud I am to meet his son."

This was something I had not known. I took my little stool away to a corner and tried to efface myself, so these two could know each other. The blue cat Beau stood guard at the door, but he did not bend his supercilious look upon us today.

I saw all hesitancy go out of Justin, and even the realization that the man he spoke with was an invalid. In a few moments they were talking earnestly of Justin's father, of the sudden way in which he had left New Orleans and the stigma of spying that had stained his name.

"If you knew my father," Justin said, "will you tell me whether you could ever believe him a spy working against the South?"

"Of course he was no spy," said Papa. "And I doubt there was a man who would have thought him so. Though of course tempers must have run high before the firing upon Sumter."

Justin agreed grimly and my father led the talk away from the South, asking him questions about Colorado and his life in the West.

I was content to watch and listen. It was enough to have this unexpected chance to observe Justin openly, to study the way his fair hair grew above his ears, the way it dipped at the back. I watched his hands as he moved them in speaking and remembered with sweet pain the time his grip had lost itself in my hair. I was of course memorizing him for all future time.

But Justin had come to talk to me—whatever that might portend—and in a little while he turned to me with a question in his eyes.

"Perhaps I could see you in the parlor for a few minutes," I suggested.

He rose and told my father good-by. Then he followed me along the gallery to the dim and shuttered parlor. I sat stiffly on the little palisander sofa and waited to hear whatever he had come to say.

As usual he moved about the room, speaking to me as he walked. There was no softness in his face now. The anger, the sense of violence suppressed were there again, yet he was trying to hold himself in check.

"I was too hasty when we talked the other day," he said curtly. "I have realized since that whether this marriage is right for you or not is none of my affair or concern. Clearly you seem to be good for my brother. Do you still mean to go through with marrying him?"

None of his affair or concern, my heart repeated. It was difficult to hear his other words.

"Of course," I said faintly and waited again.

He paused in his pacing and faced me, his hands gripping the back of a chair. "Very well then, I'll set my brother up in an office of my new company in the North. We are opening a branch on the Ohio River. Will that suit you?"

"We will go anywhere out of New Orleans," I said.

"Well, then? You don't look very happy about it."

"Courtney and I will be most grateful," I told him stiffly. "When we are settled we will be able to bring my father and mother North to live with us."

"Courtney in the same house with your mother?" he asked.

I nodded. "My father is truly recovering for the first time since his accident. Mama knows now that she belongs to him."

"And I suppose you'll be enough to hold Courtney's attention," he said. "But get your hair out of that ugly knot and—"

I rose abruptly. "What you are doing for us does not

give you any right to dictate my appearance."

"Of course not," he said. "I'm sorry." His tone softened. "Sorry for many things, Skye." He held out his hand in a sudden gesture. "Sorry this has to be good-by."

His sudden kindness was nearly my undoing. A rush of feeling went through me and my attempt at indignation was forgotten. I could not let him go like this. There was more I must say to him. But even as I fought to control this betraying surge of emotion, I heard my uncle's step on the stairs coming up to the gallery.

"Hush," I warned Justin, and tried to gesture him out of sight. Since the dinner party, the very name of Justin Law had become enough to anger my uncle. If he found him here now, there would surely be a clash.

The gallery shutters were closed, the room dim, but the door to the hall stood open and my uncle in passing glanced in. Justin had not moved. He stood in the middle of the room looking as if he would welcome an encounter with Robert Tourneau. Uncle Robert saw him and paused in the doorway.

"Good morning, M'sieu Law. Why was I not informed of your presence in my house?"

"I came to see Miss Cameron," Justin told him.

"A gentleman does not call on a lady without the consent and knowledge of her family, m'sieu. And you, Skye—"

"It was a business matter," Justin broke in.

I held my breath, hoping he would say no more. I did not want Uncle Robert to know what we planned until the last possible moment. Then there would be no way to stop us. But Justin was less afraid of my uncle and less cautious than I. He went right on.

"I have decided to take my brother into business as my partner. He will manage an office on the Ohio River. So he and Skye will be leaving for the North right after their marriage."

Uncle Robert stared at him in angry amazement. "What nonsense is this? Courtney will do nothing of the kind. He is obligated to me for the very clothes he wears. He will do exactly as I say!"

"If he's in debt to you I shall pay off his debts, naturally," Justin said. "I too owe a debt, but of a different sort. I owe it because of my father, whose good name you destroyed."

"It was I who got your father out of this city with a whole skin." Uncle Robert was very nearly shouting now. I had never seen him so disturbed.

"After you spread the rumor that he was a spy," said Justin. "This much, at least, I know."

Uncle Robert pointed to the door. His very beard seemed to bristle with rage. "Get out of my house! Get out and never set foot in it again. I should have known better than to accept one of your repute. A scoundrel, a murderer!"

Justin didn't wait for him to finish. He strode to the door without another look for either of us. But as he passed me I saw his face and knew that he was relishing this scene of anger and violence. He was in an element to which he was accustomed and which became him well. His steps were light and sure upon the stairs.

Uncle Robert turned to me. "Go to your room, Skye! You had no business receiving that man alone. I will speak to you later. You may forget this nonsense of going North with Courtney. I shall not allow it."

He went out of the room and crossed the hall to his study. I wasted not a moment, but flew to the windows that opened on the street gallery. With shaking fingers I unlatched the shutters and stepped out into the hot sunlight of late morning. I had to see Justin again before he was gone from my life for the last time.

For a moment I feared that he had vanished along the banquette beneath the gallery. Then I saw his broad shoulders, the wide brim of his gray hat as he crossed the street.

"Justin!" I called softly. And again, "Justin, wait!"

Several vendors looked up at me with interest and amusement, and one of them signaled Justin across the street, called me to his attention. He swung about and wove his way back through the noisy traffic to a point beneath my balcony. With the same mocking bow I remembered from that day on Gallatin Street, he swept off his hat. "At your service, mademoiselle."

I pressed my hands against the iron rail, caring nothing for the attention I might attract. "I must see you again," I whispered. "There's something I must say to you."

Blue mockery was alive in his eyes. "I'll be on the docks around three o'clock this afternoon, Miss Cameron," he said and turned away from me to cross the street.

I stepped back from the blazing sunlight of the gallery into the dim quiet of the parlor. The docks! Always this man was friend and enemy, confusing, dismaying. No lady would walk alone upon the docks, but I knew I would be there that afternoon. Nothing would keep me away.

Twenty-One ☀

I returned to my father's room with Justin's words still ringing in my ears. Papa smiled and gestured me to the chair near his bed.

"What did you think of him?" I asked. What my father thought of Justin Law meant a great deal to me at that moment.

Papa closed his eyes, and I was glad not to have him watching my face as he spoke.

"There's strength in the man, and honesty," he mused. "And there's anger in him too. I think he has been misused in some way."

"He has been in prison—for murder, they say." I spoke faintly.

"The West is a rough country," my father said. "Men live by cruder laws."

"But—murder?" I persisted, pressing the blade of the ugly word to wound myself more deeply.

"I think that's not the whole of it. He seems a man after my own heart. As he is, perhaps, after yours, lassie."

I looked away quickly, not wanting him to read my feelings. "He is going to make it possible for Courtney and me to leave New Orleans, Papa. Courtney will be in charge of an office Justin is opening in the North. Later you and Mama can join us there."

"So there's generosity in the man too. And is this what you want, Skye?"

With all my heart I longed to tell him the truth. But my father must never know that I married Courtney for anything but love. I forced the trembling from my lips, made myself answer.

"It is what I want, Papa."

"Yet I think you are in love with Justin Law, lassie dear. It grieves me to see you hurt again. Why do you marry Courtney, if it is his brother you love?"

I answered quickly. "No, no! I don't love him. Truly he

is not a man a woman can happily love. And he's not for marrying. He has told me that."

"Men have spoken such words before. And if you do not love Courtney—"

"I love Courtney," I told him. "It is a different love. I've promised myself to make it a good marriage. If we can only get away from this house, away from New Orleans, then that will be possible."

"Once you wanted to run away from New England," Papa reminded me. "Now you are downcast because you're marrying the man you say you love, and not another. And again you want to run away. This is a puzzling thing for a man like me to understand."

"I am like other women," I said. "I cry over the wrong things and I want a moon I wouldn't know what to do with if I got it. Doesn't every girl dart in contrary directions when marriage is upon her—wanting and not wanting?"

He spoke thoughtfully. "You mustn't let Robert Tourneau force you into what he desires, if you find it wrong for you."

This was dangerous ground. "No one is forcing me. Papa, there is true gentleness in Courtney, and oh, but I want a man who is gentle!"

"Of course," he said. "And I would want no other for you."

I bent and kissed him lightly, then went out of the room before he could draw me back to dangerous territory. It was true that I wanted a man who was gentle. A man who was strong and violent and sometimes frightening, yet could be gentle and tender as a woman if he chose. And there were words I must speak to such a man.

When the noon meal was over I put on the golden-brown dress that shimmered with an orange flame. I loosened my hair upon my shoulders and pinned it back with silver combs in the style Delphine had shown me. Then I took from its nest of tissue paper in my armoire the little hat of pale fern-green. My mother had never missed it that day I'd picked it up from the floor in her room.

This time when I faced my mirror with the hat in my hands, I was not afraid. With my hair upon my shoulders the small bit of fluff was made for me. I would never be conventionally beautiful like my mother, and I knew now that it did not matter. The girl who looked gravely back at me from the mirror was arresting and had a distinction of her own. She was gaining the courage to be herself. If I could never see Justin again, then at least I would have him remember me as he liked me best.

174

I waited my chance and slipped out unnoticed. But I was no more than a square from the Tourneau house when a small figure dashed toward me across the street. It was the boy, Lanny Fontaine.

"What good fortune, mam'zelle!" he cried. "They watch me so closely that it is very hard to escape. Today my chance came and I have hurried at once to see you. But I feared to approach your house too closely."

I could only regard the child with dismay. At any other time I would have welcomed his company, but now I must get to the docks quickly and by the shortest route possible, lest I miss Justin altogether. My own problem was urgent and uppermost in my mind.

"Is anything wrong at home?" I asked him.

"No, mam'zelle," he said. "It is only that you are my friend and I hoped to see you."

I couldn't walk away from his beseeching look. I would have to figure out what to do with him when I reached the docks.

"Then come with me," I said hurriedly. "I'm going to meet someone by the river."

His eyes danced as he walked beside me. "Ah, I would like to see *la belle rivière*. I've not seen it since I came to New Orleans. Thank you, mam'zelle."

He must have sensed the urgency in me for he made little attempt to talk as we hurried along, darting across streets between the wheels of vehicles, under the noses of horses, weaving our way along the usual thronged banquettes. When we reached Jackson Square we turned toward the river, walked quickly past the French Market and across the railroad tracks. The Mississippi was very near now, but we could not see it, though it was higher than the town. The levee and the sheds along the docks hid it from our view.

As we climbed steps leading to the docks that were built along the levee, my heart began a deep, anxious pounding. Would Justin really be here? And if he was, would I be able to say the things I had come to say? Anxiety urged me along and I was hardly aware of the boy as he walked beside me.

In a few moments we were out among open wooden sheds and warehouses, on a boardwalk above the water. But now I could only stop and stare about me in helpless bewilderment. Here at the very edge of the Vieux Carré was a world completely foreign. Masted ships were anchored, sometimes two or three deep, along the docks. There were luggers and fishing vessels and steamboats—a world of rope and canvas, foreign faces and the sound of foreign speech mingling with the native French and English. The river lapped muddy and brown at our feet and the gulf wind blew in our faces.

I gazed anxiously up and down the long stretch of docks.

This was wholly a man's world, but though curious glances were flung our way, no one spoke to us, and Justin was nowhere in sight. Not knowing which way to turn, I stood for a moment watching the river.

At our feet the current ran quick and strong, marked here and there by small whirlpools and eddies, the far shore line low and green, dotted with the houses of Algiers. Behind us, through an open shed we could glimpse the buildings of the French Quarter curiously below the river. Since the Mississippi was higher than the town, it was only the levee that kept it from flooding New Orleans out of existence.

I raised my hot face to the touch of a fresh, clean wind and breathed deeply, trying to still the turmoil of anxiety within me. For a little while I could stand here, waiting. But what if he did not come? What if he had been joking this morning when he had said he would be on the docks, thinking perhaps that I would never come here?

"In a little while I believe it will rain," said Lanny's voice, small and apologetic beside me.

I squeezed his hand contritely. I should not have brought him with me, when I had no heart for his problems just now. I noted the boiling of dark clouds that rolled up one edge of the sky, but I did not care whether it rained or not. With the wind and brilliant light flooding over me, I breathed the river smell, not wholly pleasant, but sharp and invigorating, and I stood there waiting.

In the end it was Lanny who saw him first. The boy's cry of recognition made me turn. Justin Law had stepped out of a shed below us, in conversation with a river captain in blue uniform and visored cap. His appearance startled me a little. Always before I had seen Justin more carelessly dressed than any Creole gentleman. His vests were often bright and there was a western curl to the wide brim of his gray hat. Today he wore the light-colored clothes commonly adopted by New Orleans men in the summer months, and a neatly ribboned straw hat which did not suit him as well as the gray. But he was still a giant, even among these rivermen.

176

Lanny, less inhibited than I, called out to him and Justin glanced in our direction, bowed slightly, and returned to his conversation. His seeming indifference brought a wave of scarlet to my cheeks. How little he must want to hear anything I had to say. Yet I must wait for the moment when he would come toward us of his own accord.

Before I could stop him, Lanny dashed off down the dock to join Justin and the river captain. Justin seemed to welcome him and I saw him introduce the boy to his companion. I looked away, studying the roiling brown of the river, my mind busy with the words which must be spoken when the opportunity came.

It had been wrong to ask Justin for help without telling him the truth. There must be honesty between us if he was going to assist Courtney and me to get out of town. He must understand the truth of what I meant to do, the reason for my doing it.

Lanny called to me, waving excitedly, and pointing to a nearby river boat. The captain shook hands with Justin and then led Lanny up a gangplank and aboard the boat —clearly for a tour of inspection. Justin came toward me alone. So the problem of Lanny had been solved as simply as that.

I watched the man who approached me—this stranger of whom I had known nothing only a few months before— and who would never be a stranger to me again. In all that world of river and sun and wind there seemed only we two.

As he reached my side, Justin took off the incongruous straw hat with a sudden careless gesture and sent it skimming through the air to land at a distance upon the drifting surface of the water.

"I've always wanted to do that!" he cried. "And I'm glad to be rid of the thing."

The wind ruffled his bright hair and beneath it his face had a look of laughter in it— laughter without mockery— that I had never seen before. Somehow the tension in me lessened and I heard myself laughing too, a sound that rang strange and deceptively carefree in my ears. The straw bobbed away on the river's surface, sailing toward the Gulf.

At the sound of my laugh, Justin turned toward me. "You've worn the green hat and you can laugh out loud. New Orleans is having an effect on you, Skye. How foolish you were to think you needed to rival your mother. You need only be yourself."

"I know that now," I said.

"Why did you want to see me again?"

"I had to talk to you. If you are to help your brother, then you must know the truth about us. I am not marrying him for love." Now that I'd spoken them so abruptly, the words sounded callous in my ears, though that was far from what I intended.

Justin's expression was cool again, watchful. He waited for me to continue.

"You've met my father," I said. "You know how fine and brave he is. He is recovering from an illness of the spirit and that is more important to me than anything else in the world."

"I like him," Justin said simply.

"Yet if I don't agree to marry Courtney, Uncle Robert will no longer keep my father in his house. And there is nowhere else for him to go. Nowhere at all."

Justin said nothing, but his gaze did not leave my face.

"There has never been any pretense of love between Courtney and me," I went on quickly. "This is a marriage arranged in the Creole fashion. But I will do my best to make it a good marriage, for my part of the bargain. This is what I wanted you to know."

I turned from him, lest he see the tears that sprang into my eyes, betraying too much. The dark cloud climbing the sky had blotted out the sun and a sudden splatter of rain stung my cheek. Across the river rain pelted, sudden and heavy. I could see the pin-point beating of the drops speeding toward us across the water. Yet I stood helpless and silent, staring at the swift-flowing river.

"Come along," said Justin gently. He took my arm and we moved quickly to the shelter of a shed. Both sides stood open, but the ends were closed and we could step behind a row of wooden barrels out of the wet, shielded by hogsheads and bales.

The sky had darkened and it was shadowy here in the end of the deserted shed. Once more I had the feeling that we two were alone in all this river world that was now being beaten into fury by the rain. And being alone, we drew inevitably together. Justin's hands were not to be denied. Unquestioning, unresisting, I went into his arms. He bent his head and put his mouth against my own until my lips ached with longing. This was my love. The only love I would ever know, or want to know. His arms, his mouth, told me wordlessly that I was his. He held me so tightly that I came near to crying out, though not with pain.

178

"My dear," he said and kissed me again, with only tenderness in his touch.

This was as I had dreamed it could be, with love and gentleness between us, yet with a fire ready to blaze such as I'd never known back in those cold New England days.

He kissed my eyelids lightly and once more my mouth, then held me away and looked at me. "I'm glad you told me, Skye. I've tried to make you hate me, yet I could not truly want you to, even though I never meant you to be caught in this trap."

I looked at him with love in my eyes and hardly puzzled over the meaning of his words. How could it be a trap, when a man and a woman loved and longed for each other, as we two did?

But his words ran on, sudden and bewildering. "It's been hard to keep away from you. We mustn't see each other again, Skye. What's between us is too hard to deny."

I heard him in bewilderment. He put me aside and went to stand where he could look out at the storm upon the river. I saw the rain visible beyond him like a streaming gray curtain that he might fade into at any moment, and fear went whipping through me. The words he spoke had no meaning. We loved each other. That was all that mattered.

I was wrong, of course.

He spoke to me over his shoulder without looking at me. "Marry Courtney soon, Skye. Get him away from New Orleans as quickly as you can."

"Marry Courtney!" I hated the way my voice trembled and broke. "But how can I marry Courtney when—when I—"

He turned quickly. "Forget about me, Skye. For me the record has been written. For you life lies ahead. Look—the rain is lessening. Let's get the boy and I'll take you home."

The change came too sharply after the feeling I'd had in his arms. This was some sort of dreadful dream from which I must surely waken. How could he hold me as he had and then put me so quickly out of his life? He beckoned and I went to him dazedly, too choked and confused to question. He took my hand gently in his and we stepped together into the wet, steaming world of river and docks. The shower was over and the sun glared behind thin clouds.

"Wait," I said, holding back. "It can't be like this. You must tell me why—"

But there was no time to tell me, even if he would. Lanny stood on the drenched deck of the river boat, looking for us. When he saw us, he bade his friend the captain good-by, then ran down the gangplank, skipping puddles on the dock as he came. So full of his adventure was he, so thrilled by new discoveries, that he did not notice the strangeness that lay upon Justin, or my own subdued manner. With the boy between us, we walked down the steps and across the tracks toward Jackson Square.

It seemed to me that I moved blindly, not knowing where I went, more confused than alarmed by what had happened. I could not yet believe his final words. I was glad that he kept the boy talking, while I groped for understanding.

"Have you always lived in New Orleans?" he asked the child.

Lanny formed the answer softly, as if this were a subject to be spoken of with tenderness. "Most of my life I have lived with my grand'mère in the bayou country of Louisiana."

"She was a Cajun then?" Justin inquired, though I knew he spoke absently, and that his thoughts too were elsewhere.

"Grand-père was a Cajun," Lanny said. "When Grand'mère was a young girl she ran away from her Creole family in New Orleans to marry him. Grand-père was drowned in a storm long ago—I do not remember him."

Through my daze I listened to Lanny and thought vaguely that this was how the child came by his lovely manners, his somewhat adult courtesy—through a Creole grandmother.

"And what of your grandmother now?" Justin asked gently.

"She is dead," said Lanny and glanced up at us with tears in his eyes.

It was clear that he did not want to speak of what had happened since his grandmother's death, and Justin questioned him no further.

Twenty-Two ❧

When we reached the Pontalba building where Lanny lived with Lobelia Pollock we went through the door to the lower hallway and stood for a moment below the curving sweep of stairway. It was not in me at that moment to take any decisive action of my own. I waited only for Lanny to leave us, so that I might be alone with Justin. Perhaps then I might question him, entreat him to explain what I did not understand.

Lanny touched me lightly on the arm, sensing that my attention was far away. "If you please, mam'zelle—if you could come with me upstairs, perhaps explain—"

"We'll both go up with you," Justin said. "Between the two of us, perhaps we can save you a scolding."

Mrs. Pollock lived on the second floor and as we stopped before the door Lanny indicated, I heard the sound of voices arguing within. Those were Mrs. Pollock's tones, a bit harsh and rough, then a fainter voice with a slight whine to it.

"They are angry because I have run away again," Lanny whispered.

Justin lifted the knocker and the sound of it went echoing through the hall. At once there was silence within, followed by the sound of heels clicking across a bare floor, and the door was opened so that Mrs. Pollock could peer out at us. If I had thought her eye-stopping before in her purple and plumes, I was now stunned by her appearance in an evening gown of glittering cerise, with a low decolletage and a train that swished spangles across the bare, grimy floor. The woman, undoubtedly, was dressed for her work at L'Oiseau d'Or.

She gasped at sight of us and moved as if to reach for Lanny and shut the door in our faces. Justin, however, had rudely put his foot against it.

"We've brought Lanny home," I said quickly. "We hope you won't punish him because he came with us for a little walk."

Mrs. Pollock paid no attention to my words. She stared at Justin with the same look of alarm and dismay that I had seen in her face that other time in the Square, and which seemed out of any proportion to the cause.

Something about her look, her extreme anxiety, made Justin suspicious. He pushed open the door and went past her into the apartment. From where I stood the room lay framed before me. After bright sunlight outside, the shuttered dusk made it hard to discern details for a moment. I was aware of lofty proportions and a grandeur that no spare and sleazy furniture could lessen. Across the carpetless floor stood a couch upon which reclined the shadowy figure of a woman. Over the mantelpiece behind her rose a great mirror, the glass marred by a cobweb of cracks. The chandelier which must have lighted this room in more auspicious days was gone, and the plaster rosette on the ceiling was grime-encrusted.

Lobelia Pollock, breathing a cloud of heavy perfume as she moved, stepped backward before Justin, every sequin aquiver as she fluttered her hands at him angrily.

"How dare you force your way into my rooms, sir! How dare you—"

"I will leave, madame," Justin said, "when you tell me why you run like a scared chicken every time you see me. Why do you snatch the boy away, as if I might harm him? If you will explain—"

Across the room the figure on the couch sat up with a cry of alarm and Justin broke off. There was a moment of pulsing silence while they stared at each other. It was Justin who spoke first.

"Isabelle!" he said in a cold, sharp tone.

Lobelia Pollock pounced upon Lanny and pulled him away from me. "Now the fat's in the fire for certain!" she wailed. "Go to your room, boy. At once. Close the door and stay there until I come for you. You've been naughty enough for one day."

Lanny threw me an anguished look and fled before her anger. The woman on the couch had risen and was staring at Justin as if she saw an apparition. For the first time I could see her clearly.

I know now that she was a younger woman than my mother, but at that moment she looked far older. Her hair was a metallic yellow, with darker patches betraying its true color at the roots. She was pretty in a faded way and rouge touched her lips and cheeks. Her mauve-colored dress was shabby, but still theatrical in its color and style. She looked exactly what she was—a third-rate actress out of work.

As I watched her, not understanding any of this, she raised one trembling hand to smooth the brassy yellow hair back from her forehead. Then, with a little moan, she crumpled to the floor in a faint.

"Now you've done it!" said Mrs. Pollock sharply to Justin. "Well, don't stand there. Pick your wife up and put her on the sofa."

I heard the words clearly, but I could not at first understand them. Shock and disbelief held me like a woman frozen.

Justin went to where the woman lay and lifted her in

his arms. Then he laid her upon the sofa and put a cushion beneath her head. In a moment Lobelia was there with wet cloths and smelling salts, and Justin stepped aside, plainly shaken.

"The boy is my son?" he asked Lobelia.

She paused in her ministrations and stared up at him indignantly. "The boy belongs to his mother. You've no right to him at all."

"He is my son," Justin repeated softly, as if he did not hear her.

On the sofa the blond woman stirred, recovering consciousness. She struggled to sit up, her eyes wide with fright.

"Don't let him touch me!" she cried shrilly.

"Nobody's going to hurt you, dearie." Mrs. Pollock thrust her back upon the sofa. "Lie still or you'll be popping off again."

Justin did not swerve from the single course of his thoughts. "The boy is mine and I'm going to take him out of your hands."

Mrs. Pollock handed the bottle of smelling salts impatiently to the woman and faced him. "You lay a finger on the boy, and I'll call the police. They don't run things in New Orleans the way you're used to in Leadville."

Justin made an explosive sound of anger, but she had the advantage and for the moment he gave up. He turned to walk out of the room and saw me then, remembered my presence.

"Come, Skye," he said. "I'll take you home. This matter can't be worked out now."

I did not look again at Isabelle Law. Her weak, pretty face was stamped forever on my memory. I went out of the room and down the stairs at Justin's side. I still walked in the nightmare that had begun on the docks, but now I knew the full extent of the barrier that lay between us. Justin's face had a stony look about it, but I knew that he raged inwardly. He offered me no explanations and I asked for none.

Once on the way he spoke of his son. "Lanny—I never knew, I never dreamed. Fontaine must be the stage name she took when she left Colorado. The boy was named Napier after my Creole grandfather—Napier Lance Law."

He said nothing more and I felt too numb with shock for talking. At the gate of the Tourneau house, he murmured, "I'm sorry, Skye," and went quickly away before I could find words to answer him.

As I went upstairs to my own room, all my capacity for feeling began to revive. Always before I had believed that it was Justin's own nature which held him back from marriage. It was some prejudice he had against marriage which must surely be overcome with time. Or perhaps his reluctance was due to the prison smirch upon his name, to the feeling that this would be too much for a wife to accept. Now I knew the truth, and the truth was an insurmountable wall between us.

I thought in those moments that I must have tasted the depths of self-torture. The face of Isabelle Law kept returning to me, and I wondered when and how Justin had cared for her. There was the thought of Lanny to hurt me too. I loved him more than ever now, as his father's son, and suffered because he must remain in such hands. Perhaps Justin would be strong enough to take the boy into his own keeping. The thought of that would bring me some comfort at least.

As I say, I believed I had reached the depths of torment. But there was worse in store. That afternoon I heard the sound of Caro's voice raised in excitement and I went out on the gallery to see what was happening. Uncle Robert stood below me in the courtyard speaking to Delphine, and with him were Isabelle Law and Justin's son, Lanny. Clearly I heard him instruct Delphine to give them a room across the courtyard from mine.

Unbelieving, I watched Delphine lead the way upstairs. When Uncle Robert followed and retired to his study, I hesitated only a moment. I had to know what this meant. I had to know why my uncle had taken such a step. For Justin's sake, I had to know.

Caro was chattering happily to Lanny as Delphine showed his mother the room. I left the gallery and went to the door of my uncle's study.

He called to me to come in and I think he knew by my face when I entered that I would not be easily put off. He could not know what prompted my feeling about the matter, but he knew I was in earnest.

"Why have you brought Justin's wife to this house?" I asked, without preliminaries. "How did you know she was in New Orleans?"

"Please sit down, Skye." He was suave as ever, unruffled. "Do you presume to question my actions? What is this to you?"

"I'm asking for information," I said.

184

Uncle Robert moved his hands in a gracefully vague gesture. "Ah, well—a woman's curiosity. Monsieur Justin's wife is the daughter of an old friend of my childhood. She has asked for my protection. After all, you brought the boy here yourself. That was when I first saw him and learned his name. I knew Madame Law had used the name Fontaine on the stage."

I felt that what he was saying was only partially true, and I waited for more.

"New Orleans is a rough city, as you yourself have discovered," he went on. "This poor woman is alone and she feared some violence from her brutal husband. Madame Pollock came to me after his intrusion this morning. It is possible that the fellow might even attempt to take the boy from his mother. In this house both will be safe. I have explained the matter to my wife and she is completely satisfied. May I ask, Skye, what it is you suspect me of? And why you are disturbed about the woman's coming here?"

I knew only that I did not trust him and that somehow this was a move against Justin. Whether or not Mrs. Pollock had mentioned my presence this morning, I couldn't tell, and I didn't care. There was no truth in my uncle at that moment and I did not want to struggle with explanations. I turned away abruptly and went out of the room. As I walked down the hall, I heard Uncle Robert laughing, alone in his study. The sound was eerie, and somehow evil.

My first thought was that I would find a way to get Lanny out of the house myself and take him to Justin. But this was not so easily managed. The servants had been set on guard, and Delphine seemed to be everywhere. Neither the boy nor his mother were permitted downstairs and I knew if I attempted to take him out of the house there would be a hue and cry before I reached the street.

Of course the household buzzed with questions about this woman who had been set down in our midst. Mama was all atwitter over the fact that Justin had a wife about whom we had known nothing. Aunt Natalie, of course, adapted herself in every way to her husband's wishes, but I believe she was distressed at having a woman of the theater put into her good Creole home.

The news that Isabelle was Justin's wife and Lanny his son came clearly as a surprise to Courtney. Since Justin's mother had not written to him he had never let her know about his marriage, or of the birth of his child, so not even Aurore knew of her grandson's existence.

Only Lanny, of us all, profited by this move into Robert Tourneau's house. Aunt Natalie, Mama and I all gave him our affection, and he delighted in a friendship with Caro and my father. His mother treated him either with apathetic indifference, or else scolded him endlessly.

I took little joy in living these days. Each morning brought pain and there was a shriveling in me at the very sight of Isabelle Law. Oddly enough, she sought me out as someone she might talk to in her lonely captivity. I know she feared my uncle and slipped out of his sight whenever possible. She had nothing to say to Aunt Natalie, nor did she care for my mother, who plainly showed distaste for her. But since I, in my lethargy, showed nothing at all, she sought my company whenever I was not quick enough to escape her.

One unhappy morning she came to my room while I sat listlessly sorting embroidered lingerie which Aunt Natalie had given me, packing the things into a chest scented with the inevitable vetiver root. Isabelle did not ask if she might come in—the door stood open and she entered. There was a limp and pallid quality about her which set my teeth on edge. She was so wispy, so easy to hurt, that I had to suppress a desire to hurt her, as she without knowing it hurt me through her very existence.

She fingered a fine linen nightgown and sighed dejectedly. "You are lucky, Miss Cameron. How well I remember my own wedding and how little I had."

Everything had been hers, I thought, turning away from her. She had married Justin.

She dropped the nightgown on the bed and went to sit in my little rocker. More brown was showing at the roots of her hair and she was using less rouge since she had come to this house. She sat in the rocker and twined her fingers nervously together.

"Justin and I had nothing in those early days," she went on. "I had run away from home with a traveling theatrical company as a stage-struck young girl. Times were bad in Colorado and the company closed. So I took a job as a waitress in Leadville. Justin and I were two lonely people a long way from home and we had the background of Louisiana to bring us together."

"You don't need to tell me these things," I said stiffly. "It must be painful to remember."

Her lips quivered. "Everything is painful to remember. Of course Justin recognized that I came from a gentle home and was above the work I was doing in that rough café. He couldn't wait until he got me out of the place. How insistent he could be in those days!"

There seemed no way to stop her. I went on with my task, trying not to hear, but listening to every word in spite of myself, both repelled and fascinated.

"Of course I'd never have married him if he hadn't had such faith in that mine," she informed me, twining and untwining her fingers. "He built up my hopes so that I was willing to put up with poverty for a while because of what I'd have later on. But Justin was gone most of the time and sodden-weary when he was home. He wouldn't give up. He and that partner of his said they'd make it pay off eventually." She pressed her fingers to her temples. "Then he committed that terrible crime!"

I glanced at her and saw her shudder. I had to ask the question that had filled me for so long.

"What happened?"

But she darted away from the question at once. "I don't want to talk about it. Sometimes I still dream about it at night. After that I was terrified of Justin. All I wanted was to change my name and get away from Colorado. I had my chance when they put him in prison. It took months to reach Louisiana, where I could leave the baby with his grandmother. Then I was free and I did pretty well for a time too."

I said nothing and after a moment she got languidly to her feet and went to my dressing table to peer at herself in the mirror.

"I'm not so bad-looking even now," she said as if to herself "After all, I'm no more than five years older than Justin. Sometimes I'm tempted to have a try at marriage again. It seems a shame for all that silver money to be wasted. He loved me once—perhaps he would again."

I must have made a sound, for she whirled away from the mirror, offended. "Oh, you needn't think I'm not attractive to men. I'm no silly young girl now. I know a trick or two to get around them. And I ought to know how to get around Justin." Her expression went suddenly dreamy. "He could never let me alone in the old days. Often he told me I was the prettiest thing ever, and the sweetest and warmest. There's no reason why that can't come again if I really put myself to it."

I could endure no more. "Please," I said, "I've a headache. I want to lie down for a little while."

She shrugged indifferently and wandered out of the room. I did not lie down. Shamed and sickened, I made myself work busily sorting and packing. I would not think of what she had said. The words must be erased from my mind, forgotten.

But spoken words that cut deeply are not easily dismissed. That night when I lay sleepless in my great bed, listening to the hum of mosquitoes outside the *barre,* I could see Justin's face clearly in my mind. But it was not at me that he looked, but at the young Isabelle. Her words returned to whisper cruelly through my mind. With my cheeks burning I could see her in his arms, held close against him. I knew just how hungrily he must have bent his head to kiss her.

The night was so hot and so long. The pictures came endlessly, tormenting me.

Twenty-Three ❦

There was no word from Justin during these last days of August. Somehow I had expected him to make a forceful move, perhaps appear at the house and demand his son. But nothing of the sort happened. Courtney said his brother was away from the house much of the time, busy launching his steamboat business. There were nights when he did not come home to the Garden District at all, but stayed in his rooms on Dumaine Street.

The fact that nothing happened troubled me. I had a feeling that Uncle Robert continued to scheme, and that with the passing of time the chance of Justin gaining possession of his son grew increasingly slight. It began to seem that everything hinged upon Uncle Robert's motive in holding Isabelle and the boy. Why had he instituted himself their "protector"? Why had Lobelia Pollock reported to him so quickly that day when Justin had gone to her place and discovered his wife? Why was it that Uncle Robert was so set against letting Justin recover his son?

The more I pondered these matters, the more it appeared that Mrs. Pollock herself knew most of the answers, and I wondered if she could be persuaded to talk. According to Lanny, she had been kinder to him than his mother had. She might be aggravated sometimes about his running away, and she might scold, but she had often intervened when his mother wanted to punish him. It was possible that she might answer a question or so. I could at least try.

Once I had made up my mind, I waited for my first opportunity to slip out of the house unnoticed. My chance came in midafternoon of a September Sunday. Since Mrs. Pollock appeared to go to the Bird at irregular hours, I didn't know whether I would catch her or not.

As it happened, I met her on the way, hurrying down St. Peter toward Bourbon, elaborately dressed for her duties at L'Oiseau d'Or, and hardly willing to pause as I spoke to her.

"Can't stop now, dearie. I'm later than usual and these Creoles love to gamble at all hours, you know. Especially on Sunday."

She would have rushed breathlessly by if I had not turned and walked beside her.

"When may I see you?" I asked. "There's something important I'd like to talk to you about."

She threw me a quick, shrewd glance. "Come along now, if you like. Once I'm at the Bird and can keep an eye on things, we can talk all you want. I've a nice private room and I'll see that no Creole gentleman glimpses you."

I did not hesitate. What Uncle Robert might think about my visiting such a place no longer mattered, and I was eager to catch her while she was in a friendly mood.

"Here, take this," she said, and removed the cloud of purple veiling from the brim of her large hat. "Wrap yourself up in that purple fog and nobody will identify you. What your doting Uncle Robert don't know won't hurt him, dearie." Her shoulders shook with a sudden gust of laughter, and spangles glittered in the sunlight, bouncing on her quaking bosom.

I tied the veil on, reassured. She might be working hand in glove with Uncle Robert, but she wasn't above playing a trick or two upon him.

So that was how I came to visit L'Oiseau d'Or that Sunday afternoon in the Vieux Carré. I must confess that I was curious, and once hidden beneath the smothering veil, I was not nearly so appalled at entering such a place as I suppose I should have been.

The house on Bourbon Street looked no different from any other, with its iron-lace balconies and charming court-

yard. Evidently a Palace of Chance which catered to the
crème de la crème of New Orleans male society must be
run with grace and decorum.

Lobelia's key let us in a side door and she hurried me
through a dim and musty hall and into a small sitting room
that was tastefully furnished. The draperies at the windows
were of rose satin and the Aubusson rug soft rose, mingled
with green. The crystal chandelier was as fine as that in any
Creole parlor, and the expensive furniture must have come
from France.

"Throw back that veil so you can breathe," Lobelia directed. "Not bad, is it? Of course your uncle knows the
best when it comes to furnishings. Personally I like things
a bit gaudier, but I'll admit he knows gentlemen's tastes."

I stared at her as I put back the hot veil. "Uncle Robert?
What has he to do with this?"

"Whoops!" said Lobelia gaily, moving toward the door.
"Looks like I've let a cat out of the bag. Not that it matters,
being as how it's all in the family. And anyway, I'm getting
a bit sick of your uncle's airs. Yes, of course—he owns the
Bird. He set me up in business years ago, and it has paid
him well. I know how to run a place like this and he can
stay out of sight. But sit down and rest your feet, dearie.
I'll be back in two shakes when I've seen how things are
going."

I seated myself on a brocade sofa and stared at the door
Lobelia had closed after her. Even though I was well dis-
illusioned with my uncle, I knew enough about Creoles to
be shocked by the information she had just divulged. There
were only certain professions with which a gentleman might
correctly associate himself—if he worked at all. Certainly
a gambling establishment was not one, though gentlemen
attended such places readily enough. I recalled what Tante
Aurore had said about Uncle Robert's obsession for acquir-
ing money—again not a Creole trait. It seemed that he was
so possessed by a driving desire to maintain his way of life
as he had always known it, and recoup his disastrous losses
after the war, that he would stop at nothing. Most gently
bred Creoles of the older generation would fade quietly away
in poverty, rather than change their concept of what was
suitable for a gentleman. This was one reason why the
American, who had no such notions, had been able to come
in so vigorously and take over the business of the city.

In Uncle Robert there was a strain of iron that did not
altogether mix with the softer metal of the Creole. So—he

was involved in this business of making money through the weakness of others, though still maintaining a surface respectability. I was sure that the surface appearance would be tremendously important to him, and that he would never be seen within these walls except as a patron. Now I could understand why Lobelia made visits to my uncle's office in the role of a "client."

Before long Lobelia returned, still breathless, but apparently in control of whatever needed to be controlled. She seated herself in a chair before a delicate rosewood *escritoire* and grinned at me rakishly.

"As I was saying, these are pretty fancy quarters for an office. At times it's necessary to have a quiet place to talk to an inebriated gentleman, or to those who have lost more than is healthy and are feeling reckless. Not that there's much trouble with Creoles. They consider it a disgrace to be seen intoxicated in public. Now then—tell me what it was you wanted to talk to me about. I can't stay for long, and I don't expect you want to either. By the way, how is Lanny, poor little fellow?"

This was my opening. "It's because of Lanny that I'm here," I told her. "He said you were kind to him and I'm worried about the way his mother treats him."

Lobelia snorted. "A fine one she is! Probably never wanted a kid in the first place."

"Don't you think the boy's father would take better care of him than the mother?" I asked.

A wary expression came into her eyes. "Suppose you come across with just what you're trying to say, dearie. I'm not much good at hedging. Speak your piece and I'll listen. What's more I won't give you away to your uncle."

"All right," I said. "I want to know why Uncle Robert has taken this unlikely interest in Isabelle Law."

Mrs. Pollock twisted her mouth wryly. "Well now, he went to a lot of trouble to keep track of those two all these years. He knew when Justin went to jail and he knew he left a wife and child outside. He knew when the grandmother in Louisiana died a year or so ago and when the boy started traveling with his mother. When Justin showed up in town he sent for them and brought them both here. He put me in charge of 'em and didn't show his face at the Pontalba at all. That's why he didn't know the boy when you brought him to the house that time."

"Uncle Robert brought Lanny and Isabelle here? But what is this to him?" I persisted.

She was silent for a moment, staring at me speculatively. "I can't tell you that, dearie, because I'm not sure. Maybe this is just a way of getting things to go the way he wants them to. You know how much he likes to run people. Though he don't run me as much as he thinks."

This seemed to be all she could tell me, and it seemed only to increase the puzzle. As I thanked her and rose to leave, she came to the door with me.

"Since you've come this far, you might as well have a peek at the rest of the place. There's a way so nobody'll know you're looking."

She grinned at me wickedly and I think she liked the idea of again flouting Uncle Robert through me.

I followed her into the hallway and now I could hear the sounds of laughter and talk from the gaming rooms, and the cries of what Lobelia said were croupiers. She opened the door of a dark little room, scarcely larger than the interior of an armoire. Her plump, damp hand closed over mine and she drew me to a place where a peephole opened into the next room.

The blaze of light blinded me for a moment. There were gas globes everywhere, glaring and harsh, and I had to blink a few times before I could see. The room before me was lavish with gilt and marble. A long table bordered with numbers and sections of red and black stretched down its center. Men stood about it, watching intently the spin of a wheel.

Lobelia whispered in my ear. "We have roulette downstairs—that's what they're playing there now. Faro's on the second floor, and keno on the third. Of course we have private rooms too, where a gentleman may have a quiet game of poker or vingt-et-un, or even blackjack, which the Americans brought in. Every now and then somebody gets the notion that it's all against the law. But they never keep us shut up for long."

A group of men on the far side of the table moved apart and I gasped. Courtney Law was setting a stack of chips before him, and I saw his face, flushed as if with wine, and his unsteady hands.

I turned from the peephole and whispered urgently to Lobelia. "He's been drinking and he'll gamble himself into further debt to my uncle. Do you suppose I could see him for a moment?"

She didn't like the idea, but at my insistence she took me back to her elaborate parlor and let me wait there for

Courtney, while she sent a servant to fetch him.

When Courtney came into the room he started at the sight of me.

"Skye, what are you doing here? This is no place—"

"What are *you* doing here?" I broke in. "What will it serve you to put yourself still further in Uncle Robert's debt? But since I am here, you can't let me leave unescorted. Will you please take me home now?"

By his own code, he could do nothing else. Mrs. Pollock saw us somewhat derisively to the door, pressed the further loan of the veil upon me, and we left L'Oiseau d'Or together. Lest Courtney be too curious, I prodded him at once with questions of my own.

"Have you talked to Justin lately? Has he said anything further about plans for you?"

Courtney nodded unhappily as we made our way along Royal Street. "He told me this morning. The new office is waiting on the Ohio River. He has our train tickets, and arrangements for us at the other end. He is being most efficient about getting me out of town, this brother of mine."

"Don't resent his help," I said. "We can pay him back later. This is the only thing we can do now."

Courtney walked stiffly beside me, his gaze fixed straight ahead. "How can I face your uncle, Skye? He will be angry, and with reason. He wants only what is for our own good. I think you do not altogether understand this. After all he has done for me, after all his past kindness, am I to take a step that will estrange me from him forever?"

I was coming to see Courtney more clearly by now. Always he would be inclined to drift a little with the tide. It would make him happy if he could please everyone, oppose no one. But life seldom permitted such a course and I knew I would have to be the stronger of the two. I, who had always admired men with iron in their natures, would have to lead a man who was made of far softer metal.

"We can't stay here and live as Uncle Robert wants us to," I said reasonably. "And you need not talk to him about any of this, Courtney. Leave it to me. I'll see him soon and make it all clear to him."

This seemed to reassure him a little and he turned to me in some relief, covered my hand in the crook of his arm. Now I could smell the odor of wine on his breath as he bent toward me.

"You are an amazing girl, Skye," he mused. "From the first you have interested me because you are so different

193

from any girls I have known. I am sure, *chérie*, that we will come to care for each other."

Somehow this was more alarming than his indifference. I had to contain a sudden desire to snatch my hand from his arm, to run away from him. In a few weeks this young man would be my husband and if I were to feel such revulsion toward him at the slightest touch, how could I bear this marriage which I had promised myself must be a good one?

"Your broken heart heals easily," I said, no longer kind.

He looked hurt and I felt sorry for him again. Always he fought confusion within himself, being torn in many ways. At least the words he had spoken to me were an effort in the right direction. I tried to smile and forced myself not to shrink against the feeling of his warm fingers clasped about my own.

I was relieved when he left me at the Tourneau gate. We did not want anyone to ask where we had been, or how we had met. But now I meant to waste no more time about making Uncle Robert understand and accept our plans.

That night when I asked to speak with him, he was in a well-disposed mood. Indeed, he told me, he would be happy to discuss whatever I liked. Tomorrow afternoon he would come upstairs and give me as much time as I pleased in the seclusion of his study.

The hours before that talk with my uncle I spent in a state of apprehension. I knew the things I must say to him. Even though I was not entirely sure about Courtney, I must make it seem that neither Courtney nor I could be shaken from the course we planned. I must tell Uncle Robert that if he threatened to put my father and mother out of his house, then we would simply take them with us. When we reached the town where Justin was placing us, they could live in our home. This might be difficult for all of us. It would be far better if we could begin our married life alone and have my parents join us later when our adjustments to each other had been made. But at least this was a way of disarming Uncle Robert.

I tried to think reasonably of these things, but every time I faced the reality of being Courtney's wife, something sickened within me. How was I to live through this wedding, when I wanted only to be Justin's wife? How was I to endure this new life? Now, more than ever, escape from New Orleans became imperative. It would be hard for me anywhere. But in New Orleans it would be impossible.

The next day dawned still and hot. A luminous yellow haze lay upon the city and the air seemed heavy and difficult to breathe. Aunt Natalie told me it was storm-brewing weather. September, she said, was the time for storms in New Orleans and probably there was a disturbance now out over the Gulf.

I found myself more nervous and tense than ever and I could hardly be still. My mother's guileless ways, and Isabelle's limp dejection, both set my teeth on edge and I hoped this weather would not have an equally nerve-tensing effect on Uncle Robert.

It was midafternoon when he came upstairs to his study and sent Delphine for me. The moment I stepped into the room I knew that he was extremely pleased about something. He was in much too benign a mood to set me at ease. As he placed me gallantly in a chair near his desk, I saw that for once the silver cover had been left off the chessboard.

Uncle Robert did not refer to the game, but my eyes were drawn to the board in fascination. There were only a handful of men left upon the checkered squares and Black's position was plain. One more move and the white king would be in check. The game was already over.

I forced my attention from the chessmen and looked my uncle full in the face. There was no purpose in hesitating, and I must not falter.

"I wish to tell you about the plans Courtney and I are making for immediately after the wedding."

Uncle Robert stroked his beard in great good humor. "Ah, yes, my dear. You will, of course, come straight home to this house where you may stay in seclusion for a suitable length of time. Naturally, a newly wedded couple does not go out, or receive calls for the first weeks of their marriage."

This, I knew, was the Creole custom. But it was not for me. "I'm sorry, Uncle Robert," I said evenly, "but Courtney and I will be leaving for the North at once. Justin has already obtained our tickets and all arrangements have been made."

He did not seem in the least disturbed and that in itself was ominous. "So? I thought it must be some foolishness of this sort about which you wished to speak to me. But it is not possible, of course."

"If you think you can hold the matter of caring for my father over my head," I began, sounding angrier than I intended,"—if you think your threat to put him out—"

He did not let me continue. "Threat? That is a strong word. Naturally I shall not put your father out of my house."

He spoke as innocently as though the thought had never occurred to him. "But you must understand, Skye, that your benefactor—M'sieu Justin Law—" his tone was derisive, "will not after all be able to aid you as he had planned."

"But he *is* aiding us!" I cried.

Uncle Robert shook his head gently. Never had his voice sounded more musical. "My dear, you delude yourself. When I have talked to him, he will proceed no further. There is one thing in the world that this man wants above all else. The possession of his son. He has been searching for him without success. Now that he has found him, he will do anything to take the boy into his own charge. And he may have him—for a price. Part of the price, naturally, will be that he does not interfere with my plans for you and Courtney."

I could only stare at my uncle helplessly. Now I was beginning to see his purpose. It was as if chains had been locked suddenly about me, leaving me incapable of speaking or moving.

Uncle Robert raised his head alertly, listening to steps in the hallway. "They must be here now," he said. "We will be able to work this out most amicably together, my dear. I've invited M'sieu Law to come this afternoon—for a business call only. And I have asked Courtney to bring him upstairs."

Courtney's knock sounded on the study door and my uncle called, *"Entrez!"* in his most cordial tone.

I sat stiffly where I was, hardly daring to look at Justin until he was well into the room. When my eyes met his I felt the old pain go through me more sharply than ever. His face was a mask, without emotion, and he looked at me as though he did not know me. But now I knew the look meant only that he must hide what he felt. Uncle Robert made no offer of his hand. He indicated a chair and after a moment's hesitation Justin sat down opposite me. But Courtney would not sit. He remained uneasily standing.

My eyes strayed once more to the chessboard. The men were set for the final play. In a moment my uncle would lift his hand and move the Black. White would be checked and the game finished. I, who was no more than a pawn, sat in silence, seeing the play, the end of the game, as clearly ordained as it was upon the chessboard.

Twenty-Four ❧

As I watched in silent apprehension, the game came to life before my eyes.

Uncle Robert toyed, as he had done before, with a slender ivory paper knife, and I was reminded of the day when he had taken a dueling sword from the wall and whipped through a few movements. How romantic I had thought him! Now he dueled with words, punctuating what he had to say with little stabs of the ivory knife, and our very lives were being attacked.

"M'sieu Law," he began, "I have asked you here to meet with my niece and with your brother because I am unhappy over rumors of your meddling with their plans. *My* plans. I shall make my position clear at once. It has been my long intention that Courney enter my law firm when he is ready, and later advance to a partnership. He has been like a son to me." He turned a benevolent look upon Courtney, who flushed. "It give me great satisfaction that he is marrying my niece, Skye, and that the two of them will make their home here in my house."

Justin spoke quietly. "As I understand it, Courtney has other plans. It's my desire to help him in what he wants to do. The planning is not altogether in your hands."

"Ah, m'sieu, but that is where you are mistaken." Uncle Robert raised the bit of ivory and tapped his thumbnail with it thoughtfully. "I believe you are not in a position to influence Courtney's future."

"What do you mean?" Justin asked directly.

"Only that I hold the means of checking any move you make which does not please me. In other words—your son."

"I shall take my son," Justin said.

"By force? I think not, m'sieu."

Justin shook his head. "Not by force. By law."

Uncle Robert remained unperturbed. "That would be foolish indeed. No court would take him from a mother who is so plainly in a position to give him good care, thanks

197

to my interest in the boy. He is a distant relative and I am happy to aid one of my own family. There is also the matter of the scandal such a struggle would make in the courts. Do you wish the boy to suffer for the things you have done in the past? Do you wish to bring such shame upon him that he will never again hold up his head in this town?"

"The past is scarcely a secret," Justin said.

"It is an old secret. People will be willing to forget, to accept the new order. But they will not if you drag your dirty linen through the public press."

I saw Justin's hands tighten on the arms of his chair. Courtney had moved restlessly away from us, taking no part in this fencing, but now he turned to watch intently.

"Of course," my uncle added, "you do not have to stay in New Orleans, M'sieu Law."

"I choose to stay in New Orleans," Justin said. "This is my home. I intend to raise my son here and I intend to live in my father's house in the Garden District."

My uncle waved the little knife at him in reproach. "You are a stubborn man. If you want your son, you will have to gain his possession by a different method."

"Now we get to the point," Justin said. "Suppose you tell me just what this bargain is that you offer me."

"Very well, you will cease to meddle in your brother's affairs, of course. You will return the house in the Garden District to your mother's name. You will take your wife and your son and leave New Orleans. There is all of America for you to live in and what you do when you leave this city does not concern me. Providing you never return."

I could not read the guarded expression on Justin's face. Perhaps he was not a good enough chess player to know when he had been finally checked. But I knew and my heart ached for him. And for myself as well.

"I will never agree to give up my father's home," Justin said, as if there were still a chance for him to bargain. "You have carried the support of that house and of my mother for long enough. I am happy to take care of both myself."

Uncle Robert's slender hand moved in the light from the window as he laid the paper knife carefully on the desk beside him. "That will not be necessary. Your mother has been happy in my care. And I have been glad to assume the duties of her nearest relative."

"Was it because of this relationship that my father put the handling of his fortune in your hands? That he left it with you in trust when he was forced to leave New Orleans?"

198

"Fortune," Uncle Robert echoed blandly, "is hardly the term for what was left in my hands. But we were friends and it was natural for him to trust me."

"In spite of the fact that he had married the woman you had hoped to marry?" said Justin.

Courtney moved in the shadows of the room, came to stand beside me. He looked angry now, but his anger was directed at his brother.

Uncle Robert answered smoothly enough. "Rather, let us say, that he trusted me for that very reason. He knew that because of my affection for Mademoiselle Aurore Le-Maitre, I would be true to this trust as long as she or I lived."

"And you have been true to it, M'sieu Robert," Courtney said quickly. "This man does not understand Creole honor."

"That's where you're wrong," said Justin quickly. "I understand any man's honor and respect it. My father—your father, Courtney—was a good and honorable man. A man who trusted his friends and would never have believed one of them could betray him."

"May I ask what inference you are making?" Uncle Robert said coldly.

"All in good time. Though I believe you may be able to guess. May I ask what became of the money left for my mother in your hands?"

"But certainly." Uncle Robert was curt. "I have kept careful records of the entire transaction. The money went into the purchase of Confederate bonds. Where else would a good Southerner have placed money at that time? My own much larger fortune went the same way."

"What of investments in England?" Justin asked.

There was a faint hesitation on my uncle's part. Then he answered readily enough.

"Indeed, there was such an investment made. A small one, I assure you. It is that which still gives Aurore the tiny income she has. It is scarcely enough to support her and her son."

"It may interest you to know," said Justin quietly, "that I have been able to uncover certain information in this city. With some difficulty, I assure you, due to a fire which caused the destruction of records. But not all were destroyed, as you may have believed, sir. My father, who had no faith in the Southern cause in spite of his great love for the South, took precautions so that only a moderate sum was left in your hands for my mother's care during the war. The rest was invested in England, where it would be safe from being wasted on Confederate bonds. Not until the war was over were you to have control of that money for her benefit."

Courtney made a choked sound, but neither man looked at him. Uncle Robert rose to his feet, his face livid with anger.

"Monsieur, do you have the audacity to call me a liar?"

Justin remained coolly in his chair. "My father was foolishly trusting, as I say. He was born to money and had made it easily. He expected to make more in Colorado. When he was rich again after the war, he hoped to return to New Orleans and clear his name of the spy charge. In the meantime he had the comfort of knowing that his wife and son were well cared for. As indeed they have been. But they have been made to grovel for every penny. They have been made to feel indebted to you, as they were never truly indebted."

My uncle put one hand to his throat as if he were choking, but Justin went on relentlessly.

"My mother and my brother have been held in your power, while you in the beginning recouped your own losses and reinstated yourself as a man of wealth, using the money which had been safely invested in England and which was available to you in your power of attorney after the war. You appropriated my father's shipping concern without payment to my mother for it and she did not understand what happened. If Courtney marries your niece, the circle will be well closed. Even discovery could not destroy you then, for Courtney would never act against you. In the beginning there would have been no whisper of a spy charge against my father, if you had not instigated it in a successful effort to send him out of town. Indeed, sir, I call you a liar, a cheat and a thief. And I think you will not hold my son from me."

It was necessary for Uncle Robert to reach for the back of a chair to support himself, so apoplectic was his anger.

"There has been enough of such slander!" he shouted, his voice cracking on a high note. "There is only one way to deal with one like yourself. It is a way which belongs to the more honorable past, but it is a way of which gentlemen still avail themselves on occasion. My seconds will call on you, monsieur."

Justin got lazily to his feet. "This is not the first time I've been challenged to a duel since I came to New Orleans." He flung a brief glance at Courtney, who stood rigidly beside me, his face white as paper. "Never do you Creoles lose your romantic notions. I've no intention of fighting you or anyone else. In your own case, I would not fight a man whose hands tremble so that he could not take fair aim with a pistol. Were you my own age, I might give you a good thrashing. But that satisfaction can't be mine under the circumstances. You will hear from me again, however. Now, if you will excuse me, I have business here in town. Courtney, you will kindly tell my mother I do not expect to be home tonight."

Justin bowed with mock courtesy to my uncle and threw Courtney a look of pity. Then he bowed gravely to me and went out of the room. My heart was thudding in my ears and for the moment I was too frightened to move. My uncle was not one to take insult without action.

Uncle Robert steadied himself with an effort, leaning both hands upon the chair back. When he could speak again he turned to the white and silent Courtney.

"My boy, you will of course act as my second, if this fellow can be forced to fight. It will give me great pleasure to kill him."

Courtney spoke between tight lips. "Justin will not fight you," he said. "And I will not be your second. But I will be glad to pick up the challenge my brother has refused. I will be happy to meet you at the Oaks at sunrise tomorrow, m'sieu. You have deceived us all too long."

Uncle Robert stared at him dumfounded. Moving a little blindly, Courtney went toward the door. Just before he reached it he saw his mother's picture on the wall—the portrait of Aurore LeMaitre as she had been long ago. He turned abruptly back to my uncle.

"I have always wondered—why do you keep that picture of my mother on your wall?"

With an effort Uncle Robert regained his self-control. "I keep it there to remind me of something I wish never to forget—the faithlessness of your mother. It is to remind me that she must pay for her miserable treatment of me. Indeed, m'sieu, I shall be most happy to meet her son on the field of honor."

Courtney bowed stiffly and went out of the room. My uncle seemed to have forgotten me. He walked to the table where the velvet-lined case lay and opened it. Almost tenderly, he took out the two pistols which lay within and regarded them proudly. The feel of them in his hands must have reassured him, for something of the blazing color went out of his face. He raised one pistol and sighted along the barrel.

As Justin had said, his hand was not steady. He put the pistol down and saw me then, sitting in my chair across the room.

"I would rather kill the other one," he said. "But the young one will do. I am sorry to deprive you of your bridegroom, my dear, but this will be necessary."

I recovered the power of movement and fled from the room. Uncle Robert had miscalculated his opponent. The game had taken a new turn and I was desperately frightened. As I ran past the dining-room door, Delphine stepped out of the dim and shuttered room.

"There's going to be a duel!" I cried. "Someone will be killed. Delphine, we've got to stop it!"

"We will not stop it," Delphine said calmly. "It is M'sieu Courtney who will die."

"You—know what has happened?" I gasped.

"But certainly," she admitted without hesitation. "I have much interest in this meeting today. And the voices were loud enough for me to hear, mam'zelle. But have no fear for your uncle. M'sieu Robert has never been defeated in a duel. Only once was he ever so much as wounded."

It was not my uncle for whom I feared, but I could see that the only way to get Delphine's help was to shake her confidence in Uncle Robert as an expert shot.

"You may have heard," I said, "but you didn't see him. He has turned into an old man whose hands tremble. He is in no condition to face a man as young as Courtney. It is Uncle Robert who will be killed."

She drew herself away from the hand I reached toward her and left me there in the hallway. I could only look after her tall figure, moving hurriedly toward the stairs in the wake of my uncle.

There was nothing to do but go to my own room and try to gather some understanding of the things I had heard and seen. I sat there rocking in the breathless stillness of that yellow afternoon, and no more than twenty minutes passed before Delphine came to my door.

When I called to her to enter I was shocked by her appearance. Almost always she seemed cool and remote and controlled. She might condemn the actions of others, but she did it without emotional involvement, as if from some Olympian height. Now her golden skin looked a little gray and her lips trembled when she tried to speak.

"It is as you say, Mam'zelle Skye. M'sieu Robert is an old and shaken man. It is to be hoped that by dawn tomorrow he may recover himself. He has been greatly enraged by that American *canaille*. Yet he is a man of experience in the duel."

In a few moments she would talk herself back into a state of confidence in Robert Tourneau.

"We must take no chances, Delphine," I said. "Somehow this duel must be stopped. If the police knew—"

She looked at me in horror. "Would you bring the disgrace of arrest upon this house?"

I knew then I would get no help from her. Whatever had to be done, I must do myself. Justin did not know that Courtney had picked up the glove he had left in the ring. Surely Justin would stop Courtney when he knew what had happened. If, as he said, he was not going home to the Garden District tonight, then there was a chance that I might find him at the lodging he kept in town and let him know what had happened.

Once Courtney had pointed out to me the place where his brother had taken rooms. I would go there and try to see him. There was no other way. I walked out of the house boldly that afternoon, and I think not even Delphine could have stopped me, even if she had tried.

The rooms were on Dumaine Street—what in New Orleans were known as *chambres garnies*, furnished rooms for gentlemen only. The passage to the courtyard stood open, but as I hurried through, Justin's landlady—no Creole, but one of the outsiders who had lately moved into the Quarter—came to meet me. She looked like the sort who would deal firmly with any situation of which she disapproved and she asked me my business curtly. No lady could properly visit a gentleman's rooms, and she meant to have no nonsense in her respectable place.

But I was as determined as she, and I played the Creole *grande dame* haughtily. It was a matter of the greatest importance, I assured her. If the gentleman were not home at present, I would wait. And down I sat on a bench in the courtyard. If she wanted to remove me, she would have to use force. Apparently she thought better of the matter and went off, muttering to herself.

This was no tidy, well-cared-for court like that at the Tourneau house. The tropical growth had fairly burst its bounds, thriving in unkempt profusion among weeds and long-untrimmed shrubbery. I think I studied every inch of it that afternoon as the shadows grew long and I waited for Justin. I stared at the dry fountain, graced by a one-armed nymph; I noted that the bricks of the passageway were green with that mould that grows instantly in any damp shady spot in New Orleans. Apparently no *marchand de brique* came here weekly to sell the brick powder which kept courtyard and passageway at the Tourneaus' so brightly free from the slippery green.

And all the time, while I tried to occupy my mind with trivialities, I could see Courtney lying stretched beneath an oak tree in the park, his life snuffed out needlessly, foolishly.

When it was nearly suppertime Madame returned and stared at me with disapproval. "When he don't show up by this time, miss, he won't likely show up till a whole lot later. No use you wearing out that bench and yourself with waiting. My other gentlemen will be coming along soon and it won't look right—you sitting there."

I knew then that my mission was futile. He wouldn't come until late tonight, when he returned only to sleep in these rooms. But if I could not see him myself, I could at least leave him word of what had happened.

"If you will loan me pen and paper," I said, "I will write Mr. Law a message."

She brought them to me, happy to be rid of me at last, and I wrote a note, beseeching Justin to stop Courtney from keeping his rendezvous at dawn the following morning. Then I sealed the envelope and told the landlady that it was a matter of life or death to get the message into Justin Law's hands. Her promise seemed sincere enough and there was nothing else to do but go home and hope that it would finally reach him.

The feeling of an impending storm was still in the air when we sat down to supper that night. Uncle Robert was absent from the meal. Aunt Natalie said he had a most terrible headache and could not eat. Plainly she had no inkling of what had happened. Often, she told us, when there was this oppressive sense of a storm stirring out on the Gulf, he felt like this. It was to be hoped the storm would not come inland.

With Uncle Robert absent, Aunt Natalie and Mama, innocent of my knowledge, indulged in the usual light gossip. Only Isabelle and I sat silent. Inwardly I fumed with impatience for the meal to be done with. It was difficult to sit there and dissemble. As far as I was concerned, I hoped a good-sized hurricane would break over New Orleans. A storm might stop the duel as nothing else could. Any sort of delay might furnish the way to stop it permanently. Nothing tempted my appetite that night, and I sighed with relief when the long meal was over and I could hurry away.

At nine o'clock in the evening, Delphine came looking for me. The night was sultry and still, and I had left my windows open, but she spoke so softly that even I could hardly hear her words.

"Where did you go this afternoon, mam'zelle?"

I told her without hesitation and for once she did not quote Creole convention and shake her head over my behavior.

"It is useless, mam'zelle. M'sieu Robert will not be stopped."

"It's Courtney I'm thinking of!" I cried. "He's the one who must be stopped."

"If M'sieu Justin goes to the Oaks tomorrow morning to stop his brother, he will perhaps choose to fight himself," she said thoughtfully.

This had never occurred to me. "Oh, no! He wouldn't do that. He has said he would not fight a duel."

Delphine went on, as if to herself. "I believe this would be more dangerous to your uncle than facing the boy. Let us pray, mam'zelle, that M'sieu Justin will find some means to stop this evil thing without any fighting at all. I myself shall go to the Oaks in the morning."

"*You* will go?"

"*Pourquoi non?* Why should I not? This, mam'zelle, is not the first time women of my race have gone at dawn to the Dueling Oaks in the park. Men have died in the arms of such women in the *ancien régime.*"

I shuddered. "Don't talk like that. No one is going to die tomorrow. I can't believe they will fight a duel. It's too ridiculous."

"The graves in the cemeteries do not laugh, mam'zelle," Delphine said. She turned gravely toward the door, but before she could pull it open, I made a decision.

"Delphine—I'm going with you!"

She looked at me as she had that day when I'd wandered unknowingly into Gallatin Street. "Ladies of good family do not behave in such fashion, mam'zelle. It is impossible."

I slipped between her and the door. "Forget that I'm supposed to be a Creole lady who can't do this, and can't do that. I'm a Yankee, and you know what you think of them! As a Yankee I shall go with you in the morning. If you don't take me, I shall tell everyone, summon the police—"

Delphine looked as though she might strike me, but she

could not release herself from the disciplines of long training. "Like your maman, you must always have your way. But I shall not call you in the morning. If you are ready when I am ready, it makes no difference to me what you do. I take no responsibility for your behavior. Nor do I answer for what your uncle will do if he sees you there."

She went out and closed the door quietly behind her.

I sat down in the little rocker and swayed gently back and forth. My thoughts were in a turmoil, but I knew I would go with Delphine if I had to sit up all night to manage it.

What I intended to do at the Dueling Oaks tomorrow was not clear, but something, surely, would offer itself.

Twenty-Five ✸

All that night I dozed and woke and dozed again. Often I heard the sound of the Cathedral bell tolling the hour. Night still shrouded the courtyard when I arose and dressed. I was fully wide awake and alert to every sound.

There were no stars to be seen out my windows, but the storm, if it was to strike New Orleans, had not broken. The courtyard was hidden by mist, thick as custard and motionless. I heard Jasper when he went out to bring the carriage for Uncle Robert. And though he moved softly, I heard my uncle too when he came downstairs. The sound of horses reached me clearly from the street and when I was sure he had gone, I sped lightly past my father's room.

When Delphine let herself out the gate into the thick yellow murk I went with her. Delphine had made her own arrangements. A shabby carriage awaited us a square away from the house down a cross street. I wore a heavy veil over my hat, but Delphine had not troubled to disguise her identity.

Lamps at the corners shimmered in the gloom, but shed little radiance. Above us the iron lace of the galleries shone black and wet when light from the carriage lamps touched it. As we turned onto the wide Esplanade and jogged northwest toward the park, the mist began to drift into stringy wisps and I saw faint gray dawn in the sky behind us over the river.

"What are we to do when we get there?" I asked Delphine anxiously.

"We may only watch, mam'zelle," she told me. "There is an old house among the Oaks, very dilapidated, but it will serve to shield us from view."

I shivered and sat back in the carriage, wondering if we would be in time.

We had left the old Creole part of the city and I knew that this had once been a country road leading to the Allard plantation. But the plantation was now part of City Park and houses encroached along the road. When we crossed Bayou St. John the buildings disappeared. We had reached the appointed place.

The carriage stopped and Delphine got out, instructed the driver to wait for us here. Then we moved together into the misty-gray shadows of live oak trees. The black trunks were vast in circumference and branched thickly overhead. Spanish moss dripped from every tree, and a strand of it touched my hand, dry and gray as withered skin. I followed Delphine beneath the trees with my heart thudding in my breast.

She had chosen an approach that would not be used by the men and we were able to walk unseen toward the old house that huddled in tottering ruin among the trees. The roof looked as if it might come down upon our heads, but Delphine moved with confidence.

"Often the wounded and dying were brought here after a duel," she whispered as she led me toward a paneless window where we could look out upon the scene, well shielded in shadow.

Dawnlight, murky though it was, now slanted between the great live oaks, lighting the scene clearly enough. There seemed to be seven or eight men moving about on the grassy expanse between the trees, and it looked as if an excited argument was going on. Beside the principals, there would of course be seconds and doctors. The group seemed to center around a figure which lay still upon the ground and I grasped Delphine's arm.

"They've fought already! Look—someone has been wounded!"

"Be calm, mam'zelle," Delphine said, but for once her own voice trembled. "I believe it is M'sieu Courtney on the ground."

207

I saw Justin then in the hazy group. So he had come! But perhaps too late. "Do you think that Courtney—" I began.

"Wait, mam'zelle. I do not think they fight as yet. See— see what is happening!"

My uncle was removing his coat, and I saw that Justin also removed his. Delphine whispered in anguish close to my ear.

"It is the barbarian who will fight M'sieu Robert, mam'zelle! It is as I feared. The brother has put M'sieu Courtney out of the fight."

Justin had of course come here to stop Courtney from fighting, and perhaps the only way he could manage that was to knock Courtney down. Now it was clear that he intended the thing Delphine had prophesied—to take his brother's place in the duel.

The mists were lifting, whisked away by a wind that set the long strands of gray moss swaying as if with a life of their own. I could see the participants more clearly now. The seconds were advising Justin and my uncle. One of the doctors still knelt beside the prone figure of Courtney, but he rose quickly to watch what was happening. The distance was measured in paces and Delphine's lips moved as she counted silently.

"Ten paces," she said. "A man with a steady hand cannot miss."

Justin's hand would be steady. If he chose he could kill my uncle, unless he himself were killed first.

"Will they fire more than once?" I whispered.

Delphine shrugged. "Who knows? Sometimes honor is satisfied at first blood. Sometimes it is a fight to the death. It will be arranged. M'sieu Robert has preference for an exchange of three shots."

Three shots—three chances to kill or be killed!

The seconds led Justin and Uncle Robert to their positions and I could only watch, frozen and helpless. So tiny now was the strand of time that hung between life and death. The two men stood facing each other, pistol muzzles down toward the ground. The pale light of dawn caught the murderous blue-black gleam from the barrels. The waiting was unbearable.

We heard the signal plainly: "Ready! One—two—three —fire!"

The explosion I feared crashed through the quiet grove. I saw Justin stagger briefly, then stand erect again. A spread-

208

ing stain of crimson showed against his left shoulder. At once the seconds approached Uncle Robert to learn if he was satisfied and would call off the duel. He shook his head angrily. Justin did not move at all. Delphine whispered tensely, "The American did not fire."

Uncle Robert cocked his pistol with his thumb and raised it again, but I saw that Justin's arm still hung at his side. He did not raise his gun to aim.

Delphine pounded one fist in the palm of her hand. "Kill him, kill him!" she whispered.

Again a shot exploded through the grove, but this time Justin did not sway and I knew the shot had missed. Delphine raised her two fists and shook them. "Only one is shooting. The other awaits his turn. Oh, but this is wicked, wicked!"

Again the seconds tried to interfere, but Uncle Robert shook his head. He looked pale in the morning light.

"Go on!" Justin ordered curtly, though I could see that his left shoulder was wet with blood.

Uncle Robert seemed seriously shaken by having missed. Once more he cocked his pistol, but even at this distance I could see his hand waver as he tried to take aim. Now I understood what a shattering thing Justin was doing—though at what great risk to himself! Uncle Robert knew now that Justin would not fire until his opponent was through. Then Robert Tourneau must stand unarmed and face the careful aim of Justin Law. It was a cruel thing, perhaps, but it took great courage, for first Justin must face three bullets without firing, his own pistol pointed at the ground. Delphine leaned in the window, her fists clenched, willing Justin to die. And I stood beside her, shaken and sick, praying that both would live.

Uncle Robert took his time, trying to correct his aim. Beyond the duelists, movement caught my eye and I saw Courtney sit up to stare dazedly at what was happening. Above his head the moss strands dipped and swayed in the rising wind.

My uncle steadied his arm, pulled the trigger. The smell of gunsmoke drifted again through the glade. But again he had missed and I thanked God with all my heart.

Now it was Justin's turn and I remembered the time he had said that when he had a score to pay, he paid it, for good or for evil. Was he truly a cold-blooded murderer as they said? The sound of his pistol being cocked was startling in the breathless quiet. Uncle Robert was plainly a brave man. He faced Justin, his shirt a white target against the dark trees. And Justin was young, his hand would not waver.

From where I stood it seemed as though he aimed directly for Uncle Robert's heart. I wanted to cry out, "No, no! No matter what he has done, don't kill him!" Beside me Delphine was as a woman carved from granite.

The shot rang out, but Uncle Robert did not fall. I almost wished that Justin had wounded him at the first shot. Then perhaps this dreadful affair might be stopped. Surely, if both men drew blood—but again Justin's arm came up, his pistol was cocked, the shot fired.

Uncle Robert swayed, tottered, but there was no betraying spurt of blood and I had caught the singing of the bullet through leaves, the spat of it as it struck bark. Twice Justin had missed, but a third shot remained. My knees turned to water and I leaned heavily upon the splintered window sill for support. Delphine did not move at all, but I heard her praying softly aloud.

Again the dreadful routine was repeated. Again the sound of a shot shattered the peace of the grove and this time Uncle Robert cried out, clawed at his breast and fell face down upon the grass. The third shot had clearly found its mark. Yet I could not believe with my heart the thing my eyes told me had happened.

Delphine swung herself over the sill of the broken window and dropped lightly to the ground—sped across the grass toward the group that gathered about Uncle Robert. I was too weak to follow her with such dispatch. I chose the door, but I hurried too, with no thought for the impropriety of my presence at the Oaks that morning.

Justin stood alone, his pistol hanging loosely in his hand, watching the seconds and the doctors as they knelt beside my uncle. He saw Delphine's whirlwind approach before he saw me. Then he turned and looked incredulously in my direction.

I ripped back my veil and ran toward him. He tossed the pistol to the grass and reached for me with his good arm. I clung to him, hid my face against his shoulder. No matter what I had seen, I did not believe that Justin had meant to kill my uncle.

"You wouldn't shoot to kill!" I wept against his shoulder. "It was an accident. I know you didn't mean to harm him."

He held me tightly. "I got your message, Skye, and went out to the Garden District at once. But Courtney didn't return home at all last night. So I came here this morning to stop him in any way I could. I had no other choice than what I did."

"I know," I said, clinging to him. "I understand." Then I remembered his wound and raised my head. "You're hurt. The doctor must help you."

"It's nothing," he assured me. "Only a grazing of the flesh."

"Is—is my uncle dead?"

"I don't know," Justin said gravely.

Courtney got to his feet, rubbing his jaw as if it pained him. Uncertainly he moved toward Justin. Before he reached us, the small group around my uncle opened to let Delphine in and even the doctors seemed to know and respect her, for she was allowed to kneel beside Uncle Robert as they examined him. It was one of Uncle Robert's seconds who spoke first. He stood up and looked in Justin's direction, puzzled.

"There is no wound," he said. "The bullet did not strike him."

"I never intended that it should," Justin said. "Do you think I could not have killed him if I'd wanted to?"

"But, monsieur—" the second began doubtfully, and Justin spoke curtly.

"Take it that I missed, if you like," he said. "It makes no difference to me. I meant to frighten him well and apparently that's what I've done."

The man gave him a look of cold disapproval. No Creole ever thanked you for breaking with proper tradition.

From where she knelt beside Uncle Robert, Delphine looked up at the others. "It is without doubt his heart. He knew he should put no stress upon it. Often, often, I have warned him. But he lives and we must take him home at once. Will you permit this, M'sieu le Docteur?" When Uncle Robert's doctor nodded, she spoke to the seconds. "Please— you will carry him to the carriage, messieurs."

Two of the men picked him up and bore him from the dueling place. Delphine followed, her head held high. She did not glance our way, but brushed past close to us without a word.

"And now will you see Courtney's doctor?" I pleaded with Justin.

"Wait," he said, and I saw that Courtney was approaching.

After a quick glance of astonishment at me, Courtney stopped before his brother. "Had I stood in your place," he told Justin, "as I intended to do, one of us would be dead by now—M'sieu Robert or myself. I would not have missed, I think, but I would have offered a less nerve-racking target to my opponent." Suddenly he held out his hand. "Sir, I thank you. I've long misjudged you. Will you accept my apology, brother?"

The words were stiff, formal, but Justin flung an arm about his shoulders in a quick embrace. Before anything else could be said, one of Justin's seconds hurried across the grass to us, with the doctor following. He held out his hand in congratulation to Justin.

"You are fortunate to be alive, m'sieu. May I suggest that we leave this place at once? It is likely that the police will get wind of the affair and be upon us at any moment. A duel with pistols is not a quiet matter. Naturally this lady" —he bowed to me—"must not become involved with the law."

He added, as though it had been my main concern, that no gentleman present would ever permit my name to pass his lips as having been present this morning. *Quelle horreur* should my name appear in print in the newspapers! In my state of weak relief I wanted to laugh. Always the Creole must be a Creole and true to his code, so I thanked him as sincerely as I could. But as far as I was concerned, I didn't care if they blared my presence from the rooftops. Courtney, however, was plainly of the same mind and took my arm protectively.

We waited only for the doctor to examine and bandage Justin's slight wound. By that time it was clear that there was another reason for hurrying. So concerned had I been with the events before me that I had not glanced at the black, scudding clouds overhead, or noticed my skirts whipping in the wind. I'd held to my hat automatically and paid no attention to the gusts that tried to snatch it from my head. But now, even as I looked toward the heavens, cold drops stung my face. This appeared to be no summer shower like the one which had caught Justin and me once before.

Together Courtney and I ran toward the carriages. I longed to go with Justin, but Courtney was the man I was going to marry; he had the right to be my protector. I was bundled into his carriage and we set off toward home in the wake of the other party.

That drive became a race with the elements about to break in fury over New Orleans. The driver whipped up his horses and we clattered at a great rate toward the Vieux Carré, to reach home before the storm really started.

To my surprise, Justin stood on the banquette outside the Tourneau house, bidding the other members of his party good-by as we drove up. When we left Courtney's carriage, he came into the passageway with us.

"If no one objects," he said, "I'd like to wait downstairs in the anteroom of your uncle's office. I want to know how matters go with him. Believe me, Skye, I didn't intend what happened."

"I know," I said, and could only put my heart into my eyes as I looked at him.

"I too will remain," Courtney decided. "You will bring us word, Skye, of your uncle's condition?"

Only a little while ago he had wanted to kill Robert Tourneau. Now he was concerned about his health.

I nodded, but there was something else I must know from Justin. "If—if he gets well, what will you do? I mean, if you have proof that he used your mother's money—"

"I want only to regain my father's business," Justin said. "Otherwise I'll not expose him. I've no desire to hurt his family, or submit those near to him to public disgrace. He did not, after all, leave my mother in want. She has been cared for with my father's money all these years. Her suffering has been of the spirit, not the body, and there's no reparation for that. From now on, I'll take care of her myself. Perhaps she will make a home for my son."

I knew then how very much I loved him. When I turned away we did not say good-by. He was still in the house. I would see him yet another time. For the moment I forgot Courtney as if he did not exist.

Twenty-Six ❀

I found the household in a turmoil. Delphine and the doctor had arrived and supervised the matter of getting Uncle Robert to his bedroom. Aunt Natalie never went to pieces as Tante Aurore did. She was bustling about upstairs and down, arranging whatever could be arranged for the sake of Uncle Robert's comfort. News of the duel had sped through the house and there was concern on every face. I found a maid and asked her to take Justin and Courtney a pot of coffee. And I sent Justin a fresh shirt of my father's.

When the girl had gone on these errands, I stood on the rain-lashed gallery for a moment watching the miniature storm in the courtyard. The wind whirled through the small patio, whipping the banana leaves to shreds. As I stood there Lanny rushed toward me and flung himself into my arms. I had never seen him so wild with excitement and I drew him into the dim and quiet parlor, away from the storm.

"Mam'zelle!" he cried. "Is it true that M'sieu Law is my father? Maman says this is so and that my father is a murderer. She says that he has now killed M'sieu Tourneau."

I put my hands gently on his shoulders and looked straight into his eyes. "It is true that Justin Law is your father, Lanny," I said. "But it's not in the least true that he is a murderer. Uncle Robert has not even been wounded. He is ill, but your father did not try to kill him."

Beneath my hands I could feel the boy quiver. "But my mother says there was a man in Colorado whom my father killed."

Anger against Isabelle rose in me. Why had she chosen this time to tell Lanny things that had so long been withheld from him?

"Come with me," I said to Lanny. "I'll take you to your father now. You mustn't believe any lies you've heard about him. He is a father you can be proud of."

We went downstairs together and into the office where Justin and Courtney waited. I saw that the two brothers had been having a talk that must have cleared the air, for Courtney seemed moved almost to the point of tears.

"I've brought your son," I said to Justin and gave Lanny's shoulders a gentle push that took him toward his father.

He stepped forward uncertainly, unsure of how to meet a long-lost father. Politely he held out his hand in greeting. Justin was so big, so towering beside the slight, small boy. But he took the boy's hand in his and drew Lanny toward him with a tenderness I had seen before. I had one glimpse of Lanny's shining face and the pride in Justin's eyes. Then I touched Courtney's arm and we went together out of the office.

The passageway of the porte-cochere was a windy place with the storm howling at both ends and trying to tunnel through it. My skirts whipped about me and there was a roar of wind and rain in my ears.

"Everything possible is being done for Uncle Robert," I said. "Perhaps it would be better if you went home to your mother. If any rumor reaches her——"

He nodded. "You're right, of course." But he stood there looking at me strangely and when I would have turned away, he took my hands and held them gently. "I can see the truth in your face. I began to sense it this morning at the Oa's. You love my brother, Skye?"

There was no reason now to hold back. "I love him," I said, and suddenly I knew that I must carry the words farther than that. "I love him and I can never marry anyone."

Courtney kissed me lightly on each cheek. "I could wish life had set us a different pattern, Skye."

I knew now that his gallantry was part of him and truly sincere. My affection for him was greater than it had ever been.

"You'll go alone to the place in Ohio where Justin wants to send you," I said. "Away from my uncle, you'll find yourself."

He nodded. "I will find myself, and then I will return. Never could I be happy too long away from New Orleans. But now I must get home to my mother. I've a carriage waiting for me, if the horse is not drowned."

He turned toward the street and the storm and I watched him go, glad that neither he nor Aurore would ever again have to grovel before Uncle Robert's wishes.

Slowly I climbed the stairs. When I reached the top Isabelle came hurrying toward me and I saw that she looked almost hysterical with terror.

"Where is Justin?" she shrilled at me. "Tell me where he is! Tell me quickly!"

Anger for what she had revealed to Lanny stirred in me and then, strangely, was gone. She was too pitiful to make me angry. I answered her in as calm a tone as I could summon.

"He has come back to the house to see how Uncle Robert is. He is downstairs in my uncle's office."

She recoiled as though I had struck her. "In this house? Now? What shall I do? If he finds me, he will kill me! Just as he has killed your uncle."

"He's not looking for you," I said quietly. "And no one has been killed. For the sake of your son, as well as your own sake, you must control yourself."

She twisted a soggy handkerchief between her fingers and her eyes were wide with a frantic fear which had no reason in it. One thin hand grasped my arm.

"Help me to get out of this house! I must escape from him and save my life. There are ferries across the river. I can hide myself in some town where he would never think to look. Oh, please help me!"

I looked at her in all her misery and unreasoning despair and I could not despise or hate her, as once I had done. Long ago she had been young and pretty and sweet. Justin had loved her. These things she had somehow destroyed. This morning I had stood beneath the Dueling Oaks and watched life spin itself into the frailty of a cobweb. And in those moments something in me had changed, had gained in perspective and proportion. I could not think of Isabelle as Justin's wife, but only as a human being in great misery and need.

Gently I took her arm and led her along the gallery to her room. "You mustn't make yourself ill," I said. "Here, lie down on the bed and be as quiet as you can. It's storming terribly outside and you couldn't possibly go into it."

She seemed to relax a little under my soothing, though there was still a wildness in her gaze.

"No one wants to hurt you," I assured her. "Not Justin, or anyone else. You must believe me."

"You don't know!" she wailed. "You can't know!"

I brushed the damp brassy hair back from her eyes and felt no repugnance, as once I might have done. The smoothing of my hand seemed to calm her a little and I hoped she would fall asleep.

"Lie here and be still," I told her. "No one will harm you. I'm going to find Delphine now and send her here with something to help your nerves."

"I don't know why they let him out of prison!" she murmured. "I don't know why!"

There could be no reasoning with her in this overwrought state. I held a glass of water for her to sip and then I went upstairs to find Delphine.

She came out of my uncle's room with a tray and I told her quickly of Isabelle's condition. Delphine was plainly impatient and not inclined to trouble. But she agreed, at my pleading, to give her something to quiet her so she wouldn't disturb the rest of the household—in particular my uncle, who was now sleeping quietly.

"Watch her," I warned. "She has some foolish notion

of going out in this storm. She's hardly in a sane state."

When Delphine had promised to do what she could, I went downstairs to my father's room. Mama was with him and she looked up anxiously when I entered.

"I thought you'd never come, Skye. I'd have gone to look for you earlier, but your father would not let me. Is it true there has been a duel?"

I nodded, feeling a little numb now, after all the currents of emotion which had washed over me.

"Can you tell us about it, lassie?" my father asked.

So I told them all that had happened at the Dueling Oaks in the gray dawn. My mother's gasps alternated between excitement and shock. Papa listened with sympathy, yet with the delight of the Scot in a rousing good tale of derring-do. When I told of how Justin had kept Courtney from fighting and of how he had conducted himself in the duel, Papa exclaimed that he would have liked to witness the affair himself.

Having told the story, I felt limp with reaction. I'd had nothing to eat that morning, yet I felt I could not bear to swallow food. I said I would lie down for a little while and went into my room and stretched out on the bed.

But the oblivion of sleep for which I longed would not come. What was to happen to us now? How was I to live? Justin was still under the same roof. If I chose, I could go downstairs and see him again. But what would that avail me? Each new parting cost me more than the last. While I lay there, Delphine brought me a bowl of rich soup and stood over me until I ate. Yes, she said, she had seen to Madame Law. I need trouble myself about nothing. I must sleep now and regain my strength.

Still I did not sleep and after a time Lanny came tapping at my door. I went to let him in and tried to smile a welcome. His bright face told me how successful the talk with his father had been.

"I am to live in a big house in the Garden District!" he cried. "And there I will have another grandmother. One I have never met. My father says she is a kind lady who will love me."

"That's true," I said. "And you will love her." Lanny's coming might well mean a new life for Aurore Law. "But what of your mother?" That was a question I had to ask.

Lanny sobered. "She is to come there too, if she wishes. My father does not desire to harm her, mam'zelle, as she thinks—though I do not believe he likes her very well.

217

Just now I went to her room to tell her she need have no fear, but she is not there. And her cloak and umbrella also are missing. Do you know where she may have gone?"

I stared at him. Had Isabelle escaped from the house after all? On foot in this storm, she would be a pitiful object. I must discover what had happened at once.

Leaving Lanny in Papa's room, I ran upstairs, to find Delphine pacing the corridor outside Uncle Robert's door.

"Do you know where Mrs. Law is?" I asked her. "Lanny says his mother is gone from her room."

Delphine looked at me without expression. "I do not know where she is at this moment, mam'zelle. I called to her attention the severity of the storm, but she insisted that she must leave the house."

"Delphine!" I cried. "You didn't let her go outside?"

Something seemed to flicker in Delphine's eyes. "What was I to do? She pleaded with me, being in fear of her life." Calmly Delphine told me what had happened.

I could see the whole thing clearly. Delphine had helped her with her cloak, handed her the umbrella, kept a guard over her as she led her downstairs. I could see the moment in that windy passageway when the storm must have reached for Isabelle with angry fingers, yet had frightened her no more than the delusions of her own mind. Delphine had opened the gate and let her out upon the street.

"Do not concern yourself, mam'zelle," Delphine said. "What becomes of her is of no consequence to anyone."

Her words filled me with horror, yet I could see how it was with Delphine. All her loyalty belonged to Uncle Robert. She might also use her wisdom to help those whom she respected as she did my father. But since Isabelle was of no further value to my uncle, it had been easy to do the primitive, ruthless thing. She would never understand that I must be bound by a different law.

I turned away from her surprise at my concern and ran downstairs to the office, where Justin sat drinking his coffee. He had changed from the stained shirt and now wore his jacket buttoned loose over his wounded shoulder, the sleeve hanging empty and free. He jumped up at the sight of me.

"Skye! I've been longing to see you, to talk to you."

But there was no time for talking. "Isabelle has run away into the storm," I told him quickly. "She thinks you mean her harm and she persuaded Delphine to let her out of the house. I think she intends to take a ferry across the river. But she's in a weak, half-crazed state and I don't know what will happen to her."

"I'll go after her at once," Justin said, as I fully knew he would.

He was wounded and I hated to see him go into the storm, yet I knew without question that this was what he must do. When he had gone I went upstairs to my own room and locked the door. Quietly I sat in my rocker thinking.

In me, as in Delphine, there was a primitive being. There was a woman who wanted to echo Delphine's thought. *Let her go. She does not matter to anyone. If she never comes back then it will make all the difference in my life.* Yet I listened to the voice in a detached way, knowing that it had nothing to do with me, could never truly shake me.

And that was a strange revelation. For I knew that the girl I had been in New England would have thought only of her own desires, her own loves and hates. Yet a little while ago I had smoothed back the hair on Isabelle's hot forehead and had felt only compassion.

Who was I? When had I begun this growing? When had I changed from girl into woman? This morning at the Oaks? Or earlier still? It did not matter. There was a new strength in me and I knew I could meet and face whatever must be faced. Never again would I be hopelessly caught in such a trap as my uncle had woven around me. There would be defeat for me only if I accepted defeat and bowed under it. In that moment of strange clarity I felt closely akin to my father. Like him, I had gone down to the dark shores, and I had turned my back and walked away.

I bent my head and covered my face with my hands. There were no words to the prayer that flowed through me, but with all my being I asked for the one thing a man or woman might pray for—strength to meet any trial that lay ahead. Strength for Isabelle, for Justin, for me. Even for my uncle. Compassion was a warm, enveloping thing that dissolved all that was hateful and ugly. When Uncle Robert recovered, he might well be a broken man, but whether he was or not, I could only pity him for the empty shell he had made of his life.

The hours of that stormy day were long and no word came. By evening the rain had abated a little and the roofs of New Orleans ceased to run torrents of water. Still there was no word of Justin and there was little chance now that word would reach us before tomorrow. Perhaps he had crossed the river in search of Isabelle.

All night long I stayed up waiting, and in the early hours of dawn I heard him at the gate. I flew downstairs to let him in and saw that he was alone, wet and cold, his face a little gray in the pale light.

I asked no questions. "Come upstairs," I said. "There's an empty room off the gallery." It was Isabelle's room.

Delphine came out of her quarters, a wrapper over her long nightdress, and for once no tignon concealed the shining black hair that hung in a braid down her back. I asked her to make coffee, warm some food, bring them upstairs. She gave me a startled look, but went at once to do my bidding.

In the small bedroom, I helped Justin out of his jacket, pulled off his boots, brought a dressing gown of my father's so that he could rid himself of wet clothes. When Delphine came in with a tray, he drank the thick black coffee, but he wanted no food. He must talk to me first, tell me all that had happened. I tried to persuade him to rest, and let everything else wait. But this he would not do.

Delphine stayed in the doorway, as if she had every intention of remaining, but for once I was stronger than she. I told her to go away and shut the door in her face. Then I sat down beside the bed and held Justin's hand in my own two.

Evenly, without emotion, he began to tell me—not what had happened the night before, but how he had met Isabelle in the beginning and what had occurred long ago in Colorado.

For all that she was an actress in a traveling company, Isabelle had been a girl from home. She had Creole grandparents on one side, and so had Justin. She was a pretty thing, older than he, but young in manner. She was eager for pleasure and a softer life than she had been able to lead. Already she was tired of the theater that had seemed so glamorous to her in the beginning.

I sat very still and listened with all my being. I could imagine how welcome Justin's interest must have seemed to the young Isabelle. He had been no more than a boy, lost in the rapture of first love. So surely had he believed that the mine his father had left him would come in and make him wealthy that he had convinced her too. Mainly, perhaps, because that was what she wanted to believe.

So they were married and Isabelle had entered a life for which she lacked the stamina. She had lacked, too, the ability to love in spite of circumstances. The child had been a further burden for her, and Justin knew his wife began to look in the direction of the stage again.

In marriage she had revealed her narrow self-interests and a disturbing tendency to fly to pieces when faced with responsibility. When a wealthy mineowner in Leadville began to pay her attention it went to her head. She must have believed his avowal of love and have seen in him rescue from the life she had been forced to live with Justin. With her tendency to hysteria and her quickness to move in impulsive rage, she had been unable to accept the moment when her lover lost interest in her and was attracted to someone new.

Justin had been working too hard, and had been too bone-weary and desperate in his own efforts to keep going with the mine, to have any suspicion of his wife. He had idealized her, had seen in her what he wanted to see, as a young man often will. Feeling that his own mother had betrayed his father in refusing to come west with him, he had looked to Isabelle to restore his belief in women.

Then one day he came home unexpectedly to find tragedy awaiting him. Isabelle had shot her lover in a frustrated rage and was in a state of utter terror. In spite of his own horror and shock, there seemed only one course of action for a young and chivalrous man. He himself must take the blame. He must save Isabelle at all costs.

I listened, my eyes brimming with tears. He had borne so much, been betrayed so grievously. There was a bitter note in his voice as he went on.

"She recovered fast enough when she found she wouldn't be held to account for her own actions. During the trial she refused to admit that the man who was killed had been her lover. In the end it looked as though I had shot an unarmed man on sheer, unjustified suspicion. Only a faint doubt which remained against Isabelle saved me from the gallows."

In an even, emotionless tone he went on to tell me what must have happened afterwards, as far as he could piece it together.

Isabelle had waited until he was safely behind bars. Then she fled the state with her baby son, took a stage name and managed to play her way through the South until she could reach Louisiana and leave the little boy with her mother. By that time she must have wanted only to escape Justin forever and dissociate herself from the possibility of being arrested for the crime. This much Justin had been able to learn since he had come to Louisiana and found friends of the child's grandmother to inform him. Only when the grandmother had died a year or so before, had Isabelle once more accepted the duties of motherhood and taken the child with her on the road.

"Thank God he was not in her hands for long," Justin said. "I believe his grandmother must have been a fine woman."

Of course the mine had eventually proved valuable beyond all hope. His father's partner had been scrupulous and honest. He did not try to take advantage of the fact that Justin was in jail. And he never believed in his "confession." Years later this same partner had met an old fellow who had followed the will-o'-the-wisp of lost mines all his life, and who had a story to tell.

On the very day of the murder this man had gone to Justin's house, hoping for a handout. The door had stood open and when no one answered his knock he walked in. The sight that greeted him was so horrifying that he fled at once, not wanting to be charged with the murder himself. But it had been on his conscience all these years that he had lacked the courage to speak up for an innocent man. At length he came back to Leadville and sought Justin's partner to tell him the story. At the hour when he had stumbled upon the body, Justin was in another part of town. He could not have committed the act. It was obvious now that he had lied to save his wife. The old man remembered details so clearly that those who listened to him were impressed. In the end Justin had been given a pardon. Since no one knew where the wife had gone, nothing further could be done. It would probably not be possible to prove at this late date that Isabelle had committed the crime with which her husband had been charged.

"My chief purpose in coming to New Orleans," Justin finished, "was to find some trace of my son. But I also wanted to see my mother and brother again and discover just what had happened to the fortune my father must have left with Robert Tourneau."

I longed to comfort him with my love, but there was still more to be told.

"You—found her last night?" I asked softly.

He brushed a hand wearily across his face. "I found her. But too late, Skye. And the fault is mine."

I held his hand tightly and listened to the rest of the story. Justin himself did not know too clearly what had happened. Probably Isabelle sought only to escape across the river, to hide herself in some small, unlikely place where no one would be apt to seek for her. She feared his anger because after she had left him in prison to take the blame for her crime, she had disappeared with his son. He had every right to hate her, and her own conscience must have whipped her with fear.

Ferry crossings on the river were delayed by the storm. The Mississippi had turned to a raging muddy torrent and when Isabelle reached the dock she found others waiting there in the rain. She was more frantic than they, however, driven perhaps by the guilty terror that was in her.

"I know," Justin said, "that she was convinced that I meant her bodily harm, though I had never laid a finger on her in violence. It could be that Tourneau put the thought in her mind, where it found ready soil in her knowledge of how she had cheated me. When she saw me there on the dock she struggled to get aboard the boat that was readying itself to leave."

Justin had called to her to wait, but she had fled from him, hurled herself to the dock's edge. Whether she slipped, or whether she acted with intention, no one could tell. Justin had heard the cries of those who saw her fall, but he did not realize that she had gone into the river until he too reached the edge of the dock where he could look down upon the turbulent water. The current was strong, but she had gone in where the flow pinned her against the side of the ferry—or she would have been lost forever down the river.

"I started to go in after her," Justin said, "but men on the dock held me back. A sailor from the boat had already thrown in a life belt and jumped in to rescue her. When they were hauled on deck she was unconscious. I worked over her myself until the water was driven from her lungs and she recovered consciousness. Then I found a carriage and took her to the hospital."

All night he had stayed with her, but the doctor had said the struggle was too difficult for her weak and fluttering heart. She had died just before dawn.

Afterwards he had come directly here.

He stopped and I put his hand against my cheek. I did not beg him not to reproach himself, for I knew that would be futile. Justin too had found compassion in the long stormy hours of the night.

He reached out and put his other hand upon the brightness of my hair. "I can remember what she was like when I first knew her. So pretty and young and gay. And I can remember my own youth. All I had hoped for and wanted of life centering about Isabelle and me. It was like that, Skye."

I felt the tears wet on my cheeks. I could remember too.

That a dream might be mistaken did not make it any less poignant to look back upon.

He moved his hand across my hair and then beneath my chin, tilting my head so that he could look into my eyes. "Will you want to make your home with me here in New Orleans?"

"My home is where you are," I said and knew this would always be so.

He sat up and I went into his arms. He held me close and tight for a moment before he let me go.

"You must rest now," I said. "Go to sleep. I'll come back the moment you want me."

The room was dim and quiet, its shutters closed against the rising sun. I drew the door softly to behind me and stood upon the gallery for a moment, looking down upon the brightening courtyard.

The storm was over, the sky clear overhead. New Orleans was wakening to a new day.